Breadcr

and

Bones

A Honsham Forest Village Cosy Crime

Lorna Clark

First edition independently published in the United Kingdom 2023.
ISBN (Paperback): 979-8-3927609-0-9
Typesetting design: Matthew J Bird

A CIP catalogue record of this book is available from the British Library

For further information about this book, please contact the author at **www.lornajclark.co.uk**

Dedicated to David and Heather Wakefield, with thanks for their friendship and wise advice.

Honsham Forest Village *is a small market garden in Norfolk.*

It is worked by up to twelve resident adults in need of quiet or refuge.

Residents

Amber Single parent of **Daniel** (9 months). Brought up in care system. Victim of domestic violence.

Alex Widower. Boyfriend to **Jen**. Maintenance-man. Owner of Mungo, a black Labrador.

Clifford Partner to **Will**. In charge of outdoor work.

Jazz Of West Indian descent. Son of **Wilma**, a GP and **Ogden**, a paediatric consultant.

Jen (age 37) Divorced. Mother to **Lily** (age 14) and **Mark** (age 13). Girlfriend to **Alex**.

Meadow (age 73) Administrator/manager of Honsham Forest Village.

Peter Son of Sally. On the Autism Spectrum. Expert on tomatoes and tomato growing.

Sally Divorced. Mother to **Peter.** Chief cook.

Teddy Ex-offender.

Will Partner to **Clifford.** Works in kitchen.

CHAPTER 1

A lex turned white. 'It's a skull.'
'Oh hell. Is it human?'
'Yes.'

We stood there staring, my stomach turning, until Alex said, 'We need the police.' I could see him shaking. This was one of the few times I regretted having no mobile with me. I grabbed hold of his hand, wishing I didn't feel nauseous.

'Are you alright, sweetheart?' he asked. I nodded, trying to organise my thoughts. How could this happen in such a peaceful place? I walked back down the hill to the bench where Teddy was sitting.

'How are you feeling?'

'Crap,' he replied. 'Do you think this will go on my record?'

'I don't think it can. You were just the one who found it… It could have been any of us.'

Before this, we'd been enjoying our cups of tea outside in the warmth of the autumn sun, looking up the hill at the rectangular plot of orange pumpkins.

We took Teddy back to the courtyard and he disappeared indoors, closely followed by Alex.

My tea shook and overflowed as I picked the mug up. Alex came out and sat down beside Meadow, the administrator. He had a brief discussion with her and she knocked on the table.

'Quiet everyone. I'm afraid Teddy has dug up a skull. We've called the police, and I suggest that everyone stops work for today, except for cleaning your tools. Don't go anywhere near where Teddy was working.'

'What about your children?' she asked me. 'You'll need to catch them as they get off the school bus and tell them what's happened. I don't want them frightened by a police presence.'

At fourteen and thirteen, it was unlikely that either of them would be frightened but I understood what she was saying.

Normally I felt a sense of calm and tranquillity when the metal entrance gate was closed. But not today. As I walked towards it later, I could see that about half of the top area of ground was taped off and there were a number of police and plain cars around, including one outside the open gate.

'Not again,' Lily said, as she got off the bus. 'What's happened this time?'

'Teddy dug up a human skull.'

'Cool. Can I see it?' Mark asked.

'It's a crime scene,' I said. 'Anyway it's just a skull, you must have seen one in biology.'

'Only a plastic one. Do they know who it is yet?'

'It only happened half an hour ago, so no one knows much yet.'

'This is so much more exciting than living in London. Nothing ever happened there,' Mark said.

'Little brother, you have no feelings. I don't think it was very exciting for the person that died.'

'Sorry.'

I took them back to the apartment where they made tea and helped themselves to biscuits, then I went to check on Meadow.

She was worried. 'I hope it's an old burial site.'

'Teddy was double-digging to get rid of the brambles, so it was shallow,' I said, 'not deep enough for a proper burial ground. Jazz said they'd dug up a baby doll earlier, but they took no notice as they thought the area may have been a waste tip at some time.'

'Sadly, the police will dig it for us now,' she said, 'and wreck our asparagus bed.'

'I know. Would you like me to make you a hot drink?'

'Yes please, my dear. I can't do much in the kitchen using this walking frame.'

'Would you like me to stay with you? You look as if you need company.'

'I'm concerned about Teddy. He looked so poorly,' she said.

'He'll probably feel a bit better by suppertime, but he's had an enormous shock and the police will want to talk to him.'

'And he doesn't like them. He seems to think they were responsible for his prison sentence, but they had nothing to do with it. He's settled so well here, I don't like him being upset like this.'

By suppertime we had heard no more. The media, of course, had photographed the police car at the now closed gate, but nothing had been released to them. There was just a short piece on the news but, after Meadow being attacked in the summer, they felt justified in suggesting some outrageous theories of what may have happened behind our big metal gate.

Teddy managed to get himself to supper but still looked pale and only picked at his food. Just as we were clearing the dishes away, a tall elderly man, whom I recognised as DI Watson, came in search of Meadow.

I walked him over to her apartment. 'Would you like me to leave?' I asked.

'No. If you're happy to stay, then it will save me repeating myself,' he said. 'The skull appears to have been buried within the last ten years and it's female. Can you think of anyone who thought she was in danger during that time?'

'Not really, the years seem to run into each other now. Would you like to see the register of residents and visitors?' she asked.

'Can I take it back to the station with me?'

'Is that really necessary? I mean, would a photocopy do?

'I suppose it will have to.'

A few days later, DI Watson returned to speak to Meadow. Again, I asked if she'd like me to stay and she indicated that she would.

'Well,' he said, 'we've managed to trace everyone in the register from that time, except for one person. There were less than a hundred, but it wasn't easy, believe me. People move house a lot more than they used to when I was younger.'

'Who couldn't you find?' Meadow asked.

'I don't know if you'll remember her. She was only here for one night. Nicole Hanson.'

Meadow pursed her lips. 'I remember her well, actually. She's the only person I've had to ask to leave. She upset a lot of people here.'

'How?' he asked.

'On the surface she was pleasant and polite. I thought she was okay until some of the other residents complained. First it was Sally, our cook. Apparently, Nicole owned a restaurant and Sally's cooking wasn't of the standard she was expecting.'

I was surprised. Sally's cooking might be traditional, but it was excellent. I had never had cause to complain.

'So I suggested to her that she may like to work for a while with Sally and help her. That didn't go down well. She said there was no way she was working with "that woman". She stalked off, went over to Sally and verbally abused her. I called her back in and she suggested that I didn't know what I was doing. I'm afraid I tore her off a strip for being so rude.' Meadow rubbed her temples. 'I thought that would be it, but then Clifford and Will came to see me. She collared them, told them they were living in sin and should be ashamed of themselves. If they couldn't see what they were doing, then they should go to a doctor and get treatment.'

What? Clifford and Will were a kind and gentle couple who worked hard. They were at the Village to get away from attitudes like that. I was protective of my friends.

'Anyway, I told her she had to leave. She argued about it and said she could make this place much better. Do you know she actually questioned my authority to send her away. I made sure that she knew my husband, and I were equal partners and gave her half an hour to be off the premises before I called the police. Not long afterwards, I saw her dragging her suitcase up the lane toward the gate.'

'What age would you say she was?' he asked.

'In her early to mid-sixties I think.'

'Can you describe her?'

'She was about five foot six and thick set. A miserable old-fashioned woman. She could be charming if she wanted to but we didn't see much of that here. She came to us in the summer in a blue dress and matching jacket. Oh, and flat lace up shoes.

She was wearing a large-linked silvery chain too. I'm afraid that's all I can tell you.'

'There were no missing persons in this area around that time,' he said, 'but we're checking nationally. There was something strange though. The person who she listed as her next-of-kin – a chap called Ross Childs – had no idea who Nicole Hanson was. She might as well have picked his name randomly from the telephone directory.'

With that, he left.

'I wonder if she was using a false name,' I said.

'It's possible,' said Meadow. 'She was the sort of character who might not want to be traced. Everything was about her. She seemed so charming at face value, but she had no ability to empathise. Snowy was very ill then and she didn't seem to care at all, just asked if I had the authority to evict her without my husband's permission. I always was and always will be able to do whatever I feel is right. I didn't have to ask anyone first.'

'Hey. Don't get yourself upset. Would you like a smoke?' I asked.

'I think I would, although now my elbow is better, I can manage by myself. You don't have to mollycoddle me, my dear.'

'I wasn't, just thought it may help you to relax.' In less than a minute the musky scent of her 'smoke' filled the room and I felt light-headed.

'I'm sorry,' she said, 'I shouldn't get myself so worked up.'

'You have reason. It's obvious that DI Watson isn't thinking of taking the investigation of the listed next of kin any further. Would you mind if Alex and I went out to see him? He may talk to us but not to the police, in case something she's done rebounds on him.'

'That's a thought,' she said, 'after all, you did a better job than the police in discovering who was attacking me in the summer. I don't think they'd have caught him so quickly if you hadn't intervened.'

'I'm just glad we did,' I said.

I went to the community kitchen and made DI Watson a mug of tea. 'Thanks for this,' he said, 'today seems to be dragging.'

'Is there anything I can do to help?'

'Not really. I suppose being here brings back memories of last time. Did you know I was suspended for leaking information? I was innocent but the mud stuck. Meanwhile, I'm wondering where to go with this skeleton. If we can't identify her, I'm in a real mess.'

'So you've found some more bones?'

'Yes. Thanks for the tea and sympathy. Much appreciated.'

After he'd left, I remained at the table, thinking. I hadn't intended to get involved, but it seemed that I might be in a better position to get Nicole's next-of-kin talking. The police wouldn't have told him there had been remains found, but it wouldn't be long before the media found out. If he was hiding something, or was frightened, he may be prepared to talk to someone not connected with them. I decided to discuss it with Alex when we walked his dog that evening.

CHAPTER 2

Alex and I had been growing closer over the past three months and I wanted him to be with me if we were to do anything. He was in favour of getting involved but insisted I talk to Meadow again.

She was hesitant. 'I'd like to know whose skeleton it is. I didn't mind you trying to find out who was threatening my life but I'm not so certain this time. Obviously, I don't have any say in how you use your own time. If you decide to help, you must let someone know where you're going. You realise, my dear, if the skeleton is Nicole's, the man listed as next of kin could be her killer?'

'Yes,' I replied. 'But we don't even know if her death is suspicious. We just want to give her a name and see her properly buried. We'll let Jazz know our whereabouts.'

'Okay, but I want to know nothing until she has a name. Understood?'

I nodded and left, feeling as if a strict teacher had reprimanded me.

I checked with Alex and we decided to visit Ross Childs on our next afternoon off. As Alex pointed out, he lived in Holt, which was less than an hour's drive away.

'You'll love Holt,' he said, 'it's picturesque, lots of old buildings, many of them flint. A lot of the houses are second homes, so there's a lot of independent shops and cafes.'

'We may have to stop on the way home for coffee and cake,' I said.

'We may well do,' he smiled. 'Your real problem will be thinking of a reason to visit Mr Childs. He'll be wary as the police have already contacted him. I don't know what they asked him, but he didn't offer any information.'

'Have you got any ideas about our reason for going?' I asked.

'Not really. You could check on the exact date she was here and say that it's normal to check on people after a certain length of time. Perhaps we could suggest, when we get there, that we may be looking for a donation or we're having a reunion or something like that. You're the assistant administrator, so it would seem logical coming from you.'

'I'll work on that one,' I said. 'I don't want to antagonise him.'

'He might have had second thoughts about what he said to the police and be glad of the opportunity to open up.'

'I hope so.'

When I telephoned Ross Childs, I mentioned that the Village was following up on previous residents and he seemed eager to help. I mentioned nothing about the remains being found, and he didn't question my story. He suggested we came to see him on Wednesday afternoon, which suited us well.

'Do you think we should make a list of questions?' I asked Alex that morning.

'No, let's just see how things go. It's probably better to have just a leisurely chat.'

Ross welcomed us at the door. 'Come on through. It's a beautiful day, I thought we could have tea in the garden.'

It was a bit chilly, but the garden was surrounded by tall flint walls which seemed to radiate heat. After a few minutes he came out with a tea tray.

'How long have you lived here? I asked.

'Probably about twenty-five years. I loved the enclosed garden at first sight and the shops nearby. I work outside most of the summer, even on days like this, and then use the summer house or the local cafes when the weather's not so good.'

'What's your work?' I asked. 'Garden design?'

'I feel flattered. I designed and landscaped this garden, but that was in between books. I'm a crime writer.'

'Oh dear,' said Alex. 'True or fictional?'

Ross laughed. 'Fictional. I was in the police force for thirty years and then decided to retire. I know all about police procedures at the time I left. At first, I decided to try to keep my knowledge up to date, but I realised that it would be much easier to set the books in the period I knew. There's enough research to do without learning new procedures.'

'I've been told that authors don't make much money. Is that just a rumour?' I asked.

'It's true, I'm afraid. I've heard of people who do a lot of social media and advertising work and they make a considerable amount. Obviously celebrities do, people follow them because they have the right name. I love the writing side but can't be bothered doing all the rest of the marketing stuff.'

'Do you write under your own name?' Alex asked.

'No. I decided that it would probably be better to write under a pen name as I didn't want any come back from criminals. I use the name Ross Carpenter.'

'I'll have to look for your books,' I said. 'I love a good crime novel.'

'What about you?' he asked Alex.

'I usually read spy or espionage stories, but I haven't been able to settle to reading much since my wife died.'

'I understand that,' he replied. 'My wife died six years ago and I couldn't concentrate at all, no matter how I tried. The words made sentences, but I couldn't take them in.'

'I know what you mean,' said Alex, concentrating on his tea.

'So how can I help the pair of you. I've never been to Honsham Forest Village, but my step-sister has.'

'Do we know her?' I asked.

'Penelope Brown.'

We both shook our heads. 'Did she use another name?' I asked.

'Yes, numerous ones. She kept changing them because she didn't want her reputation to follow her.'

'How do you mean?' Alex asked.

'Put it this way… When my father married her mother, she was horrible to me and my brother, Rupe. We weren't good enough for her. We were just normal boys who had been brought up to work hard and be polite. If we didn't please her, she would go running to Mummy and we got the blame. As we got older, we deliberately wound her up. Dad could see how awful she was to us and I think he would have liked to have done the same.' He sipped his tea.

'She was sixty when she came out and had nowhere to go. Although my wife was sick, we felt sorry for her and offered her lodgings here. It was a mistake, she hadn't changed at all. We insisted she paid rent for the room and something toward her food and she managed to get summer work locally. She could be really nice to people at times and cow-towed to the wealthy summer visitors. She was waitressing and earned more tips than wages, until she came across someone she wanted nothing to do with. She was so rude, just like she was here. She lost numerous jobs and as Penelope Brown's reputation spread, she simply used different names,' he said.

'Her continuous criticism was getting us down, so one day I threw her out. That was when she went to Honsham Forest Village. I didn't know where she was until a day later when she rang me to arrange a taxi to collect her. She thought she was coming back here, but no way.'

'That must have been awful for you,' I said.

'I didn't hear anything more of her after that. I expect she's managed to con her way into council accommodation by now.'

'You didn't get as much as a birthday or Christmas card from her?'

'Never. Now would you like some more tea and cake?' he asked. 'I feel I need to sweeten myself up after talking about her.'

The cake was delicious, so neither of us refused his offer. When we left, a short time later, it was with reluctance.

CHAPTER 3

'What do you think?' Alex asked on the way home. 'I'm confused. Her attitude sounds like Nicole Hanson, but he talked about her coming out. That was the bit that concerned me. If she was gay, why would she be awful to Clifford and Will?'

'That's what confused me, too. I think I'll have a chat with Clifford to make sure it wasn't Will exaggerating. He's a bit of a drama queen.'

'I'll see if I can find anything more about Penelope Brown online, although it's a common name and there are probably a lot of them around,' I said.

There were so many questions we should have asked, but it had been just a friendly chat. Ross told us to come back at any time but to ring first. If Penelope was in the habit of changing names, she may not be traceable. The pressure was on because Ross would soon find out that someone had been buried at the Forest Village. He probably still had contacts in the police and it would be in the media soon. He would probably be annoyed with us for not being open with him.

That evening I had a chat with Sally who said she would put up the flags if the skull belonged to Nicole Hanson.

'The police asked me about her,' she said. 'I just said that I thought that someone who owned her own restaurant might want to share some cooking tips with me, but she just ignored me. I don't want to run her down if she's still alive. You do know that she's the only person who's been evicted from here?'

I nodded, 'She must have been bad for Meadow to do that. Normally she would try to work with a visitor to help with her attitude.'

'Yes, lovey, but she knew that Snowy had cancer at that time, although none of us did. She would have wanted to spend as much time with him as she could and may not have had the time or energy to deal with Nicole.'

'Did you think Nicole might be gay?' I asked.

'Well, I didn't think of that. I can't see either a man or woman fancying her. But having said that, she dressed beautifully, except for her lace-up shoes. Looked as if she was wearing her Sunday best and used a napkin exquisitely. That sounds a strange thing to say, but she brought her own cotton one to meals and dabbed her face delicately. I suppose she didn't want to ruin her makeup. She had a solid frame, but she gave the impression of being very feminine indeed.'

Peter came walking through. 'Look for a white transit van.' He gave a registration number and a date, but I didn't catch them.

'He often does that sort of thing because he thinks it's of interest. But I tend to ignore it unless it matters,' she said.

Alex told me Clifford backed up what Sally said. He was positive she wasn't gay. I spent my spare time next morning online, hunting for Penelope Brown. It was impossible – there were too many to draw any conclusions. I could see we had to get back to Ross again, but would it be a good time to tell him about the skeleton?

I noticed that DI Watson was on the site again. I opened my window, 'Would you like a cup of tea?'

He came straight to the door and I let him in. As the kettle was boiling, I asked him whether he was making progress.

'Not really,' he said, 'but cases can often be slow to start with. Someone must be missing her, unless she was homeless.'

'Do you know whether it was a natural death?'

'It's unlikely,' he smiled. 'But the media are on to it now and we won't be able to hold back much longer. We'll have a press release shortly.'

This worried me. To be fair to Ross I would like to tell him before he found out from the news. We should have told him the full story at the start, but the police had asked us to keep quiet.

'A member of the public may come forward.'

'Maybe.' He didn't sound hopeful.

We talked for a while and, when he'd finished his tea, he thanked me and left.

When I found Alex in the workshop, he unplugged his drill. I told him the situation and how I was worried about Ross finding out about the skeleton before we had a chance to tell him.

'Can you phone him? I could be free tomorrow if you are... and don't forget our class this evening.'

I had forgotten. Alex had enrolled us for a breadmaking course in Honsham, thinking it would be good to do something together away from the Forest Village. I was finding it therapeutic and a good way of making new friends.

I made the phone call immediately and Ross agreed to us meeting him the following day.

Afterwards I went to collect Meadow for lunch. She was making good progress, but found she had less energy as the day progressed. I didn't want her struggling, so she agreed to use the wheelchair this time.

'Do you want to do your hair before we go across, or should I do it for you?' I asked. She still had her long hair from her hippy days, although it was grey now.

'Would you mind. I think I fell asleep on the sofa.'

I brushed it carefully, 'Ponytail, plait or loose?' I asked, 'It's still quite windy out there.'

'Ponytail, I think.'

'How's the pain?' I asked. 'Can you transfer to your wheelchair or would you like help?'

'I think I could do with some help. I'm beginning to feel my age, I'm weak and weary.'

I helped her into the wheelchair and pushed her to the communal kitchen. I'd not heard her saying that she felt weak and weary before and made a mental note to check with her when I took her home again. I wasn't aware that she was overdoing things, so she should be getting better.

The evening class started at half past five to allow time for the proving. We were kneading our dough companionably when I said to Alex, 'I think we've got it wrong.'

'It looks the same as all the rest,' he replied.

'No, not the bread. Nicole Hanson. When Ross told us he felt sorry for her when she came out, we assumed he meant out of the closet. I think he's playing with us. She could have come out of hospital, or a nursing home or prison. I don't think she's a lesbian.'

'Keep kneading, you might think of something else. We didn't know he used to be in the police force when we first met him. He may be trying to help us think in a way that will solve the problem and find out more than he is prepared to reveal at the moment. I don't think he's trying to mislead us, just getting us to ask the right questions.'

'Do you think it would be okay to go in with a list of questions this time?' I asked.

'I think a list in our heads, not written down.'

'When you think your dough is ready, you can put it in the proving oven and we'll meet in the pub,' our instructor said.

This was a big part of bonding as a class. We all sat around one table and ordered drinks and food. For some class members who lived alone, it was the social highlight of the week.

After we'd eaten, the tutor reminded us that our bread should be almost ready for the next step. We returned to our classroom and spent some time cleaning up our worktops.

'How do I make such a mess?' I asked Alex, 'I always have to sweep flour off the floor.' I looked at his immaculate area and couldn't work it out.

CHAPTER 4

The following morning Meadow looked tired, but said she was fine and told me to stop fussing. I walked back to her apartment with her after she had her 'smoke'. She could open the tin herself now her arm was better. I missed the musky smell that filled my nose when I opened it.

'What did you think of the bread this morning,' I asked. We always left ours in the community kitchen on a Wednesday evening, so that it could be eaten at breakfast.

'Did you see me cut a second slice?' she asked. I nodded. 'Well, I think you know my answer. I prefer wholemeal to white anyway, it keeps you going.'

I looked at her in puzzlement. 'That can be taken two ways. Which were you referring to?'

'Both. You know it's such a small thing, but I appreciate being able to walk to the bathroom. Most people would take that for granted, but not me. Now I can eat and drink what I like without worrying if someone will be about to help me,' she said.

'Until you pointed that out just now, I had never even thought about it.'

'I get miserable and melancholy as we move towards winter, my dear, so I've decided to think of something I'm grateful for every day.'

'If you feel low, you will tell me, won't you? One of the women in our breadmaking course is like that and she said nothing helped her until she bought a SAD lamp.'

'What's that?' she asked.

'It's a light that compensates for the lack of sun's rays that we get in the winter. SAD stands for seasonal affective disorder,' I said. 'I take vitamin D tablets, too. I've read that when we are older, we can't store it in the way that we did when we're younger.'

'That comes from sunlight doesn't it? I was listening to a podcast where a little boy got rickets from lack of vitamin D because he spent all his time indoors on his Playstation. Poor parenting. Can you get me some vitamin D supplements?' Meadow asked.

After I had collected and delivered the mail, I reminded Meadow that I was going out with Alex that afternoon.

She grinned. 'I don't really want to know about it, but I'm glad that you're spending more time together… and you haven't had an argument for a while.'

'Don't bring that one up. You know what I'm like for upsetting people. I keep thinking that it's only a matter of time.'

'Just be thankful for each day when you don't argue,' she said with a wink.

After lunch Alex and I got into his car to drive to Holt. He said, 'If you want to drive, just tell me.'

'Do you mean drive your lovely car, rather than my clapped-out old banger?'

'Yes.'

'I'm surprised you trust me. You know what a mess I can make of things,' I said.

'I think you should praise yourself for everything that goes well and learn from the mistakes.'

'Do you know, that's more or less what Meadow was saying. Are you two getting at me?'

'Innocent,' he said, 'it's just that people seem to be less appreciative through autumn and winter.'

'I haven't noticed but it may be more obvious in the countryside.'

'Perhaps, but let's talk through what we want to ask Ross.'

Ross seemed quite happy to see us when we arrived and took us to the summerhouse for tea and cake. The doors were flung open and we could see the trees in the distance, the autumnal hues already beginning.

'I can see why you write out here,' I said.

He smiled. 'I spend nearly every hour of daylight out here. It's my special place. I've established that Alex is a local lad, but you're a Londoner?'

I told him how I'd brought the children here for the summer holiday and that we couldn't face going back after six weeks in the countryside.

'I could never live in London,' he said. 'Not now. When I was younger, I did a stint with the Met. I loved the lifestyle, but when I "grew up" I wanted to settle down in a place where the horizon is two-thirds of the way down the viewfinder. Norfolk has a wealth of sky which brings freedom.'

'I can hear that you're a writer by the way you talk,' I said.

'Now, I expect you have questions to ask me as DI Watson doesn't seem to be making much progress. You want to find out who the skeleton belongs to?'

'How did you know that?' Alex asked.

'I still have contacts. When the police first questioned me, I wasn't sure what it was all about. They only asked me if I knew

Nicola Hanson. When I said I didn't, they asked no more questions. You, however, have asked more insightful questions and mentioned Honsham Forest Village.'

'Is that wrong of us?' I asked.

'No, not at all. I would quite like to see you identify the skeleton rather than a police investigator. What can I help you with today?'

'You said about Penelope using false names. Was that her birth name?' I asked.

'No, she was christened Ruth Carpenter.'

'When you said you felt sorry for her when she came out, we at first assumed you meant out of the closet, but you didn't, did you?' Alex asked.

'No, she wasn't gay,' he said laughing. 'She came out of prison.'

We were quiet for a while.

'What was she inside for?' he asked.

'She killed a baby.'

I felt as if my blood was draining out of my feet, and everything was distancing itself from me. I struggled to breathe and went outside.

Both men were looking concerned.

'I'm sorry,' I said. 'That was a rather extreme reaction.'

'Would it help you to talk about it?' Ross asked.

'I don't think so,' I said.

'Look I'll brew another pot of tea while you recover and leave Alex to look after you.'

Alex put his arms round me. 'What brought this on?' he asked.

'I'm not sure. What Ross said was such a shock. I almost had a panic attack. I'm not certain I want to continue with the investigation if that's what we're looking at.'

When Ross returned, he poured me another cup of tea and stirred sugar into it. 'I'm sorry if I hit a tender spot,' he said.

'It's okay, I would have found out anyway.'

He nodded. 'Is there anything else I can do for you?'

'You don't happen to have a photo of her, do you?' Alex asked.

He went off to fetch one. 'You realise that this won't prove anything about the skeleton,' I said.

'Yes,' Alex replied, 'but if Sally and Clifford identify the photo as Nicole, at least we'll know if it was her that stayed at the Forest Village.'

After we'd finished our tea, Alex excused us saying that he needed to get me home to rest.

As we were leaving, Ross said to me, 'If you decide to do more research into my stepsister, I should warn you that her life is not a pretty one and you'll probably stumble onto more things that hurt you.'

CHAPTER 5

'Oh, Alex,' I said as soon as were back in the car, 'that was so embarrassing.'

'Why?'

'Just panicking like that when he mentioned she'd killed a baby. I suppose I've never been that close to murder before.'

'I know you haven't. It's a warped part of life we hope we'll never get near to.'

'We'll need DNA to find out if it is Ruth Carpenter,' I said.

'Unless the police already have some on file it's unlikely that it will do any good,' Alex said, 'but I'm fairly certain that it's one of the first things they'll check.

I closed my eyes and dozed for the remainder of the journey.

I felt Alex shaking me and woke up wondering where I was, but then it all came back to me.

'I'm going to have a rest,' I said.

'Don't worry about Meadow,' he said, 'I'll collect her for supper.'

He was so good to me.

At supper time he asked how I was feeling and I told him I was back to normal. Meadow peered at me and I foresaw the coming interrogation.

'Do you fancy walking Mungo with me tonight?' Alex asked.

'Yes, I think that would be good.'

'When are you going to tell me what was wrong with you then?' Meadow asked after we'd finished our meal and she was outside having a smoke.

'I heard something I didn't like. But you told me you don't want to know anything about our investigation, so I won't tell you.'

'Fair enough,' she said.

I walked back to her apartment with her and topped up her water jug, before leaving her for the evening.

'I'll come back to check whether you need anything later,' I said. The bright colours of her apartment and the smell of cannabis that clung to every soft surface, made me feel claustrophobic and I couldn't wait to get away.

I checked that the children were busy with their homework, put my coat and boots on, grabbed a torch and went over to Alex's.

'Ready?' he asked. 'You sure you're alright, you still look pasty?'

'It's Meadow's flat. I suppose it's because she keeps the windows shut now. The cannabis affects my head and I already have a headache. I think the fresh air will do me good.'

We walked through the woods, the fallen chestnuts threatening to wring our ankles. 'Jen, I'm worried about you. Do you think we should be pushing on with this case? I'm concerned it will hurt you and I don't want to see that happen.'

'I don't know. I think we're nearly there. It would be sad to give up at this stage.'

'But I'm worried about your health.'

Before I had chance to protest, he took me in his arms and kissed me. We'd hardly finished when Mungo's head pushed itself between us and his ball dropped onto our feet.

'Mungo, you beast,' I said as I bent to pick up his ball. 'I think you're jealous of the attention I'm getting.' I feigned throwing it behind us then threw it ahead. He started running, realised what I had done and changed direction.

'I used to get away with that,' I said, 'but he's got wise to me now.'

'Don't change the subject. I'm serious about it. I think Ross was concerned when he said that her life wasn't pretty. I don't know what we're looking at and you're fragile at the moment. I don't want you damaged by it.'

'I can't spend my life running away from things that hurt. In fact, exposure to them may help. Anyway, I think Ross knows more than he's letting on and doesn't want us to continue. He was trying to put me off.'

'You may be right, but I don't trust women's intuition. He could just be concerned about you, sweetheart. What will you do next and do you want my help?'

'I always want your help. I think I'll try to establish whether Ruth Carpenter was married and whether she had children. I wish we could find an immediate family member who's prepared to take a DNA test if hers isn't in the data base.'

'There may not be one,' he said.

'Then we'd be completely stuck. I did have a thought, though. I wonder if she would have been on probation when she came out of prison. The police could find out whether she kept her appointments with her probation officer. If she had, then we're barking up the wrong tree.' I looked at Mungo who was doing just that.

'Probably pigeons,' Alex said.

'Are you sure there's no one up there?'

'Positive. That's a happy bark and he's not looking at all worried.'

'What was that noise then?'

'Look, shine your torch up there. They probably just rolled over in bed.' I shone my torch into the trees and could see no one.

'There, what did I tell you, City Girl? I think you're still worried about the time that bent policeman found you in the woods and Mungo growled at him.'

'You're right,' I said, 'and if someone was hiding, they probably wouldn't do it so close to the Village.'

He took me in his arms and kissed me again. That exquisite kiss turned my body wild.

'I think we need to get back and find you a glass of wine. It's getting nippy out here,' he said.

'Seriously, what do you think we may find in Ruth Carpenter's history that'll be harder to take than killing a baby?'

'I'm not certain. But to find out, you might have to go through newspapers and read up on her case. It's almost impossible to find anyone's ancestry if all you have is their name,' he said.

'I should have asked Ross for dates and family details, like birthdays and mother's name. If I hadn't had that stupid attack, I may have thought about it more.'

'It wasn't a stupid attack,' he said, 'it was your natural reaction to hearing something nasty. Not stupid like thinking there was someone in the trees.'

'You're not going to let me forget that, are you?'

The following morning was spent doing my normal tasks and taking Meadow to a physiotherapist's appointment.

'I wish I didn't have to see her,' Meadow said, 'I'm coping well enough, aren't I?'

'I think you're coping, but do you want to spend the rest of your life with a frame in front of you?'

'Not really. If only my legs weren't so weak all the time.'

'Is your good leg weak as well?

She didn't reply, so I let the subject go.

CHAPTER 6

Google seemed to like the name Ruth Carpenter and threw up pages and pages. It didn't seem such a common name to me, but I was clearly wrong. I decided to add 'baby' and 'trial' to my search and this narrowed it down and found the details I needed. Whilst I always thought it was unfair of reporters to mention people's age, I was quite glad they did in this article.

I had started making notes when my stomach rumbled. I looked at the clock and left my computer on while I went to collect Meadow for lunch.

I met DI Watson on the way back to my apartment.

'Do you fancy a cup of tea?' I asked.

He came in with me and was wandering around when he accidentally moved my computer mouse with his sleeve. He looked at the screen. 'Why are you looking at Ruth Carpenter's case?' he asked.

'We think she stayed here under the name Nicole Hanson,' I said.

'And you're concluding the skeleton may be her?'

'It's possible.'

'I don't think so.'

'Why?' I asked.

'I'm afraid I can't say. What I came to tell you is that we are having a media meeting tomorrow morning. You may find you have a group of reporters at the gate after that.'

'Are we allowed to know what you will say or do we have to wait until we see it on the news?'

'The latter I'm afraid. I'm sorry but I'm worried that I may be suspended for leaking information again, so I'm being very careful what I say.'

'I can understand that. Would you like me to tell Meadow? She's not having a good day.'

'That would be helpful, thank you.'

I spent the rest of the afternoon researching Ruth Carpenter and found out that it wasn't her own baby that she killed, but one she had stolen. That was painful for me, and I wondered what sort of a woman would do something like that. The little boy's parents had paid for IVF to have a child. Not just one round, but four. They must have been absolutely devastated.

I also found out that Ruth had two children of her own, both of which she put up for adoption at birth. I felt totally confused. How could she give away her own children, and why steal somebody else's? She must have had some sort of psychological problem, like post-natal depression, but there was nothing about that in the news. Or perhaps she was an unmarried mother, forced to give her children up.

I found another mention of her. A case was brought against a dentist by women who accused him of raping them while they were under full anaesthetic. Ruth also made a claim against him, but her case was thrown out. She had perfect teeth that had no work on them, so she wouldn't have had treatment. She was fined for wasting the court's time.

I needed to find those children. From the age given in the paper Ruth must have been born in 1955 or 1956. I knew her mother remarried. It was possible she could still be alive, in her eighties or nineties, yet she listed Ross as her next of kin.

My head was spinning. I closed my laptop and decided to leave Ruth Carpenter alone for the rest of the day.

I still wondered whether I should follow this through or give up. I didn't like being hurt.

I told Alex what I had found out when we walked Mungo that evening.

He pursed his lips. 'It's almost impossible to find adopted children, because the law is set up to protect them. I don't suppose you found out why she put them up for adoption?'

'Not yet, but I could do some more digging.'

'If you want to, but don't keep at it if it's upsetting you.'

'I'm not certain how I feel at the moment. The menopause has messed up my brain and the tablets don't seem to be helping.'

'Perhaps they don't suit you, sweetheart. There must be others. Why don't we visit the doctor again?'

'I'll think about it.'

'It's cold tonight,' Alex said, 'are you warm enough?'

'I should have put my gloves on.'

'And your scarf and hat.'

'I know, but I don't like wearing woolly hats.'

'Because they might match your brain?'

I laughed. 'I don't think that was called for!'

'Seriously, you will be crying out for that hat as the weather deteriorates. The Norfolk wind is icy. Let's get inside in the warm.'

'Do you fancy wine or hot chocolate?' Alex asked.

'Hot chocolate, please.'

'So that's two of us. Is it because you're cold or because you need comfort?'

'Both, really,' I said. 'What about you?'

'Same…'

'What's wrong?'

'I have this nagging pain in my stomach,' he said. 'Sometimes it eases up, but painkillers don't help much. I suppose I thought something warm might. It's beginning to make me feel decidedly unwell.'

'You need to visit the doctor, too.'

'I thought I'd leave it for a few days and see how it goes,' he said. 'I don't want to make an appointment and find it's gone when I get there.'

'So, you're waiting for it to get worse. That's not a good plan! I'm going to tuck you into bed when I've finished and make you a hot water bottle. No arguments.'

It wasn't only Meadow I was worried about now. I was worried about Alex, too.

I checked on Meadow and then returned to my apartment where Lily and Mark were finishing their homework.

'Mum,' said Mark, 'you know the police spoke to the people who were here when the body was buried?'

'Yes.'

'Well, they've talked to Sally but not Peter. And he knows a lot about it.'

This made me angry. DI Watson was slipping up. Peter knew what he was talking about and should be listened to. I didn't have time for prejudice.

The question about whether I should continue to investigate Ruth Carpenter was answered at that moment. He was questioning for a second time everyone who was around when the body was buried. He should be talking to Peter. I was determined to tell him this when I next saw him.

The days were shortening and, although I had my house in London, I thought of the apartment here as home, nestled amongst trees showing off their beautiful autumnal colouring before dropping their leaves.

I wondered if the beauty of this place, the silence or the smell of freshly cut grass would ever become normal and I would no longer notice them.

Teddy had told me earlier that this was probably the last cut this year. We had gathered the fruit from the trees and Sally had put out a plea for help making pickles this afternoon. Alex and I had both volunteered, although we had to leave early for our breadmaking class in the evening.

Making pickles together was great fun. One of the worktops was full of home-grown vegetables. There were marrows, courgettes, tiny cucumbers, green tomatoes, onions, a huge bowl of eggs and many other healthy ingredients. I soon realised we'd be making chutneys as well as pickled vegetables and eggs.

Peter, wearing his ear defenders to protect himself against the noisy chatter, was given hard-boiled eggs to peel and the rest of us took recipe sheets for our projects.

Will did the onions and didn't cry, but the rest of us did. He was jovial and said that shallots are nowhere near as bad as full-sized onions. The smell of herbs and spices reminded me of the kitchen of my Jamaican friends, Ogden and Wilma.

'What will we do with these when we've filled all those jars?' I asked. 'We can't eat all of them ourselves.'

Alex said, 'We sell them on the market in December, the whole lot usually go. It's a good way to use up end of season vegetables that won't make up a boxful or are too small or damaged for people to buy. None of us likes food waste.'

I had been enjoying myself so much with the pickle makers that I had forgotten about the media meeting that morning until I saw the group of reporters and photographers at the gate as we left.

'Do you think anything came out of that media meeting?' I asked.

'I heard it on Radio Norfolk. Most of it was what we already knew but the police are treating it as a suspicious death,' Alex said.

'It had to be. Why bury her body here if she died naturally? That would make no sense at all. I'm beginning to get really annoyed with DI Watson,' I said. 'He's taken no notice of the information I gave him. I understand they don't have a DNA match, but he hasn't checked whether Ruth Carpenter had met with her probation officer after the day when she died – if she had a probation officer at all, which we don't even know. He hasn't asked for her dental records either and he hasn't asked Peter about the burial, which I suspect he knows something about. I'm thinking of reporting him to his seniors.'

'I wouldn't do that if I were you,' he said. 'You're not the expert. You don't know what he's doing, or why. He might be following totally different leads and complaining could cost him his job. Why not talk to him and tell him what you've just said to me? Don't get angry, though. It rarely does any good.'

As soon as we arrived at the class, the students knew we'd been in the kitchen. Apparently, we stank of onions! Quite a lot of them said that they always bought their Christmas pickles from our market stall and others said they would give us a try this year, rather than buy mass-produced pickles with additives.

During the meal in the pub, we were all happily chatting, apart from Nina, one of the quieter students. I sat beside her while we were waiting for our coffee.

'Is something wrong?' I asked.

She nodded, 'I thought I was going through the menopause, but the doctor told me I'm pregnant. Because of my age, I'm fifty-one, he said there was a chance the baby could have Down's Syndrome. I won't abort it, although I hope my body will. It's not the Down's Syndrome that worries me, it's more that I won't be able to cope with a baby. I have grandchildren and find them too much at times.' She blew her nose. 'And the child might need support all his life and I don't know if I will be well enough, or even be around, to give it. I'll love him or her, and I don't think I could bear to give them up for adoption, although that may be the best for them.'

I held her hand, not knowing what to say. 'I could take it,' I said without thinking.

A look of relief crossed her face, but then she said, 'I don't think I'll be able to let it go once I've held it.' She looked so downcast that I felt helpless to do anything apart from giving her my phone number in case she wanted to talk.

I was cold inside. How could she be in this dilemma at fifty-one, while I couldn't have another child at thirty-seven? Life seemed unfair.

That night, I lay in bed thinking of Ruth Carpenter. Should I continue investigating? It would be much easier to leave it to the police. I decided that if one more baby situation came up, I would continue. If nothing came up, then I would be free to decide what to do.

CHAPTER 7

The following morning DI Watson was on site again and I invited him in for coffee.

He told me there was usually a large number of telephone calls after a media meeting and was downcast that yesterday's had a negligible impact.

'I'm concerned,' I said, 'that you don't seem to be following up on Ruth Carpenter's probation records or getting her dental records.'

'One of my staff is working on the dental records. It was considered that she didn't need a probation officer when she was released,' he said. 'Please don't think I'm not doing my job.'

'I'm sorry, I was wrong to make assumptions,' I said, 'but I'm right in believing you haven't talked to Peter.'

'He has learning difficulties, so it would be difficult for him to remember the incident.'

I banged my fist on the table and stood up. 'He's more intelligent than the two of us put together. Just because he's not neurotypical, doesn't mean he's stupid. I never want to hear that from you again.'

The poor man. I thought he was going to cry. I calmed down and tried another tack.

'Look, how would you feel if we went to see him together?' I asked.

'I'd appreciate that, thank you.'

We walked together to the greenhouse where Peter was digging up the old tomato plants.

'Peter,' I said, 'I think you saw something one night at the top of the site.'

'Which night?'

'About six years ago. Tell us what you saw,' I said.

'A white transit van with two people digging a hole.'

He told us the registration number of the van.

'When was it?' I asked.

'Thirty-first of July, 2016. 2.30am.'

'Were the people men?' DI Watson asked.

'I don't know. It was dark. One had long hair, and one had short hair and both were wearing trousers.'

'Why were you walking about at that time of the night?' I asked.

'When I can't sleep, I go for a walk. It was warm and I was wearing my pyjamas.'

'Is there anything else you remember?' I asked.

'No.'

He turned his back to us and continued working.

We went outside and walked out of earshot.

'Alright,' said DI Watson. 'So, I was wrong about Peter. I'll send this information to the station to be checked out. Ruth used a different name when she came out of prison, which is understandable.'

'Yes,' I said, 'Penelope Brown.'

'You've been doing your research well. Thank you for putting me straight about Peter,' he said. 'You won't take this any further will you?'

'Not at the moment, although I am concerned about your attitude to people different to yourself. I won't say anything without notifying you first.'

'Thank you,' he said and we shook hands.

That evening, I walked with Alex and Mungo in the woods. I looked forward to our time together and couldn't help remembering how lonely London evenings were. Those nights I spent trying to keep Ben's dinner warm until I'd realise that, once again, he wouldn't come in until the early hours of the morning. How could I have accepted his excuse that this was work? It's not as if he was bringing home extra money. I'd still had to struggle to pay the bills and feed the family. We could have done without all of his wasted meals.

I tried to clear him from my mind but the harder I tried the more difficult it became.

I pulled on my winter coat and wellington boots, threw a scarf round my neck and toyed with the idea of wearing a hat. I decided my hood would do, not that it satisfied Alex.

'Where's your hat?' was the first thing he asked when I turned up at his apartment. ' It's not summertime, you know.'

'Why are you so grouchy? Is your stomach playing up again?'

The look on his face said it all.

'You don't have to walk this evening. I could always take Mungo up to the gate and back if you're not up to it.'

At that he doubled up and fell on the floor. I bent down to him and one look at his grey face had me reaching for the phone.

After the 999 call, I telephoned Jazz, who was with us in a couple of minutes.

'Actually, the pain's not as bad now,' Alex said, trying to sit up. 'Don't waste an ambulance. One of you could take me to the hospital.'

'No,' said Jazz. 'You need to go in an ambulance. If you were taken bad on the way, we wouldn't be able to do anything. You need an ambulance.'

'Can you look after Mungo?' he asked Jazz, 'He hasn't been for his walk this evening.'

At that point the ambulance arrived. Jazz told me to go to the hospital with Alex and he would let Meadow know. 'Ring any time if you need collecting,' he said, 'it doesn't matter if it's the middle of the night.'

The paramedics checked him over.

'The pain's nowhere near as bad as it was earlier,' Alex said, 'I don't think I need to go to hospital.'

'You need to be checked out by a doctor,' the paramedic said.

'I'll come in the ambulance with you,' I said. 'We need to get to the bottom of this. Unless you'd prefer me nagging you for the next few weeks.'

'Okay,' he said.

The paramedic continued to monitor him while we waited in the ambulance for a bed to become available.

After Alex had told the doctor how he felt and I added my observations, I was asked to wait the other side of the curtain while he was examined.

'It appears that you have a perforated appendix,' the doctor said. 'We'll give you antibiotics and take you down to surgery as soon as a spot becomes available.'

'I suppose you heard that?' Alex said.

I nodded.

'Look, sweetheart, you need to go home and get some sleep. I love having you with me but there's plenty of people here to look after me. Get your beauty sleep.'

As it wasn't too late, I telephoned Jazz and he collected me.

I had a drink and went to bed, although I didn't sleep much. I couldn't get the picture of Alex's grey face, distorted with pain, out of my mind.

CHAPTER 8

Just two days later, Alex was discharged. I collected him and settled him into his own home, leaving Mungo with Jazz in case he hurt him in his enthusiasm to see his owner again.

DI Watson was waiting for me when we returned. Once I'd helped Alex out of the car, he asked what the problem was and I explained.

He laughed. 'Thought someone had beaten him up. That's the problem with being in the force.'

Over a cup of tea, I asked how things were going.

'I expect that you really want to know about the skeleton.'

I smiled.

'I'm not allowed to tell you, but if you watch the news at lunchtime, you'll find out who she is.'

'So now we know who she is, I suppose we need to know who killed her. Did Peter's information help?' I asked.

'Yes and no. He was correct about what he saw and the date. I can't believe he remembered everything so precisely after such a long time. Even the registration number was correct. The van was stolen that night and reported missing the next morning when the owner needed it for work. It was found burnt out about half a mile from where he lived.'

'And that means no DNA, I assume.'

'Indeed, so now I have to find out who wanted her dead.'

'I thought of the children she'd given up for adoption, but they probably had a better life where they were, so it's unlikely they'd hold it against her. I also thought of the parents of the child she'd killed and the people she was in prison with,' I said.

'You're working on the assumption it was Ruth Carpenter. How did you know her history?'

'Just googled it,' I said. 'Did you know that the father of the baby killed himself after the trial?'

'No, I didn't, but I can see why. Their grief must have been immense.'

'Yes. They conceived after a fourth dose of IVF. That baby was everything to them. The wife found her husband's body,' I said.

'Obviously, I have to tell you that it is unwise to continue investigating. You could cause problems for us and you don't know whose skeleton it is as yet.'

'In exchange for my information, can you tell me how she was killed?'

'Only if you agree that you will tell no one but Alex. I shouldn't be telling you at all, but I'd like to clear this case before I retire. I could lose my job and pension if this information gets out.'

'I promise,' I said.

'Good. This is unprofessional and I don't want the media getting hold of it until we're ready. We get so many false confessions once people find out. She was shot. I don't think I should tell you anything more than that.'

'That was what caused the hole in the skull?'

'We're having a media meeting tomorrow morning, and we'll be giving them the name "Penelope Brown" and her age.'

'I'm wondering why she was buried here and how the van had access to the village,' I said.

'I'll leave you to find that out. At present I'm more concerned about catching her killer.'

I wasn't looking forward to visiting Meadow with the news, but I knew it couldn't wait until the morning. It would be best if I did it immediately. I picked up the photo Ross had given us and went over to her apartment.

'Would you like a smoke?' I asked.

'You're going to tell me something I don't want to know, aren't you?'

'Yes.' I handed her the photograph. 'Do you recognise this person?'

'I hoped I wouldn't have to look at her face again. It's Nicole Hanson.'

'It was her skeleton near the gate.'

'This was my fault. Perhaps if I'd let her stay a bit longer, she would still be alive.'

She pulled a smoke out of her tin and lit it.

'This has nothing to do with you, she was buried over a week after she left here.

'The name the police will be releasing to the public tomorrow is Penelope Brown. Nicole Hanson was a name she'd dreamt up. She changed her name to Penelope Brown after leaving prison.'

'I tried to help her, but she didn't tell me she'd been in prison,' Meadow said. 'What was her name before that?'

'DI Watson asked me not to tell anyone, but it'll come out later.'

'While you're here, Amber wants to take Daniel to a toddlers' group in Honsham. She'll need transport. I said I would ask if you would take her. I know you're having a bit of a bad time with the menopause, but you're the only person I can spare. I could have asked Jazz, but it would be obvious that a fair-haired child with blue eyes was not his child and I don't want anyone assuming they're a couple. Nor do I want her to run there with the buggy, which was what she was going to do. You don't have to go in with them, you could have a coffee or do some shopping.'

'Okay,' I heard myself say, 'I'll sort it out with Amber. Daniel needs to mix with other children.'

She took my hand. 'Thank you.'

I walked out stunned. I couldn't run away from babies and pregnancy any longer. It was time to come to terms with the menopause.

It also meant I would start investigating who killed Ruth Carpenter.

CHAPTER 9

I was still worried about Alex but after a few days he seemed to bounce back. He started complaining of boredom and wandered aimlessly around the Village. He wasn't allowed to drive yet so he walked to the gate to collect the mail with me and then delivered it to the residents' apartments. He also spent time with Meadow who confided in him that she would like to try walking with crutches when she next went for physiotherapy.

'She said she'd been an invalid for too long and wants to get rid of that frame and get back to "proper" work. Thing is, what do you think of her balance?'

'If she feels ready to move on, then it's up to the physios.'

'I was wondering if you might like a ride to the hospital with us,' I added. 'You can't come in with us, but there's no reason why you shouldn't sit in the café and have a hot drink. It'd be a change of scenery for you.'

'Yes, I'd like that. But I've only just come out of the place, so I don't know about change of scenery. I feel useless here, and I've been doing a lot of thinking.'

'Go on.'

'I think, sweetheart, that we need to visit Ross and try to find out about Ruth Carpenter's children, and the situation that

50

led her to put them up for adoption. The only thing is that I can't drive yet, so would you take us?'

I smiled, pleased that he was improving, 'I think I know the way, but you may have to give me directions, okay? You do know DI Watson says that if we were involved, it may impede their investigation.'

'We'll just have to be very careful, sweetheart. And… will you come with me to walk Mungo this evening? I don't like leaving Jazz to do it when he should be relaxing.'

I put my arms around him and our lips met. It had been almost a fortnight since we had last properly kissed.

'Hey,' he said, 'You're getting me excited,' and he kissed me again before we sank down on his sofa.

I looked at Mungo, curled up in his basket. 'He's been so good,' I said, 'I could take him out on my own if you like.'

'That's not the point,' he said, 'I'm missing our walks.'

'Me too.'

I need to ask a favour,' he said. 'I have an appointment at the doctor's on Wednesday afternoon to have my stitches removed. I'll feel a lot more comfortable afterwards, and I wondered…'

'I'll take you,' I said, 'as long as you don't want me in the room when it's done. I've nothing against watching it happening, but it doesn't seem right.'

'I agree,' he said.

'Would you like to ring Ross to sort the visit out, please I feel a bit embarrassed about having that panic attack last time.'

'But you said you'd spoken to him when he rang up to see how you were,' Alex said.

'I have but I'm embarrassed, so I thought I'd leave it to you.'

He raised his eyebrows and smiled.

The following day we were on our way to Holt. I'd never driven Alex anywhere before and I expected him to be a nervous passenger, but he seemed totally relaxed. It was a relief after all the times Ben criticised my driving.

When we'd arrived and were parked, Alex said, 'That was an enjoyable journey. You drive well. Just like a man.'

'That's sexist,' I said and punched him on the shoulder.

'Hey, be careful, I'm delicate! Don't want you to break me…'

'Fat chance of that,' I said. 'You seem to be getting over your operation well.'

'I feel good,' he said. 'I'll be glad when the stitches are out. They're pulling my skin now. Unfortunately, Meadow says I'm not to work for two weeks after I was discharged. I can't see why. If I was in my own home, I wouldn't be sitting around watching daytime television, I'd be doing little things to keep myself busy.'

'I could have a word with her, but I don't think it will do any good. You shouldn't go behind her back. But she is still confined and you could do little jobs without her noticing. Note I said "little", I don't want you lifting before you're allowed. She usually rides around on her scooter after lunch, so be careful then.'

He grinned at me. 'Do you think I can go to breadmaking class? I know that kneading uses a lot of muscles, but I can't see myself damaging myself with that.'

'You could try it. I'm sure someone else will help out if you feel it's too much.'

We knocked at Ross's door.

'Hello. Come in. How are you feeling now?'

'Are you talking to me or Alex?'

'Both, I think. It's chilly outside, would you be happy in the lounge?'

We went into a well-lit room with books lining one complete wall and an open fire blazing on the opposite side. It was warm and comfortable. Ross disappeared to make the tea.

'Do you need any help?' I called out.

'No thanks, just waiting for the kettle to boil.'

Meanwhile Alex was surveying the books. 'You do a lot of varied reading,' he called out.

Ross came in with the tray of teacups and another beautiful cake. 'My reading is eclectic. I'll read anything, but I draw the line at romance and Mills and Boon. They are definitely not my thing.'

'How do you cope with bad language in a book?' I asked, 'Yours have no swearing in them at all.'

'I'm glad you've done your research. Do you think mine are less realistic because I keep them clean?'

I thought for a moment. 'No, I don't.'

He smiled. 'That's good. I heard a lot of offensive language when I was policing, but I don't think people who read crime fiction necessarily need that. If they do, they can change to a different author.'

He poured the tea.

'Is there anything in particular you need to know about Ruth?'

'We think her mother may still be alive,' said Alex. 'We couldn't find any record of her death.'

'You're right. Elsie is in a home in Norwich and I visit her regularly. Her mind is alert, but her body is getting tired.' He sipped his tea. 'I'm glad you asked. I heard about the body and suspected it was Ruth. Elsie is her next of kin, although Ruth considered her dead and always listed me as next of kin. They have been estranged since the babies were adopted. I wondered whether you'd come to see her with me, Jen, and help break the news. I visit her regularly, but it would be good to have a woman with me when I tell her.'

'I'd be happy to do that,' I said, and we fixed a date to meet at the home.

'Was the adoption of the children forced?' Alex asked.

'No, I'd have been sympathetic if it was. Ruth was a woman who only thought about herself and wanted everything perfect. She didn't seem to understand that there were repercussions to her actions. In fact, I don't think she was capable of empathy. She could turn the charm on and say the right words, but underneath she couldn't understand what other people might be feeling.' He helped himself to a slice of cake and passed the rest round.

'She was spoilt by her mother and grandparents when her father died, but I think it was more than that. She was blind to anyone's feelings but her own.' He took another sip of tea. 'Her first baby, a beautiful little girl, had a strawberry birthmark on her scalp. It was hardly noticeable, would likely fade in the next few years, and her hair would have grown over it, but she wouldn't accept a daughter with a birthmark, so she put her up for adoption. Elsie was furious and didn't talk to her again.'

He continued. 'The next child was a son who, she said, had a disability. If she was telling the truth, I assume it would be something like cerebral palsy. She couldn't cope with that either, so put him up for adoption, too. Knowing what she was like I think she did them both a favour. Anyone for a top-up?' He poured the tea.

'Some days later she walked into the maternity department in a white coat and helped herself to a baby boy. When she took him home, he cried as babies do and she shook him. When she found him unresponsive later, she called an ambulance. They managed to keep him alive on the way to hospital, but he died half an hour after he got there.' He sipped his tea. 'She argued in court that she had saved the child's life by getting him to hospital and that his death was the fault of the doctors. She made an act of being upset, but we all knew who had killed the child.'

He put his cup down. 'She was sent to Rampton, where they were hoping to help her. Instead, she made more enemies and came out the same as she went in. The only thing different was that she was in her late fifties and didn't want a baby then.'

'I'm afraid I couldn't get through adoption security to find out anything more about her children. Do you know anything about them?' I asked.

'Only the daughter, I'm afraid. She telephoned one day before Ruth was released and asked me about her. I'd been visiting my stepsister in prison, so I had up-to-date information. My wife and I invited the daughter over for the day.' He paused to take a bite of cake. 'She's a lovely woman, not at all like her mother, except that she's quite beautiful and her looks remind me a lot of Ruth in her younger days. She's kind and is married with three children. The oldest boy is fourteen and the twin girls are twelve. She loves them and seems to have brought them up well. I'm glad you didn't find her online. She'd be in danger if people associated her with Ruth. She's in touch with her brother, but I didn't want to interrogate her,' he said.

'It would be unwise of you to give me her full name, but could you give her my telephone number and explain what we're doing?' I asked.

He smiled. 'Very wise, I'll certainly do that.'

'Does she know that her grandmother is still alive?'

'I don't think so. It didn't come up in conversation and Elsie's not mentioned her,' he said.

'I assume that Elsie doesn't know that her granddaughter has been in touch either,' Alex said.

'You're right, but with their permission it may be possible to unite them. Is there anything else you need to know?'

'Do you think her daughter is capable of murdering Ruth?' I asked.

'I suppose all of us are capable of killing someone if we are pushed hard enough. She's gentle and has been brought up as a Christian. She holds no grudge against her mother even though she knows her story. She was brought up in a happy household with parents who encouraged her to do what made her happy. She went to art college and, apparently, they subsidised her while she was there. She's an intelligent woman, grateful to her parents.' He finished his cake. 'They even allowed her an extra birthday for the day they brought her home. She knew as a little girl that they especially chose her.'

Alex looked at me. 'You're not going to cry on us, are you?'

'No. I was thinking how happy her new parents must have been when she was handed over to them. What a wonderful gift.'

'I think you both need another cup of tea. I'll go and make a pot.' Ross said.

After he'd disappeared into the kitchen, Alex said, 'He's not good with emotions, is he?'

'I think he's just embarrassed. Perhaps his wife wasn't the emotional type.'

We chatted amiably until he returned.

'There's something else I need to ask,' I said. 'Do you know of any friends or enemies Ruth made while she was in prison?'

'I couldn't say about Rampton. I was working full-time, didn't visit her as much as I should have. She was in a single room , but I would imagine she made enemies there, as she did when she was moved to Peterborough Prison'

'Do you have any names?' Alex asked.

'There was Annie Mosley who was released shortly before Ruth. But Annie was inside for fraud, not anything physically violent. Apart from her, I don't have any other names.'

We chatted on for a while and then we left. I was concerned about keeping Alex out too long.

When we pulled into the parking area at the Village, he leant over and gave me a lovely kiss. 'Thank you so much for taking me. I was beginning to get cabin fever.'

'And you thought I hadn't noticed?'

He smiled and got out of the car.

When I went to accompany Meadow to the communal kitchen for supper, she said, 'There's something you need to know. Teddy turned away a man at the gate today. He said that the Village was a crime scene, so the man wasn't allowed in and told him to ring you, should he want to meet you. It was your ex, Ben.'

My legs buckled.

He was the last person I ever wanted to see again.

CHAPTER 10

'**A**re you okay?' I could hear Meadow's voice in the distance.

As I pulled myself back from what I'd just been told, I nodded my head.

'I assume you don't want to see him. Look, Teddy has done the right thing, even if it wasn't quite the truth. He wanted to protect you and to give you some time. He may not have had much schooling, but he is an intelligent and quick-thinking young man.'

'I'll have to tell the children. He's still their father. Lily won't want to meet him, but Mark may. How do you think he found out where we were?' I asked.

Without waiting for a reply, I continued, 'Of course, it's obvious. Mark probably didn't give him the location, but I'm sure he would have described the Village. Ben would have worked it out when the news of a skeleton being found was on the television.'

'If that's the case, he may just be checking that you're all safe.'

'No way. It's only since the divorce that I've realised that anything we did together was what he wanted to do. There's no way he would turn up here because of us. I suspect he's been having another affair and his new wife has chucked him out. If

I'd have realised he was doing that, I'd have done the same, but I was naïve.'

'Will you meet up with him?'

'I'll never get rid of him if I don't. I'll arrange it when he phones,' I said.

'If you need an excuse to get away, you can always use me. I'll even come with you if you want.' She squeezed my hand.

'Thanks.'

The news had hit me hard and I struggled to eat my supper. I didn't want to see Ben again and was annoyed that he thought he could just step into our new lives. I thanked Teddy after lunch, for sending him away.

'It's alright,' he said, 'Lily had talked to me about him and I felt it was wrong to have him in the Village. I suppose he'll keep pestering you if you don't meet him?'

'Yes. I thought I'd got rid of him.'

'Why don't you meet him in the coffee shop in Honsham? I could take you and when he arrives, move to a different table. Like that, if you set a time limit, you could claim that I needed to leave at that time.'

'Oh Teddy, thank you so much. Meadow has offered to come with me, but I think it would be better if you took me. Would you mind?'

'Of course not. Talk to Lily and Mark first and if they want to see him, they can join us after school at the coffee shop. I doubt if Lily ever wants to see him again, though.'

'You're right there but she needs to know he's around. I won't meet him again after tomorrow.'

'That's good. Send him packing and if he keeps bothering you, threaten to get a restraining order against him. He won't want that on his record,' he said.

'Thanks Teddy, you're a good sort.'

As soon as I returned to the apartment, I spoke to the children. Lily reacted as I had expected, from her fiery fourteen-year-old perspective.

'He's already mucked your life up once. I expect he's been having affairs behind Kim's back and she's chucked him out. I don't know why he bothered to marry her in the first place. He knew he can't resist having sex with any pretty woman that he sees. Now he's trying to get back with you, but he'll muck up that relationship again.'

'There's no relationship now between me and him and never will be, Lily. I'm meeting him at the coffee shop in Honsham and will send him on his way afterwards. Teddy's taking me, so the meeting will be short.'

'How about you, Mark?'

'I don't want to see him either, but would you let me handle the phone call? You need to talk to Alex so he knows what's going on. I'll sort everything out with Dad.'

Once again, I was grateful to my placid thirteen-year-old, who could handle people far better than I would ever be able to. I hoped he would never become a sex maniac like his father.

Alex was waiting for me with open arms. I let him hug me and then he kissed me. I knew in that moment that I could never accept Ben back. I just had to explain to Alex what was going on.

'Is something wrong?' he asked.

'I don't know how you could tell, but yes there is. Do you think we can afford to have a glass of wine before we take Mungo out?'

He went into the kitchen and returned with two glasses of white and sat next to me.

'This afternoon when we were out, Ben turned up at the gate. I'm glad we were out; I don't know what I would have said. Anyway, Teddy told him a story and he's gone off and is ringing me this evening. Mark is dealing with the phone call. I don't want to talk to him again, let alone see him, but I know he won't go away until we've met up.'

'So, what are you going to do.'

'Meet up in the coffee shop in Honsham. Teddy offered to take me so that I can cut the meeting whenever I want to.'

'Why didn't you ask me?'

'Because you're not able to drive or stand up for me physically yet. Teddy is streetwise and can handle himself.'

'I'd like to be there. I want to make sure you're alright,' he said.

'But if it was you that took me, he would immediately assume you were my new man and make a fuss. Meadow even offered to come.'

'Would you mind if I asked Teddy to take me, too?'

'I'm afraid Ben might hurt you. You've not long had your stitches out.'

'I think I should be there.'

'I don't think you should.'

'Let's not fall out over Ben. He's done enough damage as it is,' he said. 'I'm not backing down, but let's leave it for now and go for our walk.'

I nodded, we finished our drinks and took Mungo out.

'How do you think our meeting with Ross went, now we've had time to let it sink in?' Alex asked.

'He's a nice bloke, but I'm wondering why he's answering just the questions we ask and not giving us the whole picture.'

'It could be the policeman in him. Confidentiality has probably been drilled into him. He won't refuse to give us the information we ask for, but the rest is out of bounds.'

'I guess you're right,' I said.

'I'm wondering how far you want to go with this,' he said. 'We've found out who she is, but taking the step to find her killer is going to involve us with criminals who could be dangerous. On top of that we'll probably have to talk to the woman whose baby was killed. I know you're going to be hurt emotionally and perhaps physically, too. Are you prepared to risk that?'

'I'm not certain,' I said. 'Can I wait until I have Ben sorted out before I make a decision?'

'Of course. You do know how protective I am of you, don't you?'

I nodded.

'Come here you,' he said, putting his arm around my shoulder and drawing me towards him. As our lips touched, I went weak and was glad of his support.

By the time I arrived back at the apartment, the children were in bed and Mark had left a note. 'Meet in Honsham coffee shop at 11am.'

I wanted to get rid of Ben for good. I thought I had when we divorced, but he wasn't going to let me go that easily. I didn't want to meet up with him, but I had no choice.

I went into the kitchen, took a family-sized bar of chocolate and a packet of chocolate biscuits out of the cupboard. I went to my room, undressed and took my goodies into my en suite. I sat on the floor, ate the biscuits and then started on the chocolate. Tiredness was hitting me and I started to cry. I stood up, leaned over the toilet and stuck my fingers down my throat, only stopping when the taste of chocolate had gone.

I laid in bed afterwards, thinking. I'd not made myself vomit for over a month. It was Ben's fault. I had no control over him. When he was around my whole life was out of control and I reacted badly to it. He had to go. I had to be harsh with him or he would destroy me.

CHAPTER 11

My worries that Alex might find an excuse to come with us to Honsham were unfounded. Teddy opened Meadow's car door for me as if I was a lady.

'You may be my chauffeur this morning, but there's no need to go over the top,' I said.

Teddy replied, 'Sometimes you need to be pampered.'

'Thank you.' My eyes grew hot with tears and I battled to stop them coming. 'I thought my old life was gone, sort of written off. But now that sex maniac is trying to bring it back again.'

'It's hard. Do you still have feelings for him?'

'Not anymore. When he announced that he and Kim were expecting and getting married, I drew a line through my feelings for him. I could be in danger of being quite rude to him.'

'Good for you. Perhaps when we get there, if he's not there, you should sit where you can see the door, so he doesn't creep up on you. I'll choose a seat where you can see me all the time. I'll try not to listen in, unless your voices get too loud,' he said.

'I've decided to stay softly spoken, especially if he starts getting angry.'

'Just call out if you need me.'

When we arrived, the coffee shop was empty, making it easy for Teddy and I to choose our places.

By five past eleven, I'd ordered what I wanted but was getting edgy. If I'd been one of his girlfriends, I bet he wouldn't have been late.

Other people started trickling in. Then I saw him. He looked so old.

He reached out to kiss me but I turned my head away.

'You're late and you're smoking again,' I said.

'Blame it on the nerves.'

Our conversation stopped as the waitress brought him a coffee and my second one.

'So, what does Kim think of you coming to see me?'

'We're not together anymore.'

'You've been having affairs again?'

He nodded. 'But not many.'

I laughed. 'Haven't you realised that one is too many?'

'I suppose so…. but now I don't have anywhere to live. Can I use the house in London?'

'Don't you know that there are tenants in it?'

'Yes. Can you evict them?'

'No.'

'Why not?' he asked.

'Because it's their home and their rent pays the mortgage. It's mine and the children's house and I'll sell it when we need something different. You've no right to it anymore.'

'Can I move in with you?'

'I can't believe you've asked that. No! Anyway what about your job?'

He looked down.

'Don't tell me you've lost it because you were having it off with the boss's wife? Am I right?'

'No. It was his daughter.'

I laughed. 'I can't believe that anyone could be so stupid. You'll have to get yourself another job and rent a bedsit until you can afford something better.'

'You've changed. Can I move in with you? Please?'

'No. I want you to out of my life. Is that all you've come to see me for – cheap digs?' I stood up and so did he, but he came towards me and I thought he was about to kiss me. My right hand flew up and hit him across the cheek. He staggered and fell. Everyone was watching.

I looked at the waitress and said, 'He's paying,' then left with Teddy.

We'd hardly left the shop before Teddy started laughing. 'You've got a strong right hand there.'

I smiled. 'It hurts.'

When we arrived back at the Village, Teddy looked at me. 'How's the hand now?'

'Good for a few more slaps,' I said.

Alex came out and asked how it went. Teddy grinned, 'You'd better go inside and tell him.'

As soon as we were inside, Alex kissed me and I responded willingly. 'It seems you have no feelings for him now,' he said.

'I'm afraid I had to use my right hand.'

'Did it hurt?'

'It did, but more for him than me.'

He took my hand and moved each of my fingers, then kissed it.

'Does that feel better?'

I smiled as a bolt of electricity passed through me. He pulled me closer and kissed me again.

When we drew apart, I said, 'I could do with a hot drink.'

As we walked towards the kitchen, he replied, 'Perhaps a cold shower would be more appropriate.'

We settled on the sofa with our drinks and Alex put his arm around me. 'How are you feeling now about your meeting with Ben? Or would you prefer to talk about it this evening?'

'I still loved him when I saw him, but more in a motherly sort of way. I wanted to protect him as I do the children, although I realise now that the feeling isn't mutual. I vaguely wondered if he had come to see how we were doing, but all he wanted was the house in London.' I looked into Alex's eyes, 'I'm concerned he may stop the children's maintenance payments now he's on the dole, but he should be able to get work easily enough. Car mechanics, even those who have sex with their boss's daughter, are in demand.'

'And how were you last night when you went back to the apartment?'

I looked down as a lump formed in my throat.

'Chocolate and biscuits?' he asked.

I nodded.

He put his arm around my shoulders. 'It doesn't surprise me at all. It came out of the blue and you didn't know what would happen today. I think we should treat it as a blip.' He passed me a tissue.

I surprised myself by saying, 'I know that I feel protective towards him and that that could be seen as love, but I don't like him anymore. I've made that clear to him and he won't be back.'

'Are you certain?'

'I humiliated him in front of the customers and staff in the coffee shop. He's too proud to come back. We're finished.'

Alex smiled.

When I collected Meadow for lunch, she didn't move from her chair. I asked her what was wrong and she said she wouldn't go until I told her how it went with Ben.

'I had to use my right hand,' I said.

'And did it work?'

'I think so. He was on the floor when I left.'

'I wish I'd been there,' she replied.

That evening I had a telephone call from Claire, Ruth's biological daughter. We chatted for a while and I asked what her life had been like with adopted parents.

'Great. It was good to know that they hadn't taken me on by default, but they'd chosen me. When I was three, they took me to play with a little girl called Rosie and then asked me if I would like Rosie to be my sister. Rosie and I shared everything and we still do. She's just a few months older than me. Our parents sent us to the best school and gave us everything we needed. I went to art college and Rosie trained to be a chef.'

'Did you ever get to meet your natural mother?'

'Just once. When she was thrown out from Honsham Forest Village, she rang Ross, asking him to send a taxi to collect her. I went instead of a taxi, but didn't tell her who I was. She thought I was taking her back to Holt, but Ross wouldn't have her there, so I dropped her at the housing department in Dereham. When she complained, I said that this was the instruction I was given.' She laughed.

'She'd moaned and complained all the way there. She thought she was better than everyone else and the world owed her. When she asked how much the journey was, I said there was no charge for ex-convicts. She looked daggers at me, so I told her that I was glad she had me adopted as I didn't want to grow up with the attitude she had. When I drove away and looked in the rear mirror, she was still standing on the street with her suitcase. I can't help feeling I had a much better life than I would have had with her, if I'd had any life at all.'

I couldn't help laughing at the scene she had described.

She told me that she was in contact with her brother and he was adopted by a professional couple. They always told him how precious he was to them and they paid all his university expenses.

I felt so much better after that conversation. Ruth had given them up because she didn't see them as perfect, yet they both ended up with special parents and had good lives.

The question that stood out in my mind though was whether I wanted to investigate the case further. Did I want to meet the hurt and angry people who were associated with her death?

CHAPTER 12

Alex and I discussed the case later. I thought Ruth's attacker needed to be brought to justice. I also thought that every murder victim should be entitled to a decent investigation, irrespective of the life they'd led. I didn't feel Ruth was getting that.

The problem was that DI Watson would give me no information, so I didn't know whether he had any useful evidence. So far, all we knew was that she was shot.

I decided that I would speak to him the following day. I wanted to know what he was looking at and thought I may be able to trade some information with him.

The following morning was Daniel's first day at the playgroup and I thought it would be as difficult for me as it was for him.

It turned out that he didn't find it difficult at all. We arrived at the hall where a lady at the desk was booking people in. Daniel looked around, saw the other children and his legs pounded, he wanted to be with them. Amber gave her own and Daniel's details and then the lady said, 'We have to take grandmother's details as well.' Before I had a chance to say anything, Amber was telling her.

'How lovely that you live so close, you must be a great help to Amber and Daniel.'

'She's wonderful,' Amber said.

We sat down in the circle with the others and I said, 'I thought I was just the taxi service.'

'Today you are Grandma,' she said.

Because we were new, we were welcomed when the activity started and they sang a special welcome to Daniel. He was rather surprised by the singing as Amber had already told me they didn't sing together, mainly because she wasn't sung to by her foster parents so she didn't know many songs. They sang a few which were mainly action songs.

'Will you be able to remember the words and the tunes?' I asked.

'I don't think so. Do you think Jazz will know them?'

'I'm sure he will with seven younger brothers and sisters.'

'I think I'll get him to teach them to me.'

An appeal went out for people to make tea and coffee, and I went into the kitchen with the lady who was sitting beside me.

She introduced herself as Prue. 'I come as my daughter had two little ones and it's difficult for her to get them in and out of the car on her own. She pointed her daughter out.

'She was sixteen when she had a stroke and she's weak down her left side. I didn't think she'd even get married after that, let alone give me grandchildren. Her husband is the kindest and most helpful man I have ever met, he took no notice of her limited mobility, saying that it emphasised what a beautiful person she is inside.'

'It's not often that a young man will overlook the disability and see the real person. It makes me feel like crying,' I said.

'Well, if you're going to do that, don't get tears in the cups.' We both laughed.

After we'd washed up, I noticed that Daniel and another baby were playing with the toy lorries and Amber was talking to his mother.

'I'm so glad that Daniel's mixing well,' I said to my new friend Prue. 'We live at the Forest Village and he hasn't met many other children.'

'Why don't you join us for lunch one day? He can play with my grandchildren.'

'I need to confess,' I said. 'I'm not actually Daniel's grandmother. I'm really just the taxi, but Amber treats me as her mother.'

'Does she have no parents?'

'Not as far we know. She was brought up in care and hasn't expressed any interest in finding her parents. Daniel's father was on drugs and is in prison. She arrived at the village, having been beaten up by him.'

'That's terrible. She'll gradually get to know the other mothers. Some of them are staying at the local women's refuge. She'll identify with them. But you're still welcome to visit for lunch or tea.'

On the way home, Amber said, 'Daniel loves being with the other children. Some of the mums invited me to coffee with them. Do you think Meadow would let me ask them back?'

'I've no idea. It's best if you ask her. She always says that this is your home and expects you to treat it like that. So, I don't think she'd worry as long as there weren't hordes of children running all over the place.'

'I hope you didn't mind me letting them think you're Daniel's grandmother? Just seemed much easier than trying to tell them about the set-up here, and I ain't got no one else he can call Granny'

I smiled. 'That's okay, although I told one of the real grandmothers that I was a fake.'

She looked at me. 'I don't think they even believed me in the first place. You don't look much older than me.'

I didn't reply but felt happy inside.

That afternoon I offered DI Watson tea and cake. When I asked him how he was, he said he had resigned and would be leaving the force at Christmas. It was time he retired.

He brightened up. 'We've decided to spend Christmas with my son and his wife and children. It will be the first time that we've been away for Christmas. I haven't done it before because work problems arise at that time of the year and there was always the chance that I may be called in.'

'It sounds to me as if you were over-conscientious.'

'Maybe. But you've no idea what it feels like to know that I'll be untied after thirty-five years.'

'Will you clear this case before you leave?' I asked.

'I don't think so. I'm not getting far with it.'

'How would you feel about sharing information?'

'Do you have something that may help?'

'Possibly. But before I give it to you, I would like more details about Ruth's death.'

I held out my hand. He didn't respond. 'This would be against all the rules.'

'But do you want to leave on a failure?'

'Please, don't let anyone know what I tell you. Can I trust you?'

'Yes, I promise.'

'What do you want to know?' he asked.

'Was she fully clothed when she was found?'

'Yes.'

'Was there just one gunshot wound?'

'Probably.'

'Any other injuries?'

'Maybe to the face. It's difficult to say. Anything else?'

'No, I think that's all.'

Then I gave him information about Ross.

'We've already been to see him,' he replied. 'He said he didn't know Nicole Hanson.'

'That's because it was an alias. I asked him if he knew anyone who stayed here, and he told me it was his stepsister, Ruth Carpenter.'

'I think I was too dozy to ask any more questions,' he said. 'Ross gave me tea and cake and I was struggling to stay awake. I'd not been sleeping well and it seemed to be catching up with me. On the way back, I pulled into a layby and slept for two hours.'

'That doesn't sound good. Did you get back safely?'

'I did, but it was then that I started re-evaluating what I was doing. I'm not certain I was safe to be driving. I'll have to be more careful.'

Later in the afternoon, Alex and I left for our breadmaking class. It was the first time that Alex had driven since his operation.

We were making tea cakes. Once the dough was proving we went out to the pub for a meal.

We were enjoying each other's company and I was glad to see that Nina was in good spirits, too. After the main course, I popped into the ladies. Someone was whimpering in the cubicle beside mine.

'Are you alright in there?'

'I'm bleeding.' I recognised Nina's voice.

'Is it the baby?'

'I can't lose it. I want it so much.'

'Can you unlock the door? I'll call an ambulance.'

I heard the lock move and dialled 999.

'Is there anyone we can call for you?'

'My husband,' she cried. 'But I've got the car. He can't get to me without a car.'

'Try to stay calm. Where are the keys?'

'In my bag.'

'I'll ask Alex to send one of the women in with it and he'll sort things out.'

'Can you hold my hand, please?' she asked. 'I'm so frightened. Don't leave me.'

'I won't.'

Hardly any time passed before the ambulance arrived. I stood back to let the paramedics deal with Nina.

'Jen, will you come to the hospital with me?'

'You don't think I'd leave you at a time like this, do you?' She looked relieved.

I went to collect our coats and my bag.

'You okay?' Alex asked.

'I'm fine. Not sure about Nina. I'm going to the hospital with her. Will you pick me up later?'

'Just ring. Hopefully her husband will be there soon. I've spoken to him and said we'll be back with his car in a few minutes. When I talked to him, I felt like I was interrupting something, but maybe he was just worried about Nina.'

'I don't want her to lose this baby. I know how much it means to her.'

Alex pecked me on the cheek, 'That's my girl.'

As it turned out, I was with Nina at the hospital for at least an hour before her husband turned up. By that time, she had been scanned and we both heard the baby's heart beating. It was a relief, but they had to admit her to stop the bleeding.

When her husband turned up, he said, 'What's wrong with you this time?'

'What do you mean? I'm pregnant and I started bleeding. I thought I was losing the baby.'

'I told you, you're not pregnant. Will you be home tonight?'

'They're admitting me. I'll have to stay in overnight.'

'What a lot of fuss over a little blood,' he said.

Nina started to cry silently.

'Aren't you at all worried about Nina and the baby?' I asked. 'I'm a first aider. I'm the one who called the ambulance. I know how dangerous this can be for both of them. She's made no fuss at all, and until tonight Alex and I were the only people in the class that knew. She's been brilliant this evening and not complained once. I only found out because we both happened to be in the ladies at the same time.'

'I don't want Nina to be sick, it's so inconvenient, so yes I worry about her,' he said.

'What about the baby?' I asked.

'She's not pregnant. She's been acting so strangely over the past few months, I thought she was imagining it.'

'There is a baby,' she said.

'I've heard its heartbeat, too,' I said. 'She was probably acting differently because her hormones were all over the place.'

He looked shocked. 'Are you sure?'

'They would hardly keep her in here for a period, would they?'

He looked at me, then jumped up and hugged Nina.

'Were you like this when you had the other two?'

'Yes. I thought it was the menopause at first, so I went to see the doctor and she said I was pregnant.' She looked at her husband. 'How will you feel if the child isn't perfect?'

He took her hand. 'Whatever is wrong with it, it will be perfect in my eyes.'

I was ready to slope off but a nurse came in and said they had found her a bed.

'I think it's time I left,' I said.

'Thank you for everything,' she said, 'I probably won't make the class next week, but I plan to come back as soon as I'm well enough.'

We left three batches of teacakes in the communal kitchen that evening, to be toasted for breakfast.

'Do you fancy a drink?' Alex asked when we arrived back.

'I've got the shakes now,' I said. 'This always seems to happen after I've helped in a crisis. I'm confident and in control at the time, but I feel like I'm falling apart now.'

'I'm going to make you a hot chocolate and I'll let you try one of my homemade shortbreads. You need the sugar.'

'Did *you* make them?'

'Yes. I was so bored when I wasn't allowed to work, so I looked up a recipe and borrowed the ingredients from the kitchen. They taste good to me, what do you think? '

'I didn't know you could cook.'

'I'm a man of surprises. You've a lot to learn about me as yet.'

We snuggled together on his sofa, munching on shortbreads and drinking hot chocolate.

'These are really good,' I said.

'Have you heard about the Secret Santa that we do here for Christmas?'

'No. Tell me.'

'Rather than trying to buy presents for everyone at the Village we draw a name out of the hat and we can spend up to ten pounds on a present for that person. We're encouraged to use our skills and make something if we can, but the same limit applies, ten pounds on ingredients or craft materials.' He took another bite from his shortbread. 'Obviously, if we're cooking, we don't each have to buy herbs and spices. We can take small quantities of, say ginger, from the kitchen. Then we open the gifts one by one on Christmas Day. You, Lily and Mark will be included this Christmas and anyone staying over for the holiday.'

'Can we still give special gifts to the people we are close to?' I asked.

'Of course, if we want to, but it means that we don't have to buy something for everyone.'

'Sounds a good idea,' I said, 'How soon will we get the names?'

'Usually the start of November, so we have plenty of time to prepare. And you have to remember the 'secret' part. We're not supposed to tell anyone which name we draw out, unless we need help or advice.'

'What made you think of Secret Santa?' I asked.

'Well, I thought I'd start practising in case I want to cook for someone. If I get anyone that I can't think of what I can do, food is always good.'

'I've always wanted to make sweets, but I've never tried. Could you help me with it one afternoon or Sunday morning, please?'

'Sure. You may need to borrow a sugar thermometer from the kitchen, but that wouldn't be a problem. But when you get the name, you may decide on something completely different. It might be one of your children.'

'That would be a real challenge, what could I possibly make for them? What happens if we draw our own name? Do we put it back in and choose another?'

He nodded.

'I need to ask you something serious though,' he said. 'Do you think you'll have a bulimic attack after helping Nina this evening?'

'No. They were both so happy that the baby was still alive and, surprisingly, so was I. Do you know, her husband thought that Nina was imagining it?' I asked.

'It was strange, when I gave him his car key, he asked if he should go to the hospital. I couldn't understand why he asked. That makes sense if he thought it was all in her head and she was making a fuss about nothing.'

'I'm afraid I had to be quite firm with him. I heard the baby's heartbeat.'

'That must have brought back some memories.'

'Yes. But they were good memories. I'm not going to have a problem tonight. Don't worry about that, but I wouldn't mind another shortbread. I missed my dessert.'

'And I paid for both your and Nina's main courses and drinks, so that's something else you don't have to worry about.'

'Thank you. That was kind of you. Can I repay you for mine?'

'Of course not. Enjoy your shortbread.'

CHAPTER 13

A ringing sound woke me. At first, I thought it was my alarm, but it was pitch dark. It was Meadow's emergency call. I grabbed a pair of boots and was still pulling on my dressing gown as I ran across the patio. I banged on Alex's door and shouted through his partly closed bedroom window, 'Meadow's rung her bell.'

I let myself into her apartment and found her on the floor halfway between the bathroom and the hall.

'Are you hurt?'

'Ow,' followed by a stream of expletives.

'Do you need an ambulance?'

'I need to get off the floor first.'

I heard Alex calling Jazz for back-up.

'Can you remember what happened?' I asked.

'I fell over the bathroom rug. My leg wasn't strong enough to take the sudden pressure. I grabbed the edge of the door, but that moved and I hit the ground with my bad knee.'

Jazz bent down beside her. He asked her what had happened and she replied, 'I'm not a parrot.' So, I filled him in.

'Will it hurt you if we move you or would you rather wait for the ambulance?'

'It hurts like hell at the moment. It might feel better if it wasn't crumpled under me.'

Alex and Jazz lifted her up between them and sat her on a chair.

'Grip my hands,' said Jazz, which she did. 'Now smile at me.'

'I don't feel like smiling,' she complained.

'I just need to see both sides of your mouth working. That's better. How's the knee feeling?'

'It's better than it was on the floor.'

'Can you straighten it for me?' She started to do so and then yelled out in pain. Jazz looked at Alex and nodded. He was already dialling 999.

When the ambulance arrived, one of the paramedics dealt with Meadow and the other asked me, 'How's your friend?'

'The baby's okay, but they've kept her in because of the bleeding.'

'I'm glad about the baby.'

'So am I. At fifty-one she's not likely to get another chance.'

Then his colleague sent him to get the trolley and a leg splint. I could see that getting Meadow on the trolley would be painful. It was almost as if she had saved her best swear words for a time like this and she let us have them all.

'Do you want someone to come with you?'

'Jen, would you?'

As I was getting dressed, I wondered when my trips to hospital would slow down. I had accompanied people there so many times in the past few months that the nurses would wonder if I was some sort of curse on those around me. To be honest, I was wondering the same.

When I got back to the ambulance it was obvious Meadow had been crying. I held her hand.

'Are you in pain?'

'Yes, but these kind gentlemen have given me something for it. It will start to work soon.'

'Where were your crutches when you fell?' I asked. I already knew, but she had to answer for herself.

'Beside the bed.'

'You admit it then. I'm not going to say anything except that I thought you knew better.'

I turned to the ambulance man, 'Should I get her crutches?'

'You didn't say that you used crutches,' he said to Meadow. She said nothing. There were no excuses to offer.

At the hospital, she was immediately sent for an x-ray. I could see how swollen the knee was and was worried she'd inflicted more damage on it.

I held her hand while we waited for the results to come back.

'Sorry I upset your sleep.'

'Don't worry about that,' I said. 'I've been here already this evening with a student from our breadmaking class.'

'Is she okay?'

'The baby's okay, but they're keeping her in.'

I explained what had happened. 'That must have been hard for you,' she said.

'Not really. I'd got used to the idea of her being pregnant, though that took a while. I'm not envious of her at all. All this stuff with Penelope Brown has been harder.'

'Are you planning to continue investigating, or will you stop, now you've identified her?' she asked.

'I believe that no matter what a person has done they deserve the same level of investigation into their murder. At the moment she's not getting that.'

'What did she do? You haven't said.'

'You told me you didn't want to know.'

'I did,' she said, 'but I agree she deserves as much investigation into her case as anyone else. Have you considered the possibility that whoever killed her will be hostile to you investigating? You have no authority and could put yourself in danger. You have to consider your children, you're the only parent they have.'

'I know.'

'Will you think about it for me?'

At that point, the doctor came in and said that she'd not broken any bones, but they would like to keep her in overnight and book her in for a scan the next morning.

She dismissed me and I left to phone for a taxi home.

After breakfast I went with Alex to his apartment to chat about our investigation. Since Meadow had expressed her opinion, I was having second thoughts. She was worried about my children having no mother if things went wrong, but I was considering the possibility that the killer might try to get at my children.

The telephone rang. It was Meadow, ready to come home. Her knee was still swollen and painful, apparently, but the scan showed nothing abnormal and she could bend and straighten the knee without the excruciating pain she had during the night. It seemed to be just bruising. I was relieved, but knew I'd have to keep an eye on her until she was back to her normal level of mobility. I thought about Elsie who didn't know her daughter was dead yet, and decided that I would go with Ross to tell her the following morning.

Meadow was waiting for us when Alex and I arrived and I was glad to see that she stood up with the help of her crutches. Walking was a bit of an issue as she was still having trouble putting much weight on her leg, but she was much better than I expected.

The first thing she said to me was, 'I'm desperate for a smoke.' I smiled. The world could collapse around her and she'd still be asking for her cannabis.

'You'll have to wait till we get home,' I said, 'It's not like I carry it with me. Can you imagine if we get stopped by the police? They'd smell it as soon as we opened the windows.'

'Spoilsport,' she said, pouting. 'I wonder how long it will be before I can drive again. I need to be independent.'

'We understand that,' said Alex, 'but until you can do an emergency stop without your knee hurting, I don't think it will be legal. Why don't you ask the physios when you next see them?'

'I'll need to start my Christmas shopping soon. I have to do that alone.'

'Well, there's no way you can manage carrier bags. Have you thought of that? I asked. 'Would you like me to get you a bag that goes across your body?'

'Good idea, but I was thinking of using my walker. I can sit down if I need to and there's a bag under the seat for shopping.'

'Would you be able to get it in and out of the car?' asked Alex.

'With practice, I could.'

At least she was looking forward. I had wondered if this fall might have sent her into depression, but she seemed buoyant.

That evening I talked to the children about the investigation. I told them everything I knew about Ruth. Lily seemed angry, but Mark just listened.

'How do you feel about working on the side of a baby killer Mum?' he asked. I told him I wasn't sure but explained to him that I thought she still deserved a full investigation into her murder.

'I agree with you,' said Lily. Whoever killed her needs punishment or psychological help, and I think it's probably the latter. She wasn't a nice person, but that doesn't mean she deserved to be murdered. '

'What about you, Mark?'

'If it was my mother, I'd want to know who did it and why. But what about you Mum? You can't have any more children. She's done some awful things to hers. You'd never do that to a baby. But you're strong, I guess, and fair. Murderers can't just roam around, not getting caught. It's up to you, but I'd go with your gut feelings.'

Once again, I was surprised at the maturity of my thirteen-year-old son. 'You're right. I think I know what I have to do,' I said, 'but I'm going to see her mother tomorrow morning. I'll make my final decision after that.'

CHAPTER 14

The following morning Alex entered the postcode of the nursing home into his phone, set the GPS and handed it to me. I made good time and waited in the car until Ross arrived.

We passed pleasantries and I admitted that I was nervous. I was relieved to find out that he was too, even after all his training and times that he had given bad news as a policeman.

'It doesn't get any easier,' he said and I could easily believe it.

Elsie smiled brightly as we arrived. Her room smelled fresh and clean, unlike the smell of urine that permeated the hall. She was thin but immaculately dressed and had a poetry anthology with a bookmark sitting on the table beside her. Ross went over, held both her hands and kissed her on the cheek. Then he introduced me as his friend.

'It's no good you giving me that look,' he said, 'It's not like that!' We talked about the weather and the news until a member of staff brought us some coffee.

'Elsie, we've some news to give you, and I'm afraid it's not good,' he began. 'Ruth is dead.'

The old lady gasped. 'My poor baby! 'How? What happened?'

'Someone killed her.'

I watched her face for reaction. To my surprise, I couldn't see any. 'I expect she'd said or done something to upset them. Typical Ruth! Always angry as a child. Don't suppose that changed much.' She gave a light shrug. 'Do you know who it was, then? Why they did it?' she asked.

'That's what Jen is trying to find out.'

'I mean the police,' she retorted. 'What are they doing?'

'Progress is always slow at the start of an investigation,' said Ross.

It seemed that the news we had given her had finally become real to her and she took a tissue from a box on the table.

I went over, kneeled in front of her and held her hand. 'I'm so sorry,' I said.

'I suppose it was unrealistic,' she said, 'to think she might change and visit me. I've not seen her for forty years. You know, I just couldn't forgive her for putting those two beautiful babies up for adoption!' She blew her nose. 'By the time I'd understood she was sick, she was in prison. I was told it was a secure hospital. That she was a patient, not a prisoner. Until she was transferred to Peterborough…. I tried visiting her once, but she refused to see me. Perhaps you can imagine how much that hurt me?'

'Was she your only child?' I asked, gently.

'Yes, but Ross here has become a son to me, he's a lovely boy. Ruth was always a strange child,' she said. 'No one ever laid a hand on her, but even before her father died, she was punishing her dolls. She would break them if she thought they weren't doing what she told them.' She took a sip of her coffee and put the cup back down again. 'I was always finding pieces of dolls in the house and the garden. She never cuddled them or kissed them goodnight like most children did. That's not normal, is it?'

We talked some more, until she started getting tired. As we were leaving, she said, 'Will you let me know when the funeral is? I'd like to be there if I'm able.' We assured her we would, and made sure the nursing home knew the news we'd brought, so she wouldn't bear it alone.

On the car park, Ross thanked me for coming. 'I know I've been trained but I still find it emotionally harrowing telling them a loved one has died. Never know quite what to say or do. So… thank you.'

'Elsie is lovely,' I said. 'Are you her only visitor?'

'She's never mentioned anyone else.'

'Looking at the other patients, she must be finding it hard,' I said. 'They all seem past the point of talking sensibly and she's so bright and communicative.'

He nodded. 'See you and Alex again soon, I hope.'

'That would be great.'

As I drove home, I thought how good Ross was with Elsie and how kind.

I stopped at the supermarket in Honsham on the way, keen to find out whether it stocked the ingredients I would need for making sweets. I wandered around and collected a few items then queued for the till. It wasn't until I was ready to pack them into my shopping bag that I saw the bar of dark chocolate and tin of condensed milk already there. With trembling hands, I added them to the conveyor belt with the rest.

I was shocked. All these years, I had never put anything into my bag without paying for it. What was worse was that I couldn't remember doing so. I could have been arrested for stealing! How ridiculous when I had plenty of money in my purse. What was happening to me?

I threw my bag into the boot and drove off. I remember seeing something on one of the soaps where a menopausal woman was stealing and she got away with it on medical grounds. I had to get this sorted out. Perhaps the tablets I was taking weren't working.

Alex was busy in his workshop when I arrived home, so it was Meadow that I told about what had happened.

'You need to telephone the doctor now, my dear,' she said. 'I know how honest you are. This is totally out of character. Use my phone.'

I made an appointment for the following morning.

'This has really upset me,' I said. 'If I hadn't noticed those things, a security officer could have put his hand on my shoulder, taken me to his office and called the police. I'm not a criminal. I would never do anything like that.' I could feel my eyes getting hot. 'It wasn't as if I'd put it in the wrong basket, I was using a trolley and there's no way I could mistake my bag for the trolley. Even when I was short of money, I didn't even think about stealing to feed the children.'

Meadow took hold of my hand. 'I know, and I believe you, my dear. Being menopausal can mess with your head. You say you still feel confused and forgetful and now this has happened, which shows it's not all in your imagination. You're probably not on the right tablets for you. You must tell the doctor everything so it's on your records in case it happens again. I'm certain there's something that can be done.'

'But the tablets work so well on the hot flushes,' I said.

'Menopause is much more than hot flushes, my dear. Most people don't find that out until it happens to them and there's certainly not enough in the media about it. When you see the doctor, ask her if she has any leaflets or anything. Look online and try the library to see if there are books about it. Take Alex with you if you need to.'

'Thanks. I'll do that. I don't think I can trust myself right now.'

Alex noticed that I was struggling at lunchtime and invited me back to his apartment to talk. The moment I got through the door, I burst into tears. He led me to the sofa and sat me down. Mungo came over and licked my face, then laid on my feet.

'He knows I'm upset, doesn't he?'

'Are those tears for Elsie?' he asked.

I shook my head. 'I feel so bad. I've been with an elderly woman who is facing one of the worst days of her life and I'm crying about me.'

'Why not start at the beginning and I'll listen.'

So I told him about Ross and Elsie and how he was kind and caring as he broke the news to her; how she wanted to come to Ruth's funeral, and I'd been wondering who would sort it out.

Then, taking a deep breath, I told him about the way I almost stole from the supermarket. My tears wouldn't stop.

'Why didn't you come to me as soon as you got back?'

'You were busy and I didn't want to disturb you.'

'So, you sat and worried?'

'No. I talked to Meadow about it.'

'Good. Look, I don't want to speak out of turn but… did she think it might be anything to do with the menopause?

'She did, actually, but how did you know that?'

'I read about it after my wife died.'

'I've made an appointment at the doctors for tomorrow morning.'

'I'll take you. Afterwards, we'll go back into the supermarket together,' he said.

'Would we have time to go to the library, too? Meadow suggested I do some reading about it.'

'That's a good idea,' he said.

'I'm so glad I have people to confide in. If I was living in London with no one to talk to, I'd be totally lost.'

'Perhaps it would help you to write down how it's affecting you. You never know, that may help someone else in the future.'

'I've been worrying,' I said. 'I inherited my early menopause from my mother's side of the family. I'm worried that Lily may get the same thing from me. She's working towards a career and she may leave it too late to have children. She knows about it, but somehow I don't think she will anticipate it.'

'I don't think you're giving her sufficient credit. She's a clever girl and will work it out for herself. Anyway, when this is all over you may decide to publish your notes and could give her a copy,' he said.

I wasn't so certain.

'Are you likely to punish yourself today?' he asked seriously.

'You mean chocolate and biscuits?'

He nodded.

'I don't know. It feels as if my life is out of control.'

'In that case, you can help me this afternoon. I was going to ask Teddy, but you'll do.'

'What do you mean by that?'

'Well, Teddy wouldn't keep stopping me for a kiss, like you will,' and he pulled me close and kissed me.

And then he did it again.

As soon as I had got my breath back, I said, 'I'm not certain that Teddy would appreciate your kisses anyway.'

We left his apartment hand-in-hand.

We passed a pleasant afternoon and, by suppertime, the rawness of the morning had passed.

CHAPTER 15

The following morning at breakfast in the communal kitchen, Meadow announced that there was a gentleman called Stuart joining us that afternoon. He'd stayed before, possibly four or five years ago. Alex and I were to check the apartment next to mine to ensure that it was suitable for a wheelchair user. According to Sally, I'd like having Stuart as a neighbour; he was a kind and considerate man and clever, too.

Alex and I sorted his apartment before we left for Honsham. I gave it a quick dust and made the bed while Alex moved the furniture and arranged shelves to help accessibility. We put in clean towels and stocked the cupboards up. I was grateful to Meadow for giving me something to take my mind off the doctor's appointment. I really wasn't looking forward to it at all.

'Come through, Jen.' Alex gave my hand a squeeze and I followed the doctor to her room.

'How can I help you today?'

'The menopause tablets I'm taking seem to be working well with the hot flushes but I feel confused and disorientated a lot of the time. My head feels as if it's full of cotton wool. And yesterday,' I felt hot tears spill from my eyes. 'And yesterday... I was shopping and put some of my items into my bag instead of the trolley. I don't even remember doing it. I just seem to feel out of it all the time.'

She handed me a box of tissues. 'Is anything else worrying you?'

'I'm trying to cope with knowing I won't have any more children. Sometimes I handle it well. Sometimes I think I'm handling it well,' the tears came again, 'but my brain is so clogged up, I don't really know what I think or feel.'

She laid her hand on mine.

'Jen, this isn't unusual. Sometimes we need to adjust the treatment to suit you. I'd like you to have another blood test. I'll see you in a week.'

I looked at her. 'Are you sure it won't stay as bad as this?'

'I am. I think you would benefit from counselling but I don't think you're in the right place to take it at the moment.'

'Alex and I are already having counselling through the church but I get so confused in the sessions that I don't think it's working with me.'

'Don't expect too much from yourself at the moment. I promise you can and will feel better when we sort out the medication. If you need me before next week, phone reception and I will get back to you.'

'Thank you.'

'Do you think how I'm feeling is caused by the menopause? If so, do you have any leaflets about it?'

'Yes, to both questions. But we can't really tell without blood tests. If you go back to the waiting room, the nurse will call you in shortly and give you a blood test. I'll ring you as soon as I have the results. Is there anything else I can help you with?'

'No, thank you.'

She gave me some leaflets about menopause.

Alex, put his arm around me when I emerged from the blood test. 'Do you feel like going to the supermarket?'

In the baking aisle, we collected up some basic biscuit ingredients.

'Have we got everything?' I asked.

'More than I think I need, but I'm not worried about that.'

'These must be some special biscuits,' I said, 'with all these ingredients in them.'

'I thought I'd do a hamper for each of my girls and one for my in-laws. I usually give the girls money, so these will be extras.'

'You haven't bought anything to wrap them in.'

'There's no rush, it's still only October, so the practice ones will go in my biscuit tin, and probably some in yours, too.'

'That's nice. Do you go to Sheffield at Christmas?'

'No, I usually go a couple of weekends before then and we have an early Christmas there.'

'That sounds lovely,' I said.

'Now before we go to the checkout, would you like to check you've not put anything in your bag?'

I looked inside my bag and smiled, 'All clear.'

On the way home I asked Alex why someone would withhold their telephone number. I had been wondering why Claire hadn't offered hers. I didn't ask her for it but dialled 1471 after she phoned and got a number withheld message. I could kick myself for not asking.

He suggested that she may have been using her work phone which was automatically withheld. Why hadn't I thought of that? More evidence of my fuzzy brain, no doubt.

That afternoon Alex and I both went outside when Stuart's van arrived in the parking area. Stuart opened the driver's door at the same time as the side door opened automatically. A small crane inside lifted out a wheelchair and set it down beside the driver's door. The crane then retracted and the side door shut itself.

Stuart easily transferred to the wheelchair.

'Wow!' said Alex, 'that's a fine piece of equipment.'

'Thanks. I designed most of it myself,' he said. 'I'm no engineer, though, so I had it checked out before it was constructed and fitted.'

'You're a useful chap to have around,' said Alex, 'do you think you'll have time to look at something I'm working on?' Alex always had a project on the go, something that would solve a problem on site.

'Sure, I'd love to, although I may get called away to the police station at any time.'

We showed him the apartment and brought his luggage in.

'I don't suppose we need to show you around. Do you remember where everything is from when you were last here? 'Pretty much, but I'd like a reminder of the mealtimes. Are Sally and Peter still here?'

We gave him the information he needed and chatted about residents he might remember from his last visit.

I couldn't control my nosiness. 'Why could you be called to the police station?'

He laughed. 'Do I look like a criminal?'

I shook my head, already embarrassed by my question. 'I'm sorry. It wasn't polite to stick my nose into your business,' I said.

'Don't feel sorry,' he said with a smile, 'I'm a solicitor and may be called to represent a suspect or a witness… basically anyone who asks for a solicitor.'

'That must be interesting work,' I said.

'Interesting, but not always easy. It's difficult to represent someone who is obviously in the wrong and to build up a case for them. Then if the court finds them guilty, my name is dirt. I've been lucky that no one has set his heavies on me yet. It's happened to some of my colleagues when they lost their cases, but perhaps the wheelchair protects me.'

'How long will you be staying?' Alex asked.

'I don't know, I can work from here as easily as I can from home, but I'll need to be back before the Christmas parties start. Things get quite fraught then.'

'I can imagine,' said Alex.

'It's not all as bad as I've portrayed it. Some of the clients are lovely, but worried about talking to the police. I can help them, and they always appreciate it.'

Stuart seemed such a lovely man. He spent time with Peter and they chatted together like old friends. Peter's autism had stopped me properly engaging with him but Stuart had no problems. I could see that Sally was fond of him, as was Meadow. He took Daniel for rides with him in his chair. The baby loved it. I couldn't help admiring his easy way with people and wished that I was a little less self-conscious with strangers.

On Thursday evening, Clifford stood up and said, 'We need as many hands as we can get tomorrow. It's pumpkin harvest day. Wear old clothes and wellies and bring your muscles with you. There'll be no chance of selling them after Halloween.'

'I've no intention of selling my muscles, thank you very much,' said Will, which made us laugh.

'Can I help?' Mark asked. It was half-term and I thought he might like to spend his time with his friends, but he decided to help us out instead.

'I'll be glad of you,' Clifford said.

'I'll help,' said Lily smiling. I was pleasantly surprised. I didn't think getting wet, cold and dirty would appeal to her.

'Wouldn't you rather spend time with your friends?' I asked her.

'Everyone here is my friend. I'd like to help.' What a change from the awkward teenager I'd brought here in July.

'Last year Will carved the pumpkin for our market stall,' said Clifford.

'It looked just like Meadow,' said Will.

Meadow's head shot up. 'It looked nothing like me,' she said.

'We could give it some glasses this year if you like.' Everyone laughed.

'I wondered if some younger people could do them as well?' Clifford asked.

Mark sighed, 'That's a relief, I thought I might have to buy one out of my pocket money.'

'Nice one, little brother. We'll have a go and Will can see what real competition is like.'

'And,' said Sally, 'don't forget to save the innards, because we'll make chutney with those and any damaged ones. You never know, I may even make pumpkin pie for us.'

'I've never tasted pumpkin pie,' said Mark and Lily in unison.

'Nor have I,' I said.

'Well, that's my decision made for me,' said Sally.

Outside, Alex told me that he'd never had it either. Stuart said he and some friends had tried to make it when they were students, but they may have been drinking, because it tasted terrible. 'I hope that's not how it's meant to taste,' he said, 'I don't want to upset Sally by leaving it.'

'Can you demonstrate how your wheelchair works?' Mark asked.

'Sure. But I think you'll probably be most interested in the modifications I've made.'

'Like what?'

'Well, this button helps me to get things off high shelves.' Mark's eyes were round as Stuart slowly coasted upwards, so his head was higher than mine.

'Cool. Did you design the stabiliser feet?'

'Yes. It's a heavy piece of equipment and I needed to make sure I wouldn't tip over.'

'Wow. I think you may just have become my best friend. Well second-best, Peter is my closest friend.'

Stuart smiled. 'What interests do you share?'

'I want to be an architect when I grow up, and he knows phenomenal amounts about architecture. It's a shame he couldn't get a qualification online, but he's promised to help me when I qualify. I'm not so taken with his interest in tomatoes though.'

We separated and went our own ways.

'Shall we walk Mungo together?' Alex asked.

'That would be good, but I think you've got the question slightly wrong. Shall we let Mungo walk us tonight?'

'Are you feeling better already? Or is it just a pumpkin high?'

Fortunately, the weather was fine the following day, although the wind was bitingly cold.

I was wearing gloves, but the pumpkins still held their night-time temperature and the cold and damp rapidly seeped through my gloves.

Teddy drove the tractor and trailer to the end of the field and we carried each pumpkin to the trailer. As we progressed down the field, he drove closer, and continued helping us. We had about two-thirds of the field done by lunchtime. I looked at my children who were working every bit as hard as everyone else.

'Let's break for lunch,' said Clifford. 'I reckon we'll finish by three, with the extra help from the young ones.'

At lunch, I asked if they had to be unloaded from the trailer when the market started. Clifford explained that they'd been given extra space free of charge because the pumpkins drew the crowds. Teddy would drive the tractor in and park the trailer near the stall.

'Do you need extra help serving?' Stuart asked.

'That would be useful as children take ages choosing the pumpkin they want. Can you fit any extra trays of produce in your van?' Clifford asked.

'Sure. I'll bring it round when you're loading up.'

It looked as if Stuart was going to be helpful and the children would love the tricks his wheelchair could do.

As anticipated, the field was finished at three o'clock, and the orange hue that I had admired from my bedroom, had become a dirty green. Teddy fastened a tarpaulin over the top of the trailer, and we left for tea and cake.

'What happens to those that don't sell?' I asked Clifford.

'They go to the women's refuge. There are a lot of children there and the mothers have little if any money to spend.'

I thought about those children at Christmas and ideas started to form in my mind.

CHAPTER 16

The following morning, I ached everywhere. At first, I thought it was flu, but then remembered the pumpkins. The stiffness was simply from using muscles that I'd not used much recently.

Lily and Mark were full of it at breakfast and showed photos of their pumpkins to everyone.

'Okay,' said Meadow, 'which of you modelled theirs on me.'

The carvers looked innocent until Will blurted out, 'But mine does have a resemblance...'

'No, it doesn't,' she said, 'It looks more like you.'

Will laughed and shrugged his shoulders.

'Will they be taken to the market?' I asked.

'Yes. It shows the children what can be done with them.'

'I hope they sell a lot. But will there be enough left for the children at the women's refuge?'

'Don't worry about that,' Meadow said, 'I rang them yesterday to find out numbers. There's ten children old enough to carve pumpkins; we've reserved them.'

Amber piped up, 'I've made friends with some of the mums living there. Some of them left home with just the clothes they were stood up in. I've been thinking about Christmas, it's going to be rough for the children there.'

'I expect there's a bit more to it than that?' Meadow said.

'Yeah. I ain't never done this before, but I'd like to email the businesses – ask if they'd give something for them. Christmas is so important to children.' Daniel gurgled in agreement and dribbled down his bib.

'It's a secret location. Obviously, Clifford knows where it is so he can deliver pumpkins, but traders shouldn't know the address,' Meadow said.

'I get that. I thought we could use our paper with the Village name on it. I'll make myself a badge and collect them in your car. I ain't got a computer, so I'll have to use yours.'

Meadow was quiet for a while. 'It's an interesting thought. I'd go along with that. The problem is that we won't know the children's ages or genders until close to Christmas. There's a fast turnover there.'

'I think people would understand and decide what stuff to give nearer the day. I thought about putting a sign up – tons of people will want to collect for them, but I don't want to upset the mums or those with no kids.'

'Do you think the supermarket would put a trolley out for gifts for "disadvantaged families"?' I asked, 'That makes it more anonymous.'

'I'm sure the hardware shop would do the same,' said Alex. 'They stock Christmas decorations, and we could provide a tree.'

'They're squashed in that house,' said Meadow, 'I don't know if there's room for a tree… unless we put it in a pot which could be moved around. That might work. Obviously, we'll provide the vegetables for Christmas dinner.'

'When we're making the cake and puddings, we could easily make extra,' said Sally, 'and there's a few people here practising cooking gifts for Christmas hampers. They may do a few extra.'

'What about them advent calendars? Kiddies love them, even the babies,' said Amber. Do you think places would put a basket out for those?'

'It sounds as if we have a plan. How about if you spend Monday morning with me, Amber? Meadow said. We can work on it together.' Amber grinned.

I drove to Prue's that afternoon. She greeted me and then commented that I looked stiff. I told her what had caused it.

'That sounds like so much fun,' she said. 'My grandchildren always carve a pumpkin for me and then they and their friends visit all dressed up, expecting treats. Of course, I oblige, although I don't really agree with it.'

'I don't think I do either, but I don't think they understand that much when they are young, it's just an opportunity to dress up and cadge sweets.'

'True, and then we have to cope with their behaviour when they've eaten too much sugar and colourants,' she said. 'Now would you like tea or coffee?'

We went to the kitchen together and I sat down at the table, while Prue made the tea.

'This is a wonderful house,' I said.

'My husband and I bought it together and we were a really happy family until Emily, my daughter, had her stroke. The two older girls were so good with her. It was them that stopped her giving up.'

'How did your husband take it?'

'Badly. He was wonderful when she was in hospital, but when she came out and we had to adapt the house for her, he thought it would affect the rest of his life and he left. We're still friends. When he saw that she was going to live an independent life, he wanted to move in again. But he'd hurt us all badly and

I didn't think that was an option, so we are separated but not divorced.'

Then she asked about me and I told her how and why we arrived at Honsham.

'Were you shocked when that skeleton was dug up?' she asked.

I explained our part in naming her and how I wanted to continue investigating to find out who killed her.

'Doesn't it worry you that there may be repercussions?'

'I can see why you were called Prudence,' I said, 'Yes, it does. I've talked to Lily and Mark about it and to Alex, but the police aren't doing much and I want to see that the woman gets the justice she deserves.'

'Not all murder victims are squeaky clean,' she said, 'but whether she had done something to deserve it or not, the murderer should still be caught. He could do it again. But how will you go about it?'

'I've no real idea. All I can do is to talk to people she had contact with. I've spoken to her daughter who was put up for adoption when she was born. I can't help feeling she had a better life than she would have had with her birth mother.'

'I found out when I was thirteen that I was adopted. We were looking at DNA in biology. I had brown eyes, but neither of my parents did. They'd given me a wonderful childhood and I suppose I was worried that what I knew might spoil things so I said nothing. I still haven't.' She poured the tea. 'When Emily had her stroke, the hospital asked whether any family members had high blood pressure. I didn't think I did and told them I couldn't say because I was adopted. My husband wasn't much use, he had no idea about his own family, so we don't know if it's an inherited condition.'

'Did you try to trace your birth mother?'

'No. I didn't want to be disloyal to my real parents.'

'If it was one of my children, I think I would support them if they wanted to know. There were a lot of forced adoptions in the seventies, she may have had no choice.'

'I know, and she may be out there waiting for me to contact her, but it still feels disloyal.'

I smiled. 'I look like my parents, so I've never had any doubts.'

'It does worry me though. It's possible Emily's children could have the same health issues if it is inherited.'

We talked about Daniel and Amber and the conversation turned to the women's refuge. Prue was impressed by Amber's ideas.

'I'm happy to do anything I can to help. I'm a dab hand at cooking, so cakes, sausage rolls, pies and anything like that I can do. If you're not too busy, you'd be welcome to come and help or just to chat.'

I said that I was certain she could do something and I'd let her know nearer the time.

That evening Alex and I took our usual walk with Mungo. The sky was clear and the moonlight highlighted my breath. Alex was well togged up with hat, gloves and scarf but, so far, I still hadn't resorted to a hat. I pulled my hood over my head. It must have been an extra-large man's hood on a medium woman's coat.

Alex laughed, 'Can you even see where you're going?'

'Not really. I can see the ground about a metre in front of me and that's it. Tomorrow I'll risk my hat.'

'Hooray. At long last the woman has seen what's sensible.'

'I bow to your higher knowledge,' I said. 'It may be cold, but that breeze is biting.'

'It's often like this around Halloween and bonfire night,' he said. 'I can remember when the girls were young and Millie and I took them to a fireworks display. Poppy had refused to wear her mittens and she cried with cold. She never went without them again.'

'Were they the sort attached to elastic that went through the sleeves?'

'Yes. She even insisted Millie take them completely out of her coat and put them in her bedroom.'

'I'm guessing from that description she must have been about two years old at the time.'

'Yes, the good old terrible twos! I was glad when she grew out of that stage, although she's always been dramatic. Perhaps she didn't grow out of it after all.'

'How is she now? I asked.

'She loves working at the supermarket and they've put her on a management trainee scheme. She's so much happier. She just wasn't suited to university.'

'I'm not pushing my two to go, but it looks as if they will. Lily has said that she wants to be a physiotherapist and to do the UEA course, which means she can still live at home. I think Mark will go away to study architecture, although he'll find it difficult to leave Peter behind.'

'Those two have a very strong bond, but I've noticed Stuart conversing easily with Peter, too,' Alex said.

'Sally told me he had an autistic older brother and a younger Down's Syndrome sister, so he understands,' I said. 'Their poor parents have been unlucky to have three disabled children.'

'It depends on what you mean by disabled,' Alex said. 'I don't think Stuart sees it as unfortunate at all, it's given him all sorts of creative opportunities he wouldn't otherwise have had.'

'I don't mean to sound judgemental,' I replied, 'Teddy said he charmed the children and their parents when he was selling pumpkins. Nearly all of them were sold by lunchtime. Clifford said it's a record, it's never happened before.'

'We'll have to hire him next year.'

'Thinking of the future, have you made any decision about trying to find the killer?' he asked.

'I'd like to go ahead with it, but I'd like visit Ross again before I make the final decision.'

'You like him, don't you?' he asked.

'Yes. He really cares about Elsie and is quite a softie for an ex-policeman. It makes me wonder how he managed to survive in the force.'

'Will he become a rival to me?'

I punched him on the arm, 'He's just a nice bloke, that's all!'

'So, I can come with you when you visit him,' he said.

'I don't think I have any choice. I insist you come.'

He grabbed my arms and pulled me close to him. Our lips met and I knew that no one would ever compete with him.

That week we were making a harvest pumpkin pineapple loaf in our breadmaking course. Alex and I brought the pumpkins with us as we had plenty of irregular ones to spare. This was the first cake as such that we had made, but the teacher thought it would be good to do something seasonal. Once more, we did the preparation and then disappeared to the pub.

Nina was back at class and sat next to me. She brought a gift-wrapped parcel out of her bag and gave it to me.

'What's this for?'

'Everything you did, especially saying that you had heard the baby's heartbeat. Our marriage was close to breaking point and, when my husband heard what you said, he realised that I wasn't out of my mind. Everything is good now.'

'If the baby does have Down's Syndrome, it's likely that it will be less demanding than a baby without it,' I said.

'We've talked about that and decided I won't be tested for it. What's the point? We're not going to abort our baby and, if it is a difficult one, we'll get a nanny to do the night shift. I can express my milk if necessary.'

'Do you have other children?' I asked.

'Just one girl she's married now and pregnant. We wanted more, but nothing happened, so we settled for the one child. That's why this is so strange; it still feels like a dream.'

I smiled, 'When is it due?'

'The fifth of April, I'm almost four months gone.'

'That's great. You must let us know if you're struggling with anything in class. It won't hurt me to do a bit more kneading at any time. I feel a bit guilty though. Alex finished off my teacakes the week you were ill and someone else finished yours. Alex brought yours home with him as well as mine.'

'I never even thought about it. You're welcome.'

I was pleased for Nina, but I still felt bad. I thought I had put the feeling of never having another baby behind me, but obviously I hadn't.

CHAPTER 17

I could see a pattern forming in our visits to Ross. We asked Ross the questions that we had thought of at the time, but later wished we had asked him something else. This time I was determined to sort myself out.

I had a free afternoon, so I spent the time doing research. First of all, I looked for Harriet Johnson, the mother of the murdered baby. I started at the earliest date, the time when the baby was missing and then followed her to the present day as much as I could. The media had included the name of the village the family lived in, and a photographer had taken a picture of the farmhouse itself. I went through an old telephone book to find the exact address, 'Home Farm'. They had been living there when her husband killed himself. Now, I had to find out if she still did.

The telephone directory no longer gave Harriet Johnson's telephone number, which was a bit of a blow. Had she moved or gone ex-directory or even decided there was no point in keeping a landline? I guess she'd changed her number and made it ex-directory after her husband died, as there would have been calls from the media at the anniversaries of her son's and husband's death. Reporters would do anything to get a story.

At the tenth anniversary there was a story and the same picture of the house was used. There was no implication that she was still there or any further information. Then I found what I wanted. There was a double-page spread in a magazine just after Ruth was released. It would have brought in a good sum for Harriet as it was an exclusive. It was the same photographer who took the later photograph of Home Farm. It was poorly looked after. Paint was peeling from the windows and doors and waist-high weeds were growing in the garden. I wondered what had got to her, to let the house get in such a state. The picture of her at the door showed one of the skinniest women I'd ever seen. I compared it to the round-faced photo of her earlier and wondered if she had gone downhill through sadness and loss or whether drugs were involved. At one point, the reporter asked her whether she had forgiven Ruth now that she had served her sentence, to which she replied, 'She deserved the death penalty and still does. If I met her now, I'd kill her.'

That photo was the most recent I could find. I looked at the electoral register, but she wasn't listed there either. Probably she'd opted out as she would prefer to live in anonymity, away from the world.

I started my search for her fellow inmate, Annie Mosley. This was more difficult. I found the photograph of her going to court but that was around twenty years ago. She was an accountant who was convicted for fraud having stolen forty-thousand pounds from her employer.

I could find nothing else. It seems that Harriet's tragedy was more newsworthy than Annie's theft. I couldn't even find anything about her release from prison.

This helped me to formulate some questions for Ross, but I was hesitant to trouble Harriet. It seemed that she had enough problems without me intruding, but then it may help her to talk.

At lunch, Sally announced that the following afternoon would be pumpkin chutney day. We would also be cooking and roasting pumpkin seeds and making pumpkin chutney bread. Everyone was excited as working together in the kitchen was always fun.

'Quiet a moment,' said Meadow, and she pulled a woollen hat from her pocket. 'It's time to draw names for Secret Santa. Lily and Mark have already drawn theirs, but it's time for the rest of us. Remember you are not allowed to spend more than ten pounds on the person you draw out. If you draw your own name, put it back in the hat and draw another.'

Amber looked worried. 'Will you be able to help me, Jen?'

'As long as you don't draw out my name.'

I drew out Peter and Amber picked Alex.

She looked at me and I nodded, 'We'll manage that one together,' I said.

'There'll be a general air of secrecy and people will be beavering away on projects from now on,' Alex said to me and Amber.

Amber just smiled.

Stuart turned up with us for all of the following afternoon.

'I love it how everyone works together here,' he said. 'I'm helping Peter with the apples for the spiced pumpkin and apple chutney.'

'That sounds yummy,' I said.

Will was working, with a lethal looking knife, on squashes for the pumpkin and squash chutney. Amber, Daniel and Meadow were on the pumpkin chutney bread and I had responsibility for roasting the pumpkin seeds. I was a bit concerned as I'd never done anything like it before, but with Sally's guidance I soon got the hang of it. Other people were what Sally called "floaters". It simply meant that you helped out when you were needed and provided tea and coffee to anyone who wanted it. It also meant that the floaters washed up the pans, which wasn't a popular job.

By the end of the afternoon, Peter was labelling chutney jars. He'd made the labels earlier and he had to make sure they were put on exactly level. One of the pumpkin chutney breads was cut and we all agreed it was the best we'd ever tried – even though we'd never tried it before.

Amber was full of it. She had never baked before and she couldn't believe the result when her own creations were taken from the oven.

'We're selling them on the market stall on Saturday,' Sally said.

'The ones what I made?' she asked, wide-eyed.

'Yes, you and Meadow did a good job with them.' Amber jumped up and down, really excited.

'When will we next be cooking?' she asked.

'Fairly soon as we need to make Christmas puddings and cakes.'

'Do you sell some of those, too?'

'Yes, lovey, we have orders for them already. Then there's yule logs, which we do closer to Christmas,'

'What's a yule log?' Amber asked.

I explained to her.

'I like baking. I might have to take a class after Christmas.'

'Did you learn how to cook when you were younger?' I asked.

'Nope.'

'Well, we'll have to teach Daniel while he's young and you can both learn together.'

'Thanks, Jen. That'll mean I can be a proper grown up.'

The following afternoon we were off to see Ross. I had a list of questions this time, although only a short one. Ross always seemed glad to have visitors and I knew he would have cooked a cake especially.

He greeted us at the front door and invited us in.

'How's it going in the Village then?'

'Good,' I said. 'We sold all our good pumpkins, but those that were damaged and unsaleable we made into chutneys. It's always great fun when we get together to cook.'

'It must be a special place. Living here, I get to know few people and it can be lonely. Most of the houses in this street are second homes and a good proportion of those in the town are. Being a writer, I have to shut myself off from the world a lot of the time, but sometimes I wish I could just pop in to see someone.'

'Have you thought of taking up a hobby or going to an evening class?'

'I've thought of it, but deadlines mean I have to stay at home and get on with it,' he said. 'It's unsociable work. Anyway, can I get you tea and cake?'

'I thought you'd never ask,' replied Alex.

'I suppose I haven't really thought of it before,' I said to Alex. 'Ross is retired, but he's not enjoying his retirement as he should be.'

'I don't think there's any "should" in it,' Alex replied. 'He chose to be an author, so he has to live with the hardships of it. Anyway, he may like his own company.'

'I suppose so. But he's really good at what he does, it would be a shame not to have his novels for people to read. And he's leaving a mark on the world,' I said.

'You're going to leave a mark on the world. Your children will carry the family on for generations,' Alex said.

'I just wish I could do something or invent something that will make my name in history.'

It was then that Ross came in with a loaded tray.

'Lemon drizzle cake today. I hope it's something you like.'

'My mouth's watering already,' Alex said.

As he distributed the goodies, he said to Alex, 'How's the operation site?'

'It's much better than it was in the months before the op. If I'd known what it was, I'd have got treatment earlier. I didn't want to visit the doctor, so I just pressed on. It feels good now.'

We chatted amicably for about a quarter of an hour, and then Ross asked, 'Did Claire ring you?'

'Thank you, yes.' I said, 'We had a good talk, but I forgot to ask her for a phone number.'

'She hasn't given me one,' he said. 'She works shifts, so doesn't want people phoning while she works or when she's sleeping.'

'That's fair enough. Do she or Elsie know the other exists?'

'Not yet. I will probably tell Claire at some time and she can make the decision about meeting her grandmother.'

I thought that was mean of him, and wondered if it was because he didn't want to share Elsie. Perhaps he was thinking about inheriting from her, although she would have little left after her nursing home fees were paid. But it was none of my business; I only visited her at his request.

'So, what else can I help you with?' he asked.

'It's a long shot. I've been trying to trace Annie Mosley without success. You don't know if she changed her name or became homeless, do you?' I asked.

'No, I've not heard anything about her at all.'

'There's one last question which I've been mulling over for some days now,' I said.

'Shoot.'

'If I was one of the characters in your books, would you advise me not to investigate further?'

He thought for a while. 'Yes, I would. But you should know that my characters don't always do what I tell them to. They take on a life of their own, do unplanned things and often endanger themselves in the process. Does that help?'

'I think it does,' I replied.

'Well, how about another cup of tea?'

He went into the kitchen and a short time later came out with the tray.

I was unusually tired by the time we left and stumbled on Ross's doorstep. Fortunately, Alex caught hold of me.

I remember doing my seatbelt up and nothing else until Alex shook me. 'Jen, wake up, we're home.'

'I'm just so tired. I'll lay down until suppertime,' I said.

Lily woke me and, feeling a bit better, I went over for supper. I wondered if it was my new tablets doing this to me, and if so, whether I would adjust to them.

After supper, I looked for known side-effects on the information sheet in the tablet box, but tiredness wasn't listed as one of them.

I dressed up warmly and went over to Alex's apartment.

'Are you okay now?'

'Apart from a headache.'

'I don't know whether I should give you a glass of wine, or would you prefer hot chocolate?' he asked.

'Can we leave it until we get back?' I said, 'I think I could do with an early night.'

That suited Mungo well. He grabbed his ball and led us outside, evidently intent on enjoying this walk. A little bit further on, Alex stopped and kissed me. It went right through me and I thought my legs might give way, I was in ecstasy.

'So, have you made a decision about carrying on with the investigation?' he asked.

'DI Watson says he isn't going to find the killer before he leaves and it could be side-lined as a cold case. I can't let that happen.'

He kissed me again and, when I'd recovered, he said, 'We're in it together, but we must be extra careful this time and let Jazz know exactly where we'll be and when we expect to be back.'

'Will it be that dangerous?' I asked.

'Probably not, but we have to be cautious.'

I was certain that was what Ross expected me to decide, although he was warning me against it.

We left the cold shadowy woods and leaves that crunched under our feet and went back to Alex's.

'Are you still frightened of the woods at night?' he asked and I shook my head.

'I still don't see as well as you do in the dark,' I said.

'That will come. How's the head?'

'Much better, I just needed a few deep breaths of Honsham air.'

He brought through two cups of hot chocolate and I took mine.

'Whose name did you draw out of Secret Santa?' I asked.

'My lips are sealed.'

'Well, do you want to make biscuits when we get the next afternoon off?'

'Let's do sweets first,' he said, 'It's probably better to try them in case we make a complete mess of it.'

I smiled. It was fine with me.

In bed that night, I wondered if it was the office work making me tired. Without me noticing, Meadow had passed most of her work over to me in the past month. She was there if someone wanted to talk to her, but otherwise I did everything. I couldn't begrudge it, though. I was spending less time on her personal care and had to work to earn my place at the Village. I had a strange feeling at the bottom of my stomach. Was she ill? Was she preparing me to take over when she wasn't well enough to do it?

But she was seventy-three. She had worked years past retirement age. Then I remembered the pleasure she had teaching Amber how to make a cake and seeing little Daniel's hands in the mixing bowl. She deserved to spend the time she had left with her great-nephew and his mother.

CHAPTER 18

'How are you feeling this morning?' Alex asked.

'Much better,' I said, 'I have no idea why I was so tired yesterday. It seemed to come on without warning and I couldn't have driven home like that. I know that I'm doing more admin work, but it's not that arduous. I did the salaries earlier in the week, but I used to waitress for long hours in London and didn't feel like I did yesterday.'

'Meadow saw me walking you back to your apartment. She'll probably ask to see you today.'

'That's all I need. I was going to see if she was feeling well, as over the months she's passed extra work on to me. It's almost as though she's letting go of the purse strings. I don't want her to think it's too much for me. I came here expecting that I would do admin all day when she no longer needed a carer.'

'She'll have to let go at some point. Perhaps she's preparing in advance. Anyway, she has Daniel and Amber to occupy her now,' he said.

Alex was right. After I had cleaned my teeth, I went over to Meadow.

'Come in, my dear, and sit down. You know I'm nosey, but I was wondering what you and Alex did yesterday afternoon.'

'We went out to Holt, to visit Ross, Nicole's stepbrother. He's a really lovely man.'

'Lovely enough to give you drugs?' she asked.

'What? No way. What makes you think that?'

'When Alex woke you to take you back to your apartment, your pupils were dilated.'

'Were they? I thought I was tired because I've changed HRT tablets.'

'I suppose it could be that, but I think you were drugged,' she said.

'But Ross and Alex ate and drank exactly the same as me. Alex was fine.' I was certain that Meadow must be mistaken. Perhaps my pupils were always dilated when I woke up.

'I'm not going to say anything else about it my dear, except to remind you that you are mixing with people who possibly murdered Ruth. You must be very careful.'

I took hold of Meadow's hand. 'Thank you for caring.'

'It's just that I don't think I could manage without you. I love you like a sister.'

I chose not to point out the thirty-plus years that separated our ages.

'There is something I need to ask you. Are you feeling ill?' I asked.

'No. I'm on top of the world. My leg is getting stronger and it bends well and I have a lot more energy. It's kind of you to ask, but why?'

'It's just that you have passed most of your work over to me and I thought you might be giving up.'

She laughed loudly. 'That's nonsense. I originally employed you for just six weeks but hoped you would stay longer. You're forthright and honest and very capable. I can see that you're managing it well.' She laughed again. 'It just seems sensible to have someone else who knows the job in case I'm ill at any time. Of course, I know I can't go on for ever, but I've recently found my great-nephew and his mum. Daniel's a lovely baby, but Amber missed out on so much in care. It wasn't just being moved from home to home, but never having a mother to talk things through with and do other things that mothers and daughters do.'

'Like cooking?' I said.

'Exactly. And sewing. But she missed a lot from constantly changing schools and I can help her with that. She's never really had friendships that last because, as soon as she made friends, she had to move away from them. Go and make a pot of tea.'

When I returned, she said, 'Amber's a kind-hearted girl, and I want to see her grow socially and as a mother. Of course, my dear, I also want to be part of Daniel's life. Giving up admin, which I hate, has given me the opportunity to do something more worthwhile.'

'You're very lucky,' I said, 'Amber could well have been an addict.'

'I know. That's part of the reason I want to be in Daniel's life. His father is an addict and I know it runs through my brother's line. I want to warn him about drugs when he gets older, you know, and try to put him off trying them…. And that's why I was so worried about you yesterday, my dear.'

'I understand that,' I said, 'and I'm grateful for your concern. You do believe that I wouldn't knowingly even try them, don't you?'

'I don't doubt you at all. I wish I hadn't said anything now.'

It was time to change the subject. 'I was wondering if we're allowed to invite friends here. Amber has made friends with some young mothers and a few of them are at the woman's refuge and they can't invite her there. I've made a friend, too, who would probably be prepared to bring them here.'

'Of course. This is your home and Amber's home, my dear, and you must feel free to invite people here, but preferably not your ex-husband.'

I grimaced.

'Amber is bringing Daniel over shortly so we can work on her letter. I'll mention it to her casually today. She may like to have a little Christmas party for the children. They can use the communal lounge or her apartment. I'll talk to her about that, too.'

I left the smell of cannabis and went out into the clear fresh air. The sun was shining and the chestnut and birch trees were turning golden. I was so glad that I'd taken this job away from the London fumes.

The sunshine was deceiving. Although it still held some warmth, there was a biting wind as I walked along the track to fetch the mail. There were still a few conference pears, clinging to their branches, but the cherries and plums had long gone.

The police had done their best to level out the ground after their dig, but they'd disturbed the roots of many asparagus plants. I could see where they'd been replanted and labelled, but many didn't look good. Alex told me that they wouldn't harvest those for another couple of years. The income from those plants was lost, but then you couldn't put a price on finding a murderer.

I wasn't certain how the investigation was going. DI Watson said that they were 'following leads.' I had no idea what those leads were, but they had put out media appeals for information. The major problem seemed to be that it was unlikely there would be many eye-witness reports and no CCTV as we were so remote.

My thoughts roamed freely as I walked this path daily, taking in the freshly ploughed pumpkin field, the pruned raspberry canes and the empty glasshouse.

I thought of the donkeys and how delighted they would be to see the little children Amber invited round. They loved Daniel and walked over to the fence as soon as they saw him being carried to their enclosure.

I knew that Meadow went there to share her worries with them and wondered what there was that she couldn't share with me.

Most of the men who normally worked with the plants had been diverted to tree trimming, now the nesting birds had flown and it seemed lonely around the crops. I knew that, as Christmas approached, there would be lots of work to do with root vegetables, sprouts and Christmas trees.

But it was time to head for the office to get on with my work. I was looking forward to making sourdough bread at class tonight. We started the cultures at the beginning of term. Both mine and Alex's had grown and bubbled away happily. There had been some horror tales from the others of theirs having died, but we had enough to share.

Nina was at class and we chatted away amicably. For the first time, I didn't feel envious of her. In fact, I was beginning to wonder if I even wanted another baby, with the broken nights and fraught days they brought with them. I knew that the Forest Village was a wonderful place to bring them up, but one day they would have to venture out into a world that wasn't so kind, and that would be a huge culture shock.

Nina would be bringing the baby to the toddler group, so even if she couldn't continue with breadmaking, we would still meet there. That was unless Amber decided she wanted to take herself. I hoped she wouldn't as I enjoyed the morning away and the friends I had made.

'Alex,' I said, as we were walking in the wood the following evening, 'When do you think would be a good time to visit Harriet Johnson?'

'I'd hoped you'd given up on the investigation,' he replied. 'It's too dangerous to carry on.'

'When I say I will do something, I mean it.' I could hear how sharp that comment sounded and I could feel anger rising inside me.

'Sorry,' he said. 'I wanted to give you the chance to opt out, without losing face.'

I sighed, the anger dispersing. 'It's probably going to be hardest part of the investigation, so I think we should get it over with as soon as we can.'

'What are you going to ask her?'

'I don't have a clue, but I find it easy to talk to people, so hopefully the questions will formulate as I talk to her.'

'But will she talk to a couple of strangers who turn up at the door, with no obvious reason for turning up? We're not journalists or police officers or even neighbours. If we tell her we're investigating Ruth Carpenter's death, she won't have anything to do with us.'

'I hadn't thought of that,' I said.

'Well, when you've decided how to approach her, we'll arrange something.'

'Are you angry with me?' I asked.

'No. I just don't want you to put yourself in danger. If she's on drugs, she could have other addicts in the house, who could be hallucinating and dangerous.'

He drew me to him and kissed me. 'I don't want you to be hurt. That's all.'

CHAPTER 19

I couldn't sleep that night. I had to find a good reason to visit Harriet. This was complicated by the fact that I wasn't even certain that she still lived in the same house. She could have sold it to get money for drugs. If it was sold it would probably have been by auction. If I googled it, I should be able to find out.

But what reason could I give for turning up on her doorstep? The best I could think of was to say we were neighbours and popped in to see how she was keeping.

I fell asleep with that idea in mind, but wasn't convinced it would get us through the door.

The following day, Amber and I put Daniel into the car and headed for the playgroup. As I was parking the car, he became more and more excited, almost screaming when we got him out.

'I've never seen him this excited before,' I said.

'He loves being with other children,' Amber said, laughing.

'Why don't you invite someone around for a play date?' I asked.

'That's what Meadow said. She said to treat my apartment like home. But it's not much good her saying that because I never had a home before.'

'How about inviting Emily? I know her Mum, Prue, and we could be there with you, to help you out.'

'I'm always worried that I might not know what to say to Emily. What's the story with her leg and arm?'

I told her.

'Poor bugger,' she put her hand over her mouth. 'Whoops, I shouldn't have said that in front of Daniel. How do you think I can help her?'

'The best way is to be her friend and get to know her well. Then if she doesn't want to talk to her Mum or her husband about something, she might choose to talk to you.'

'But I don't know nothing. What's the point of her talking to me?'

'Sometimes, friends just need someone to talk to, someone to understand what they're going through without giving advice.'

'I'm going to put Daniel down now. Watch his bum shuffle as he tries to get to the others,' she said.

We both laughed at him making slow but enthusiastic progress across the floor.

'See that girl over there,' said Amber. I could see a woman alone and crying. 'I think she might need a mum.'

I went over and sat down beside her. 'You look like you're having a bad day. Is there anything I can help you with? I'm Jen.'

The tears continued to fall. 'I'm Felicity, or Flip for short. But no one can help me.'

'It may help to talk about it.'

'I came to the women's refuge about six weeks ago after they fixed my jaw. My periods were all over the place, but I thought it was because of stress. I couldn't afford a pregnancy test, so I went to the doctor. I'm pregnant. I can't have another kid.'

124

'Which is your little one?' She pointed out a beautiful girl about a year old.

'My mum and dad took her while I was in hospital, but my husband kept going to their house. They had to get a restraining order in the end. They wanted me and Nell to stay with them, but I couldn't risk them being hurt, so we came here. I must have got pregnant when he raped me the last time.'

'I'm so sorry. What do you feel like doing about it?'

'The doctor said it's only a case of taking a tablet and it will be like a heavy period. I don't think I'll ever get over it if I do. I'm depressed as it is.'

'Would you like to meet up one afternoon and we can talk?'

'I'd like that,' she said.

'Do you have transport?'

'Yes, the refuge has a car park at the back, so that men can't see the cars.'

I gave her details of how to find me and the entry code, and we fixed a date for the following afternoon.'

She smiled. 'Thank you.'

I returned to Amber. 'Do you think Daniel will share his toys?'

'Why?'

'I've invited Flip and little Nell over tomorrow,' I said.

'We could rummage in the toy box in the communal sitting room for a few extras, just in case,' she said, 'Would you like to use my apartment?'

'That would be good. I'll fill you in on the way home, but it's time I went to the kitchen to help with the teas and coffees.'

Amber moved over to another mother who she recognised.

That evening as we walked Mungo, I broached the subject of visiting Harriet.

'I've been thinking hard. We could say that we are neighbours and we've come to see how she is keeping. Have you thought of anything better?'

'No.'

'Have you even thought about it at all?'

'No.'

'Why not?'

'I don't agree with telling lies,' he said.

'We don't have any alternative.'

'Yes, we do. We could drop our investigations.'

'But you were keen to go ahead.'

'I wasn't. That was you pushing your viewpoint onto me, sweetheart. Drop the case. It's too dangerous.'

I was furious. I'd done all that work for nothing and Ruth at least deserved a fair investigation.

'Leave it to the police,' he said.

'And let it become a cold case? No way.' I stomped off and went to my apartment.

The children were in their rooms so I made a lot of noise in the kitchen. Mark came through.

'I'm trying to work. What's your problem?'

'Nothing.'

'So why are you crashing about?'

'Alex wants to stop investigating.'

'And you want to carry on?'

'Yes.'

'So, you've had a row.'

'Yes.'

'Sit down, Mum. Why does Alex want to drop it?'

'He says it's too dangerous.'

'Which sounds to me as if he's saying he doesn't want you to be hurt. Am I right?'

'Yes.'

'But you've got your teeth into it and you're not going to release your bite. I've seen you like this before. He loves you and he's worried about you being hurt. If you continue, he will probably tag along to keep you safe, even if it means he'll put himself in danger. As I see it, two people in love need to compromise at times. If they don't, the relationship will break down. If you're with Alex for the long haul, you need to decide whether you love him enough to let go.'

As always, Mark made a lot of sense.

'Do you want to sleep on it or sort it out now?'

I stood up. 'I'll go and see him now.'

I knocked on his door and he let me in. I was shocked that his eyes were red and puffy.

'Alex, I'm sorry.'

'I don't want to lose someone else that I love.'

He grabbed me roughly and pressed his lips onto mine. The harshness of it made it all the more exciting.

'I thought I'd lost you,' he said. 'I love you enough to continue with this investigation, because I can't let you do it alone.'

'I love you enough to let it go,' I replied.

He kissed me again, much more gently this time.

'How about if we left the car a distance away from the house and we said that we were walking by and wondered how she was keeping?' he said. 'We wouldn't be lying then.'

CHAPTER 20

Flip arrived with Nell the next afternoon and Amber welcomed her. Daniel and Nell hit it off immediately, so I went to make tea while the women were talking.

They bonded as easily as their children did, having been through similar experiences, and there was no shortage of chatter. It was a clear sunny day so, after they had tea, they wrapped up warmly and took the children to see the donkeys and the chickens. As Meadow said, the donkeys loved seeing the children, having been beach donkeys. Amber had thought in advance to get some carrots from Clifford and the babies were fascinated watching them eat.

While the children were fussing the donkeys, Flip talked to Amber about her pregnancy and Amber said honestly that she didn't know what she would do in that situation.

'I don't think I can kill it,' said Flip. 'The Chinese count their babies' ages from the date of conception, which means this little one is already alive.'

'I'll be here if you need me,' said Amber.

'Thank you,' she replied tearfully.

Amber and Flip chatted so easily and the babies played together so well, that I was surprised how much time had passed. But the babies were getting tired, so we walked with Flip to her car. She and Amber hugged and I hugged her too.

'Remember you're never alone,' she said and Flip drove away.

'How do you think that went?' I asked as we were walking back to Amber's apartment.

'Good,' she said, 'and this little one is falling asleep.'

'You did well,' I said, 'and Daniel needs to be with other children from time to time.'

I went back to my own apartment. I kept throwing myself into the world of babies, while it still hurt that I couldn't have one of my own. I didn't particularly want one, but I would have preferred for nature not to have made the decision for me.

I made a cup of tea and drank it in peace, and then fell asleep on the sofa.

'Mum? Mum, are you okay?' I woke up and saw Mark's concerned face.

'Yes, I'm fine. A friend of Amber's visited with her baby for a play date. I'd forgotten tinies could be so tiring.'

'It would be different if it was your own,' he replied, and left to do his homework.

But would it be that different? I was fourteen years older than when the children were small and I hadn't got the energy I had then. The menopause came for a reason, but still it hurt.

At suppertime Meadow wanted to know how Daniel had got on with his little friend. She was enthusiastic about the little boy and his progress. I could see now that she wasn't unwell, but just wanted to spend time with Daniel, her great-nephew. Passing the admin over to me took a lot of worry from her and gave me employment. We were still good friends. Admin was something I could do with a different employer if I needed to, but I hated that thought. I belonged here, and I had never belonged anywhere before. It would take something enormous to make me move away.

'Would you ever go back to computer work?' I asked Alex that evening.

'Where did that come from?' he asked.

'I was wondering if you had thought of moving away and starting again?'

'No way, I love it here and I love the work I do.'

'Did you enjoy the programming work you used to do?'

'I never really thought about it, but I don't think I did.'

'So why did you choose it as a career rather than something more practical?' I asked.

'I was good at it at school, so the immediate thought was university and then a career. I didn't question it. I don't know what my parents would have thought about what I'm doing now.'

'I want Lily and Mark to be happy with what they choose to do. Lily has said she wants to be a physiotherapist and I'm not certain why,' I said.

'I know she loves running and other athletics. Has she told you if she is thinking of sports physiotherapy, because there's quite a demand for that?'

'I hadn't thought of that. I just thought NHS.'

'She'll probably have to get experience that way, but there are other openings. Why don't you talk to her about it? Do you think Mark will be happy with architecture?'

'I do, but he has that very practical side, as well, and he can't take Peter with him.'

'There's plenty of time for him to change his mind, but moving away from Peter will be a huge wrench.'

'I know. He's saving his pocket money to buy a special book for Peter for Christmas. Do you know who his secret Santa is?' I asked.

'I do and I know what he's making. It was his own decision, so I'm guiding him, not that he needs much guidance. He's a talented lad.'

'Lily hasn't told me who she drew out either.'

'I expect she's sorting something out with Jazz,' he said.

I knew it was time to ask a question that may upset Alex, but I had to do it. 'Will you come with me to visit Harriet?' He stopped walking and I looked at him without blinking.

'Do you think I'll let you go on your own?'

'She may not live there anymore, it might be a wasted afternoon,' I said.

'No afternoon spent with you will be wasted, sweetheart,' and he kissed me. I felt as if I was the happiest person in the world.

On Sunday at breakfast, we were chatting away in a relaxed way, when Stuart said, 'Anyone want to come to church with me this morning?'

He looked around, but no one was taking him up on his offer. Much to my amazement I heard my voice saying, 'Yes, please.' It wasn't what my brain was thinking and I wondered if this was a side-effect of the tablets.

'Come as you are, there's no dress code,' he said. Already I was regretting it and wondered if I could back out, but Stuart was such a pleasant chap that I didn't think I could. I'd only ever been to christenings, weddings, funerals and the odd carol service, and I'd never believed in God.

Alex looked at me strangely as I left the communal kitchen. It seems he was as surprised as I was.

Stuart was an excellent driver, even though he couldn't use foot pedals. His van had been adapted for him and he was comfortable with it. On the way, we chatted about the weather and then I said, 'I don't know why I'm coming. I don't believe in God.'

'Don't worry about it, just relax. You'll be okay.'

He stopped outside a cinema and we both got out. We went through a glass door beside the cinema door.

'The church owns this entire building. The cinema rents the lower part and we use the floors above. I think we'll sit on the first floor today.' I looked at him in his wheelchair, and then around at the sleek modern entrance hall. How was he going to get up to the first floor?

He asked me if I was okay with lifts, and I said I didn't like closed spaces. So, I followed scores of others climbing the stairs. He was there waiting for me when I reached the landing.

There were people continuing up the stairs and I asked where they were going to. He told me there was a creche and children's groups upstairs and parents usually sat in the gallery in case the children needed them.

'How many people come to this service?' I asked.

'I can see my brother. He'll tell you.'

A gangly man with ginger hair approached. 'How many today, bruv?' Stuart asked.

'Four hundred and eighty-three,' he replied.

'I brought Jen with me,' but he didn't reply.

'He has autism and keeps records of how many people are at each service, estimates how many will be there on Sundays and then counts them all. Rather, he counts the empty seats and calculates his percentage error. He does the same for the service after this which starts when we are having coffee. He slips into the back of the gallery and counts. Everyone's used to him doing it.'

People kept approaching Stuart and talking to him. He was obviously well-known.

'How do you know so many people?' I asked.

'I've been coming here as long as I remember. They're like family now.'

The service started and I tried to look as inconspicuous as possible. I didn't know the songs, but people were clapping their hands and singing at the top of their voices with a group at the front. This wasn't the solemn service that I was expecting.

'Are you okay?' Stuart asked.

To my embarrassment, I felt hot tears on my cheeks.

'We can talk about it later,' he said. But I had no idea what was wrong. It must be those tablets. I'd have to check the side-effects again.

After the service, we went to the top floor for coffee and biscuits. A woman came up to Stuart and kissed him on the forehead.

'Hi, sis. How's things?'

'I made a new friend at work. Nancy. She's on the checkout next to mine.'

'That's nice. I brought Jen with me today.'

'Hello Jen. Are you Stuart's girlfriend?'

'No, no. I'm just a friend.'

She smiled at me and said, 'I'd better find Mum and Dad.'

Stuart said, 'She's my little sister and she has Downs Syndrome. I'm the only one who has flown the nest. It was hard at first because my parents had given me everything I needed and I felt as if I was walking away from them. When we talked about it, they said they were happy for me to have my independence.

'We were all adopted, and they always said they had chosen each of us as we were special, and the biggest gift they could give me was my freedom. It was true, but I know they're always around if I need them.'

'They sound like wonderful parents.'

'They're the best. Oh, there's Prue, I must introduce you two.'

I grinned. 'Prue and I already know each other from the children's playgroup.'

I met other people, but the names didn't stay in my head. They all seemed friendly and kind.

On the way home, Stuart pulled into a layby.

'Those tears worried me,' he said, 'Is there anything I can do to help?'

'I'm not certain why I was crying,' I said.

'Has anything changed for you recently?'

'Yes, but it's something rather personal.'

'I'm unshockable. I get called out to women who've been arrested and some who've had awful things happening to them. If you don't want to talk, that's okay.'

'I thought I was adjusting well to it, but I'm not. I'm having an early menopause and I thought I'd have another ten years to have a baby if I wanted, but it's taken away any chance of that.'

'Do you want a baby?'

'Not really.'

'But you've lost the chance to choose. You need to give yourself time to grieve, you've lost something precious.'

I started crying again and he handed me a box of tissues. He put his hand on mine. 'Let the tears come, you'll feel better for it.'

'No one has told me I'm grieving. It makes sense now, and this is the first time I've cried about it,' I said between sobs.

Stuart sat there and let me cry. Eventually the sobs subsided.

'Feeling better now?'

'Thank you.'

CHAPTER 21

Alex and I took Mungo for a longer walk in the afternoon. It was good to be together without any danger of being interrupted.

'You looked as if you'd been crying this morning,' Alex said.

'Oh dear. If you've noticed, Meadow will have. She doesn't miss anything. I expect I'll get my summons after supper.'

'Are you going to tell me what was wrong?' he asked, 'We said we wouldn't keep secrets from each other.'

'I know, and it's not a secret. In church, I started crying, although I had no idea what was wrong.'

'Church can often do that to people. That's why I'm hesitant to go back again.'

'I didn't know,' I said, 'but I'll always come with you, so you're not alone.'

'That's kind of you,' he said, 'especially as you don't think you believe. Why did you say you'd go in the first place?'

'Seriously,' I said, 'I don't know, except there was something inside me that needed it.'

'Did it help?'

'I don't think so. But Stuart stopped on the way home so I could talk. I didn't want to, but then I told him about the menopause and I just sobbed and sobbed.'

'Oh Jen,' he said putting his arm around me.

'Anyway, what he said has put things into perspective, suddenly it makes sense. I seem to have been catapulted into a world of babies these last few weeks, and I thought that somehow it would help.'

'Has it?'

'In a way. I can see other people struggling and feel I can offer them something, but it's made me avoid my own grief.'

'You know you can talk to me,' he said.

'Thanks Alex, I just didn't know I needed to talk.'

We walked hand in hand in silence for a while and then I knew I had to bring up a subject which was controversial.

'I wondered if we could go to Harriet's on Tuesday afternoon.'

'We'll take my car,' he said, 'I don't think yours will get there and back.'

'Ben always bought me rubbish cars, but he always came out when I told him we'd broken down. He was good like that.'

'He's a mechanic, so why didn't he take the rubbish car? He could repair it without having to call anyone out.'

'It didn't fit his image,' I said. 'He didn't want children's detritus in his car.'

'So, what you're saying is, he's selfish.'

'I wouldn't put it that way.'

'To me, any man who kept a good car and sent the wife and precious children out in an unreliable one is selfish.'

'Everything in that marriage was about Ben, but I didn't realise until recently… It's almost as if you're jealous of him.'

'I am. I would have loved to have known you before your struggle and looked after you.'

'You mean when you could have children with me.'

'No, I don't mean that at all. I know you're grieving, but please don't take everything I say as wanting children,' he said.

'Sorry. But you had Millie then.'

He nodded.

'I think I may have to get rid of that car. I've no emergency breakdown cover and the MOT is due soon. I don't think I can afford the running expenses, and the children will expect Christmas presents,' I said.

'How about if you sell it while it has some MOT left? You can use mine?'

'Thanks,' I said, 'that's generous of you. Can you help me sell it? I've never sold a car before.'

'If I was you, I'd put it in the car auction. There's a good one in Norwich. The car's not worth much and you've presumably no service history?'

'No, Ben did all that.'

'We'll sort that out then.'

'Thanks Alex, what would I do without you?'

'I'll put you on my breakdown cover, too. But there's something I need in return – '

He turned to me and our lips met.

When I had my breath back, I said 'and will you help me muck it out?'

'That's taking it a bit too far,' he said laughing.

I was already wondering if I might regret it. If I had no car, I had no means of permanently escaping the Village if I needed to. If Alex and I fell out, I may need to make a fast getaway.

CHAPTER 22

As I thought, I got my summons at supper. 'Do you want me to come?' Alex whispered in my ear. I shook my head.

Meadow wanted to know if Stuart had upset me, which I denied. I told her what happened and she relaxed. 'I just worry about you when you're upset, my dear,' she said.

'I know, and you have to believe that I would tell you if anything or anyone here did.'

Prue, Emily and her toddlers were due to visit the following afternoon. I woke that morning to heavy rain and sighed. This was not the weather for visitors.

'You look a bit downcast this morning,' Teddy said.

'We have visitors this afternoon and the weather is awful. The children love to see the donkeys and the chickens, but it's not looking good.'

Teddy smiled, 'When you've lived in Norfolk for a few years, you'll learn to read the weather. The sun will be shining by this afternoon.'

I didn't believe him until Clifford went outside and said, 'The weather's improving.'

I wondered if this was some sort of joke between them. They were both capable of fooling me. But they were right. By the afternoon, the sun had come out and I could hear Teddy on the mower doing what he said he hoped would be the last cut of the year.

Jazz had found a hedgehog that morning who didn't look well. He said it had fly strike and was too small to survive on its own. Meadow had told him to take it to the wildlife hospital as soon as possible in her car.

I'd never seen a hedgehog close up, except when they were killed on the road, and was warned to be careful as most of them had fleas. Daniel scrutinised the creature carefully, but Amber made sure he didn't get too close.

Alex told me that he had made hedgehog houses to put around the site, and asked if I'd like to help set them out with him the following day. This was something new to me, so I said I would. I knew there'd be a backlog of admin as I was taking Amber and Daniel to the playgroup, but I figured I could get the urgent tasks done and leave the rest for the following day.

I hadn't forgotten our breadmaking course that evening. Interestingly we would be making bread rolls shaped like hedgehogs.

When Jazz returned he said that they examined the little hedgehog at the wildlife hospital and it looked as if it would survive. They were giving it a bath to get rid of the fly eggs and maggots. They would nurse it to health. Like a family, the whole community wanted news when Jazz returned.

Alex walked with me to collect the mail and I took the opportunity to ask him what the smaller boxes going up around the site were. He told me about bug hotels, with cut canes, straw, and bark pieces in them. The boxes made good places for the bugs to hibernate over winter. There was also an old tree trunk, cut to about waist level, with holes drilled through the bark. He told me that was for solitary bees and how important the insects were as they don't use pesticides in the Village.

He also told me that in late spring the wildlife hospital comes and releases hedgehogs on the site, so our little one may be coming back. Hedgehogs eat slugs which otherwise would eat the leafy vegetables. It amazed me that nature was so clever. I'd previously talked to Alex about the beehives and he explained about the wild flower meadow beyond the donkey paddock which was good for bees and beneficial insects.

The honey produced was really tasty. Only the surplus was taken from the hives, but it sold on the market as did all the wonky fruit and veg that supermarket producers may discard. The Village market stall offered a lot more than most shops, at a price that could be afforded. The locals loved it.

Stuart had been such a hit with the children that he went to market each Saturday while he was staying.

I was beginning to learn that there was a lot to show our friend's children when they came to visit. Alex even said that those who were toddling would be welcome to make their own bug boxes.

'Why aren't you selling these and the hedgehog homes on the market stall? Children are encouraged to be aware of the environment nowadays. You could sell readymade bug boxes or fill-your-own. They would be lovely for Christmas presents.'

'That's a good thought. How about coming with me to a garden centre to look at what they've got and how much they cost?'

'That's a date,' I said.

I was glad to get in from the rain. It had eased down slightly and I had protective clothing on. Why was it that I always seemed to take wet weather so seriously? Then I remembered.

In London, my only winter footwear was a pair of boots that were at least ten years old and leaked. I should try to forget what I had learnt in London and replace it with lessons from Honsham.

As Clifford said, the weather was improving and by the afternoon only a few puddles reminded me of that morning. The sun was shining and, even in November, there was warmth in it.

Emily drove into the courtyard and parked the car. Amber, Daniel and I went out to meet her, Prue and the children. Daniel's excitement grew as he waited for the children to be taken out of the car. The first thing he did when we returned to his home was to pass toys to the other children. I was worried he may get selfish, being the only child among us, but I was wrong. Amber and Emily chatted away together in the kitchen, making tea, and I had a chance to talk with Prue.

'I've been thinking of trying to find my mother before it's too late, although it could be already. I need to know about health problems in the family, not just for my children but for my grandchildren, too,' she said.

'Do your children know you were adopted?'

'No, I've never had any cause to tell them. My adopted parents are still alive and I'm wondering how the children will feel when they find out they're not their real grandparents.'

'Is that why you've been putting it off?'

'I think so.'

'You accept your adopted parents as your own, don't you?' She nodded. 'Why shouldn't they accept them as grandparents in the same way?' I asked.

She smiled as Amber came in with a tray of tea and biscuits.

I'd almost forgotten how much mess children can make, but the three of them did well. The oldest was toddling, so he soon took control of distributing the toys and I loved the way they were playing together.

After a while, Amber asked who would like to see the donkeys and the chickens, and we put their coats and hats on and made our way across.

About half an hour later, we came back into the warm and had more tea, and then it was time to leave. The children were tired and the oldest girl cried when they left.

'I'll tidy up,' I said to Amber, 'while you put Daniel down for a sleep.'

I'd enjoyed my afternoon and realised I didn't want to isolate myself from children. I still questioned the appropriateness of talking to Harriet, but having made such a fuss about it earlier, I thought I should continue. I knew I would regret it if I didn't.

At class that evening I noticed that Nina had begun to grow with the baby. She mentioned that she would soon have difficulty reaching the workbench and we all laughed.

The hedgehog rolls were fun things to make. They really did look like hedgehogs, and I thought how much children would love them. No matter how hard I tried to divert my thoughts away from children, they kept coming into my head. It was probably because I was worried about visiting Harriet.

The following day, we set off after lunch to the address I thought might still be Harriet's. We had taken the precaution of telling Jazz where we were going, just in case.

'How are you feeling?' Alex asked.

'I'm not certain. Nervous though. In the newspaper photograph she looked as if she was on drugs, which made me think that she will still be hurting.'

'Or she could have let go of the hurt and replaced it with bitterness or anger.'

'That's true. Whatever emotions she has, it's not going to be easy to talk to her.'

Alex stopped the car. 'We're about a quarter of a mile away. I think we should walk from here. Are you alright with this? It's not too late to change your mind.'

'I'm okay,' I said, 'let's get going.' I'm sure he knew, as well as I did, that I wasn't okay.

We saw the house without any trouble. The garden was untended and the windowpanes were dirty and looked as if they might fall out of the frames at any time. Paint peeled off the door and tiles were missing from the roof.

'Do you think anyone actually lives here?' Alex asked.

'Let's knock and see,' I replied, more bravely than I felt.

The doorbell push had fallen off so Alex banged on the door.

There was no answer, so he tried again.

Still no answer.

'Let's try the back,' I said. As walked past the kitchen window, we could see washed crockery on the draining board. Alex banged on the back door, but still there was no reply. We peered through the window, but there was no sign of life, so we went back to the front again.

'I hate to say this, but we're being filmed,' Alex said, pointing out a camera. 'I don't think there's anyone at home so we might as well leave.'

We walked back to the car. 'Well, that was a waste of an afternoon,' I said.

'Not necessarily. We passed a garden centre on the way. Let's go in there and get a hot drink. I don't know about you, but I'm perished.'

The garden centre had a clean and expensive café, where we had tea and cake. We were feeling warmer and much more positive.

'While we're here, should we look in the wildlife section?' I asked.

We looked at their bug hotels, but Alex was scathing. 'They're not a good quality. You'll be lucky if they last a couple of winters. The wood isn't even treated.' His eyes opened wide when he saw the price.

'You're on to a good thing here, Jen. We wouldn't charge anywhere near as much as this, and there's no fill-your-own option. Let's look at the hedgehog houses.'

They were mass-produced and, once again, he wasn't polite about them – especially the price.

'I suppose they're looking to cash in on the Christmas present market,' he said. 'I'll have a word with Meadow and see what she thinks. I could do different types of nest boxes, too.'

'It will be a service to the local people,' I said, 'but don't forget your caretaking duties have to come first.'

He grinned at me. 'I never forget that, but the Village has about as many bug hotels and hedgehog houses as it can take and I still have time to spare.'

'So, it wasn't a wasted afternoon,' I said.

'Definitely not.'

'I just wish Harriet had been in and we could have got it over and done with.'

He kissed me in the middle of the garden centre!

CHAPTER 22

At suppertime, Stuart asked if he could have a chat with Alex and me and we arranged to meet him in his apartment. I was worried I might have done something wrong, but he said it was nothing like that.

We sat together on his sofa.

'I know you're interested in genealogy,' he said, 'I've been going through adoption records and believe my birth mother's name is Ruth Carpenter.'

I gasped.

'If it is her, I know her background, but I wasn't able to find out whether she changed her name after she left prison and I need to find out whether Penelope Brown and Ruth Carpenter are the same person. Do you think you can help me to find out?' he asked.

'Yes,' said Alex, 'we've been looking at her history, but we understood her son was called Michael.'

'Ross could have made a mistake,' I said. 'I'll go next door and get my file.' I was confused. Could Stuart have got it wrong? But surely a lawyer would have double-checked everything?

'If it is her, you know the worst about her?' I asked.

'I know that she stole and killed a baby boy,' he said.

I went back to my apartment and returned with my laptop. 'Ross definitely said her son's name is Michael.'

Stuart shrugged, 'My date of birth is ninth of December 1978,' he said.

'That's the day she gave birth to a son with a disability,' I said.

'I have spina bifida and that would have been obvious at birth,' he said.

'Has your sister contacted you?' Alex asked.

'No. I haven't been able to find her.'

What was going on? I trusted Ross, as an ex-policeman, to tell the truth but I didn't think Stuart would make a mistake about something so important to himself.

'I'm confused,' Alex said. 'We've been visiting her stepbrother, and he said that her children were Claire and Michael. Claire actually visited him and his wife when Ruth was due to be released from prison.'

'Could she be someone, who just said she was Ruth's biological daughter, or who had made a mistake?' I asked. 'It's strange, though, that she knew she had a brother.'

'That information could have been taken from newspaper reports,' Stuart said.

'Claire telephoned me. She said that she had collected Ruth from our gate when Meadow chucked her out and taken her to the housing department in Dereham. Claire seemed pleasant and friendly.'

'Did you get a phone number for her?' Stuart asked.

'No, the number was withheld because she works shifts and doesn't want people phoning while she's asleep or at work.'

'That's convenient,' Stuart said.

'You think she was a trickster, don't you?' Alex asked. 'I'm surprised that Ross would have been fooled. I thought police were taught to recognise that sort of thing.'

'It's not always obvious, sadly,' Stuart replied. 'Do you think it's my mother's body that Teddy dug up? Are you planning to try to find out who killed her?'

'Yes, to both.'

'How can I help?'

'Praying would be good,' said Alex. 'We've been out to see Harriet Johnson, the mother of the stolen baby, but there was no answer when we knocked.'

'That was brave of you, Jen. Will you keep me up to date?'

'Of course,' Alex said.

'Thank you.'

We left his apartment, and I had to say that I felt more muddled than I had before.

As soon as we left Stuart's, I collected my gloves and hat and went over to Alex's where Mungo was waiting with his ball in his mouth. It was a cool night with no breeze at all.

'We'll have a frost tonight,' said Alex, 'first of the season. It's a frost pocket down here, but it'll be good for the sprouts and the parsnips.'

'How come?' I asked.

'It changes the flavour.'

'Are you serious?'

'Yes, it's true and it's a full moon. We'll hardly need our torches tonight.'

'What did you think of our conversation with Stuart?'

'I can't see Stuart making a mistake about his mother and he would never choose to be related to such a distasteful person. I believe him.'

'So, you think that Claire is unreliable?'

He nodded.

'But why would she tell anyone that she was Ruth Carpenter's daughter?'

'To get more information, so that when Ruth dies, she can sell her story, or perhaps inherit.'

'I looked that one up. Once a child is adopted she can inherit from her new family, but not from her birth mother. Unless the birth mother puts her in her will. You're probably right about selling her mother's story. Think of all the information she could have gleaned from Ross and his wife when she visited them that day,' I said.

We walked in silence for a bit. 'So, are you going to tell me which name you drew out for Secret Santa?' Alex asked.

'Which bit of Secret Santa, don't you understand?'

'Fair enough,' he said and grabbed my hand. 'Mungo's waiting for us to throw his ball.'

Neither Mark nor Lily told me whose name they had pulled from the hat, but Lily spent much more time than normal in her room and Mark often disappeared when he had done his homework and it wasn't to see Peter. Amber and I worked together practising making biscuits for Alex's secret Santa. Of course, the trials were taken to the kitchen for people to have with their tea or coffee.

The men were doing more maintenance work outside, pruning trees, clearing brambles in the woods, rotovating fields, digging potatoes and root vegetables, but it was accepted as a quiet time when work could stop at lunchtime. There would be madness as the Christmas period drew nearer, and we all knew that.

The clocks had changed and darkness came early. I began to understand why farm workers used to work daylight hours as winter approached. I watched squirrels using every minute they could hunting for nuts, and partridges and pheasants moving onto our site, sensing that they were safe from shooting parties when they lodged with us.

One afternoon, Alex suggested it was time we tried making sweets. I had found recipes online and borrowed one of Sally's jam thermometers, so we were all set.

'Let's try just two recipes to start with and if we have time, we can do more,' he said.

We decided first on a plain fudge and I was surprised how long it took. I had bought some clear cellophane bags to bag it up after it had cooled.

'I was thinking of sending some to Wilma and Ogden, they do so much for Lily and Mark.' Wilma and Ogden were Jazz's parents who held an open house almost continually and had welcomed my children as their own. 'Of course, we'd have to taste it first,' I said.

'Good idea,' replied Alex, 'quality control is absolutely essential.'

'Then we could try some peanut brittle and chocolate peppermint creams, then truffles, toffee, chocolate brownies, rocky road, chocolate pretzels and…'

'That will take at least a week,' Alex said laughing. 'You've bought the bags, but how are you going to present them? In a carrier bag?'

'Ah, I need to get a basket or tray or something.'

'Why don't you ask Sally to pick up some cardboard trays when she goes to the wholesalers? You could cover them with Christmas paper. In fact, you could make a mixed hamper with sweets and biscuits.'

'You're right. Ogden and Wilma cook mainly Caribbean food, but I don't remember having any biscuits when I went to see them. Perhaps their national dishes are short of them.'

'You'll need labels, so that the recipient knows what's in each bag. They've got them in the hardware shop, would you like me to get you some?'

'Yes please. I'm looking forward to Christmas this year for the first time since the children were young.'

'Why?'

'We never had money to do Christmas with all the trimmings and what we did have, Ben would spend in the pub with his friends.'

'Or elsewhere?'

'One year I was putting his socks away and I found a jeweller's box in his drawer with a pretty necklace in it. I thought he had bought it for me for Christmas, but he hadn't.'

'For one of his mistresses?'

'Yes,' and I burst into tears. Alex put his arms around me. 'How could I have been so naïve?'

'He didn't deserve you. You're too good for him,' he said, 'and he had the cheek to expect you to take him back.'

He held me as I cried and, when my tears dried up, kissed me.

CHAPTER 23

I had been looking forward to the next playgroup. I felt, as a "grandmother", I was beginning to fit well into the group. That week there were no more crying mothers and Amber said she would keep a look out for anyone who looked as if she needed help. There was one solitary dad who came along each week, Malcolm. He told me he was a househusband and didn't worry that he was the only man. The thing that did concern him was how he might appear to the women from the refuge, those running away from domestic abuse.

Flip and I talked about it and she and Amber suggested he sat with them. Both had been abused, but could see how gentle Malcolm was with his baby, that he was not threatening at all. In fact, by the end of the morning, they had started laughing with him.

After coffee break, Prue was washing up and I was drying when she asked me if I could help her locate her family, as apparently I'd implied I'd be better at it than she could be.

'Of course,' I replied, 'would you like to come over tomorrow afternoon?' I could see how grateful she was. 'Do you know what your mother's name is?'

'Yes,' she replied, 'it's Ruth Carpenter.'

I felt myself go pale and I was glad she was working hard at the washing-up and didn't notice.

'Have you any pictures of you as a baby?' I asked.

'Yes, my new parents were taking them all the time. Would you like me to bring the album?'

Fortunately, the group was closing as we finished cleaning up and I could take Amber and Daniel home. Daniel usually fell asleep on the way and Amber took him straight inside in his car seat, meaning I didn't have to stay and talk.

When we got back, I hunted out Alex and told him about Prue.

He replied, 'Let's not jump to conclusions. Carpenter is a common surname and Ruth isn't unusual in that generation. We probably need to get her date of birth, don't we?"

'Should we involve Stuart at this stage?' I asked.

'Yes, we'll talk to him after lunch,' Alex said. 'I think he needs to be with us when we find out. It would be wrong to keep it from him. He's sensible enough to look at it objectively. Also, he's good with people and will help if she's upset,' he said.

'I've not told him about his grandmother yet,' I said. 'He should know about her, as well.'

The following morning passed slowly. Stuart popped into the office to see if I was okay and I told him he had a grandmother alive, which delighted him, but he was still concerned about Prue.

'The name "Ruth Carpenter" is just two words on a piece of paper to Prue. If she is my sister, she'll need to know what our mother did and I don't know how she will take it. I'm worried about her. When Emily had her stroke, I was there for her, as I was when her husband left her. I helped her to fill in the forms she needed for both her own and Emily's benefits. She hit a really low point when her husband left her to cope with things alone,' he said. 'I considered moving in, but her home couldn't be adjusted for both of us. Prue and I are drawn to each other. If she is my sister, that may explain the attraction between us.'

'Would you like to be with us this afternoon when we tell her?' I asked.

'I think I should, although I hate to think of her being upset again.'

'You're a good man, Stuart.'

He smiled at me. 'I do my best.'

Time couldn't be stopped and at two o'clock I heard her car. Alex went out to meet her. He introduced himself and asked if she would mind if he and Stuart helped with the research. She seemed happy enough. Alex went into the kitchen to make a pot of tea and Prue opened the album. 'This was the first photograph my parents took. The adoption hadn't been finalised then.'

'How old were you in these?

'About two weeks. Mum and Dad took me on almost as soon as I was released for adoption, which would have been around the end of October 1977.'

'You were a beautiful baby,' I said, noting the birthmark on her head. 'When is your birthday?'

'Fifth of October. It's hard to believe this little thing grew big enough to have babies of her own.'

While she was speaking, I nodded to Alex and Stuart.

When she'd finished and Alex was pouring the tea, Stuart went over to Prue. 'It's going to be hard to believe, Prue, but you and I have the same mother. We are brother and sister.'

She looked at Stuart and then Alex and me. I laid a family tree in front of her. She started weeping. 'This isn't some sort of joke, is it?'

'No,' we all said together.

'When you told me your mother's name yesterday, I wondered if it could be a different Ruth Carpenter, but the dates all fit.'

'You went quiet and stopped laughing. I wondered what was wrong,' she said.

'I think you need to know that she wasn't a nice woman,' said Stuart. 'You were given away because of that birthmark on your head, I was rejected because of my disability.'

'No!' she said.

'It gets worse,' he said. 'Do you want to know anything more?'

'I think you had better tell me.'

Stuart took a deep breath. 'She wanted a perfect baby, so she went into the maternity department at the hospital and stole one.' Prue gasped. 'When the baby started to cry, he was no longer perfect, so she shook him to stop him crying.' Prue's eyes filled with tears. Stuart continued, 'Later, when she found him unresponsive, she called an ambulance. He died in hospital. Ruth claimed that she had saved the baby's life by getting him to hospital, but the jury didn't agree. She was imprisoned.'

Stuart stopped to wipe his eyes and blow his nose. 'When she came out of prison, she changed her name to Penelope Brown.'

Prue was sobbing. 'That's the name of the person buried here.'

'Yes,' said Stuart, 'that's part of the reason why I came to stay here. I thought it was our birth mother.'

'There are people here who met your mother,' Alex said, 'and they can back up what Stuart has said. She really wasn't a nice person, that's why Meadow insisted she leave. We can introduce you to them if you want.'

'No,' she said. 'I hoped to find my mother, so I could get some idea of the family's medical history. I don't expect I will ever know now.'

Stuart was still holding her hand. 'We have a grandmother who is alive. Jen says she's lovely and her memory is good. She can tell us about our mother as a child. Would you like to come to see her with me?'

'I'd like that. I can tell you now that I have always been attracted to you Stuart. The fact that we're siblings probably explains it.'

'I've suddenly realised that I have nieces,' Stuart said.

'You've nine great-nieces and nephews, too. I'm sorry to tell you so close to Christmas, but your Christmas list has just grown very much longer.' Prue replied.

Stuart smiled. 'I can't wait to meet them all,' he said. 'But, on a serious note, we don't know who killed our mother yet. The police are still investigating.'

He looked at me and Alex.

Alex said, 'We're not happy with the quality of the police investigation. It was Jen and I who found out who she was, although we're happy to let the police take the credit. They're not getting anywhere near to finding her killer as far as we can work out. We don't want it to become a cold case, so Jen and I have been looking into it. We'd like to continue if that's okay with you two?'

'I don't want anyone getting hurt,' said Stuart sharply. 'Some of the people she mixed with may be dangerous.'

'That's why we always let someone know where we are going and when we expect to be back,' I said.

Prue looked at Stuart, 'Can we go out for a while?'

The two of them left. Alex and I sat on the settee together. 'I feel completely drained,' I said after a while.

'Me, too,' said Alex. 'Do you think they'll be alright?'

'They have each other now. Our major problem is delaying their visit to Elsie as she is sure to tell Ross and I think we should let him know first that Claire is an imposter.'

'Do you want to call him and see if we can visit him tomorrow afternoon?' he asked.

I think I must have telephoned when he was busy. He was complaining of deadlines to worry about and visiting would be inconvenient until after Christmas. I handed the phone over to Alex, who explained our concerns about Claire.

Alex was quiet for a while, and then said, 'Well, I think Elsie should know because Stuart and Prue will be wanting to visit her. Okay. Bye.'

'How did he take the news?' I asked.

'He didn't believe us. He said we were amateurs who'd probably got it wrong. I wasn't even going to try to convince him. He's obviously under a lot of strain at the moment. I haven't heard him in that sort of mood before.'

'At least you told him that Elsie should know. I don't suppose he'll be able to visit her to tell her in the near future. Could we have got it wrong? Do you think Stuart and Prue are stringing us along?'

'Knowing both of them and their backgrounds, I'm certain they're not. We both saw Prue's baby pictures.'

He picked up the album and opened it again, then took it to the window. 'That birthmark is genuine and it's on all her baby pictures. Stuart wouldn't risk his career for some sort of confidence trick. I still believe they are genuine.'

'And they know I've met their adopted parents who could give me their dates of birth. It's too risky for it to be a pretence.'

After about half an hour they both came back in.

'Did that help?' I asked.

Prue's eyes were red and puffy. She walked to me and gave me a hug, 'Thank you so much, Jen. You've put that missing link back into my life, and I've found my brother. That sounds stupid. I've known him for as long as long as I can remember but only as a friend. He's the sort of brother anyone would be proud to have.'

I could see Stuart's eyes watering, too. 'Thanks Jen and Alex,' he said, then hid his face in his handkerchief.

Alex and I took it as time to disappear into the kitchen and make another pot of tea.

'Don't hurry,' he said, 'they need a bit of time to compose themselves.'

He wrapped me in his arms and kissed me. 'If we never find the killer, we've helped two people and that's what counts.'

I nodded, 'But if we don't want stewed tea, we need to go back into the lounge.'

Eventually Stuart took Prue home. He didn't think she was fit to drive, and said he'd arrange for her car to be returned the following morning. Alex was only too pleased to oblige.

CHAPTER 24

The following evening was our breadmaking class, so we decided to leave visiting Harriet again for another day. I was wondering whether we should have skipped the class and taken another chance on Harriet. It was troubling me more each day.

That evening we made rye bread, a solid heavy bread which felt much like I did when anticipating the next afternoon. I knew we had to try to see her but my gut told me otherwise.

That afternoon, it was pouring with rain, a dark dismal day. We walked to the house which looked even more sombre than it did before. I had visions of metal buckets inside catching water from the leaks in the roof.

Alex hammered on the front door again. There was no reply, and no lights on indoors.

'Perhaps she works during the day. We could go back to the garden centre for tea if you want and come back later in the afternoon.'

'It's a thought,' I said, 'but I think we should check the back first. The dripping water could be muffling our knocks.'

As we rounded the corner, Alex stopped. 'There's someone on the ground.'

Harriet was almost unconscious and very wet. When I spoke to her, she opened her eyes and her pupils were dilated. I pushed her sleeve up and there were numerous needle scars and fresh bruising.

'The back door must be unlocked, she has no keys on her,' I said.

Alex was looking down on us. 'She doesn't look as if she's fit to walk, I'll carry her in.'

He carried her without any strain and followed me through the backdoor. I tried the doors in the hallway and when I found the lounge, he laid her on the sofa.

'I don't like to go upstairs,' I said, 'but she needs this wet clothing off and something to cover her up.' I looked around the room at the needle strewn tables. It was perishing cold, but she was too far gone to even shiver.

'Do you think we should call an ambulance?' he asked.

'I think we should, to be on the safe side, although it will probably be a waste of their time.' I handed him my phone. 'Then can you go up and find a duvet?'

When I heard his footsteps on the bare stairs, I took off her clothes and dropped them on the floor. I met Alex at the bottom of the stairs and took the duvet from him. 'Don't come in yet, she's naked.' I turned her onto her side and covered her up. How could someone this thin still be alive? She was killing herself. From what I'd read about addiction, I thought that unconsciousness was probably a welcome relief for her.

We waited until Harriet was being looked after by a paramedic. I almost ran to the car, I was so desperate to get away.

As we sat drinking tea at a garden centre, Alex said, 'Ruth didn't just kill Harriet's baby and husband, she's killing Harriet, too.'

I nodded. 'I wonder if there's a good time to catch her or whether she's always like this in the afternoon.' I was thinking aloud.

'I think there's someone else living there. One of the bedrooms was much like the lounge, with needles everywhere and a dirty unmade bed. The other was clean and tidy, but obviously being used – there were books beside the bed and folded clothes on the chair, women's clothes.'

'That's interesting. Perhaps we should go back at a different time of day or at the weekend,' I said.

'We may meet some dangerous undesirables. I don't think it's a good idea.'

'Nor do I, but I can't leave it like this. I'll come on my own if you don't want to.'

I thought we were about to have another argument until he said, 'I'll have to come with you, because you'll never find the way on your own.' The tension was broken.

I punched him on the shoulder, 'Cheeky.'

We both laughed.

I still felt shocked about the state of Harriet's body when I arrived home. I wondered if there was a way of helping her but I knew that once addiction took hold, it was unlikely that anyone could help her until she decided she needed help. She was only in her sixties, but her corpse-like appearance made her look over ninety.

'When should we go back again?' I asked Alex.

'We're tied up this weekend with baking, so I suggest we go on Saturday week.'

I didn't want to leave it that long but was aware that we had commitments which we must keep.

DI Watson was on site the following afternoon. His nose was red, he was rubbing his hands together and stamping his feet.

I opened my door, 'Do you fancy coming in to warm up. You look frozen.'

He smiled and came straight across. 'I'll never understand Norfolk. It looks nice outside but as soon as I put my feet out of the door, the icy wind attempts to bite off all my extremities.'

'Where do you originate from?'

'Cornwall. My wife and I were discussing returning when I retire. The problem is that we have friends here and we'd have to start again if we moved back. We left over thirty years ago, and no one remembers us.'

'When you retire, you won't have to wear a collar and tie. It may be simpler to just buy some warm clothes.'

'You have a point,' he said, 'but what about you? You're not local.'

'This time last year, I was in London. I don't remember it ever being really cold there. I think it was because the buildings sheltered us from the wind.'

'Which comes to Norfolk directly from the Arctic,' he said. 'Will you go back?'

'Never. Alex and I went there to tidy up my house for rental and I hated it. I've got used to the quiet isolation here. It would take a lot to make me move away.'

'What about friends?' he asked, 'Don't you miss them?'

'I didn't know what real friendship was until I moved here, and the children love being in Norfolk. How's the investigation going?'

'We've a few people that we need to interview, who I hope will move us forward.'

'Will you be happy to retire if you don't solve it?'

'Not really. But time is against me. From what people say about Penelope Brown, she deserves to have been killed.'

I tried to keep my calm. 'No one deserves to be killed.'

'Well, I happen to think that if we'd lived in the days of capital punishment, she'd have been executed anyway. And that's less than she deserves.'

I could hardly believe what I was hearing but refused to let him wind me up.

Fairly soon afterwards, he left my apartment.

As I looked out of my window, I saw two policeman putting Will and Clifford into a police car. Meadow came out and said something to Clifford.

A few minutes later, I heard Stuart's phone ring in his apartment and realised that Meadow must be asking him to go to the police station.

He knocked on my door a bit later and said, 'I'll probably be late back for supper. If I am can you let Sally know for me?'

I agreed, but I couldn't forget Will's tear-stained face.

The remainder of us were quiet at supper. Sally's eyes were red and downcast, and Meadow pushed her food around on the plate, eating very little.

Meadow broke the silence. 'You all know how gentle and sensitive Will and Clifford are. Nicole was awful to them just because they were gay. I know that they didn't touch Nicole or Penelope or whatever her name was, even though they may have had cause. Clifford would never have thought of retaliation. Even if he did, Will would have told us. He's such a drama queen, he couldn't keep it to himself. I wouldn't be surprised if tomorrow morning he is here at breakfast regaling us with what happened at the police station. Stuart is with them and I don't think there's anyone better to have on your side.'

I wondered how ethical it would be if he had to formally act for them, being Ruth's son.

'I understand that everyone is upset, especially Sally,' Meadow said, 'so I suggest that we make sure no one is left alone this evening. Sally, you're coming over to me this evening when you've cleared up in here. I'm sure someone will volunteer to help you.'

'I will,' I said and, true to my word, helped her with the dishes, cleaned the table and washed the floor.

'She was an awful woman,' Sally said. 'She must have upset thousands of people during her lifetime.'

'DI Watson knows that, but he's retiring soon. I suppose he's going to interview a few people, just to make it look as if he had done his job, and then let the case go cold.'

'It's not so much Will that I worry about, lovey, he's like a big boy. He used to be an actor and he talks everything out in a dramatic way. It's poor Clifford I feel for. He's quiet and holds his feelings close. This could destroy him.'

'I hope not. I'm sure that Meadow will keep an eye on him, she's good at listening and encouraging people to talk, very much like Stuart,' I said.

'You've noticed that about Stuart? He's a wonderful man.'

'You'll be alright with Meadow this evening, will you?'

'Yes, lovey. But only if Mark will be visiting Peter. He hasn't been doing that quite as much as he used to.'

'It's nothing to do with Peter. He's working on his secret Santa, I've no idea what he is doing, but I expect he's talked to Peter about it.'

'There's no doubt about that at all. They tell each other everything. Peter's asked me if he and Mark can go out together to get things for his secret Santa. I don't usually let him because it can be too noisy for him, but I trust Mark to look after him.'

'They'll be fine together,' I said, 'They want to go to the cathedral at the same time.'

'I thought so, lovey,' she said. 'I suppose this will be the first of many outings. The pair of them are mad about buildings.'

'That didn't happen until we came here. Peter's been a good influence on Mark.'

'That's something I've been waiting to hear his whole life. Thank you so much.'

We went our separate ways and I could feel the annoyance with DI Watson rising inside me again. He saw Peter as a half-wit, which was far from the truth, and he took two innocent men to the station for questioning, when he could have done it here. I felt tempted to report him, but didn't feel I could.

I heard Stuart's van arrive back at around eleven o'clock that evening. Voices told me that Will and Clifford came home with him.

I opened the door. 'Would you like a hot drink?'

'Thanks for offering,' he replied, 'but I'd like to get to bed. Will and Clifford are no longer suspects,' he said.

I smiled and breathed a sigh of relief.

CHAPTER 25

At breakfast the following morning, Will was talking to anyone who would or wouldn't listen to his story. Clifford was quiet, and hardly said a word. I heard Meadow ask him to come and see her after breakfast and hoped she could help him.

Will's monologue began to annoy me after a while and, as much as I loved him, I took him to one side and said, 'Sally was crying about you last night, you know. It really got to her that someone could think you capable of murder. She was so worried. Can you talk about something else?'

'Oh no. I didn't think. My enormous mouth has never learnt to control itself. I'll get them going on Secret Santa.'

He went over to Sally and kissed her on the cheek.

'What's that for?' she asked.

'To say I love you like a mother and to thank you for caring.'

Sally took out her handkerchief and blew her nose.

'Come on now, don't cry.'

'And don't you let your breakfast get cold!'

Stuart took in what was happening. He was quiet, just watching and listening. As he left after breakfast, he said to Clifford, 'You know where I am if you need to talk to someone.'

'Thanks, mate.'

I did my admin duties and noticed Clifford leaving Meadow's, so went in to clean her apartment.

'I'll soon be able to do this myself,' she said.

'But I've got to earn my pay,' I said.

'Make us coffee and sit down.'

'Is something worrying you?' I asked.

'No. I was concerned about Clifford, and I'll keep an eye on him for the next few weeks. It was a terrible shock for him and he felt he had to hold up for Will's sake. Apparently, Stuart was wonderful. He reassured them that they weren't being arrested, just being questioned, and his logic made DI Watson look rather foolish.'

'I'm glad about that, but I need to tell you something, Meadow. We believe that Stuart and my friend Prue are Ruth Carpenter's children. I'm afraid Prue had a terrible shock when she found out what her mother did, but Stuart helped her.'

'That's tough for her. But it explains why she and Stuart look so similar.'

'Do they? I hadn't noticed.'

'If I'd have known that, I wouldn't have sent Stuart with Will and Clifford. Why didn't he say something?'

'Because nothing has been proved, so ethically I don't think he did anything wrong. They're both going to have DNA tests to confirm they are related and, if so, it's highly probable that Ruth Carpenter is their mother. Dates of birth tie up with the family tree I've constructed, so I don't think there can be a mistake,' I said.

'You've done well,' she said. 'What I wanted to talk to you about is the refuge and Amber's project. I can see that she's missed out on schooling, or more likely that she's had lack of continuity in her schooling. I'd like her to go to college to brush up on her basic skills. I haven't said anything to her yet, my dear, but do you think we could cope with Daniel while she's out?'

'Easily,' I said.

'Good. We probably won't be able to get her on a course until next year, but as long as we can cope, that's fine. She's a dab hand with the computer and has lots of ideas. We've had a wonderful response from local businesses, even the strange woman with the pink and purple hair has offered to make baby carriers and bags for the mothers.'

'You mean the upholsterer I thought Alex was having an affair with that time?'

'Yes,' she said, 'and you'll have a chance to meet her when you collect the gifts, because I think we'll need two of you.'

'The supermarket has put out a trolley for donations of Advent Calendars and when they have enough, they will change it for gifts for deprived families,' she said.

'The hardware shop has offered as many decorations as they need, as well as three hairdryers, which is thoughtful of them. The craft shop has put out a trolley, similar to the supermarket, and people are putting handmade toys, knitted garments and blankets in it. Apparently there has been a huge response.' She looked at a list on the table. 'The post office has said we can have as much wrapping paper, Sellotape, labels and cards as we want, stationery and colouring books, all that sort of thing. The WI are baking for them and will provide jams, marmalade and stockings for the children. The butcher will give turkeys, sausages, and anything else they need, the greengrocer is giving fruit and the chemist has put out a trolley for toiletries, make up, nappies etc.'

'Wow! The residents should have a fabulous Christmas after all.'

'But that's not all, a number of the shops have suggested having trolleys out for donations most of the year. They want us to let them know if there's anything specific they need.'

'Amber's idea is a hit,' I said.

'Clifford has always taken the van to the refuge and it looks to me as if we may have more than one van load this Christmas, that's why you and Amber will both be needed to collect it.'

'Does Amber know about this?'

'Yes, but she's not one to boast. She's a lovely girl and I couldn't choose anyone better as a mother for my great-nephew.'

I kissed her on the cheek and she wiped her tears away.

A little later I had a phone call from Jazz's mother, Wilma.

'Would you and Alex be able to pop over after lunch?'

'Of course. Anything wrong?'

'We'll tell you when we see you.'

'It's not one of my children, is it?'

'No. Nothing like that, but please come.'

'We will. See you then.' I put the phone down. Something was definitely wrong. I'd not heard Wilma like that before. She sounded as if her nose was blocked and I thought she'd been crying.

I left the office and went to look for Alex. His workshop was crammed with hedgehog homes, bug hotels, and nesting boxes.

'Wow!' I said, 'You've been working hard.'

'I have! I'm using up all my offcuts. I just hope they sell at the market, because I'm running out of room.'

'You should be alright if Stuart is going.'

'Do you mean that he could take a lot in his van or that he's a good salesman?'

'I was thinking more of his selling ability, but his van will be useful, too,' I said.

'You don't usually hunt me out in the morning. Is something wrong?'

'I think so. I had a phone call from Wilma. She sounded upset and asked if we could go over after lunch. I get the feeling that she and Ogden want to talk to us before the house fills up with children home from school.'

'That sounds serious. It's not about Mark and Lily, I hope?'

'First thing I checked, but she said not.'

Immediately lunch had finished, Alex and I drove to Honsham to our friends' house.

Ogden welcomed us at the door. He was usually a lively and laughing man, but he looked as if he had shrunk and his shoulders sagged.

He showed us into the lounge where Wilma had prepared a tea-tray for us.

He passed an envelope over to us, addressed to 'The Head of the Jenny Lind', the children's hospital in Norwich. Ogden was a paediatric consultant there. We pulled the contents out.

The letter said, 'You killed my baby. Yours will be next.' The handwriting was shaky and I put the letter to my nose.

'This smells odd. Is it drugs? Have you taken it to the police?'

'Not yet. I didn't open it until late morning, we weren't quite certain who exactly it was meant for.'

'Can we have a copy of the letter and the envelope please? Then you need to contact the police and let them deal with it,' Alex said.

'I think you should take it seriously, you know. Your children stand out by their skin colour, if you don't mind me saying. I wouldn't want to think they were in danger,' said Alex.

'Can you think of a death of a baby from a drug addicted mother?' I asked.

'I can't. We've had addicted babies in the neonatal ward and they go through hell, poor little souls, but usually Social Services don't allow their mother access to them while she's being rehabilitated, or at all.'

'Perhaps the mother became addicted after she lost her baby,' I said.

'That's possible. Although we've been assuming the mother wrote the letter. It could be the father,' Ogden said. 'It could also be a miscarriage, but that wouldn't be dealt with by the Jenny Lind. I can't help feeling that the baby was born alive, as otherwise the letter would have been sent to the maternity department.'

'I'm not certain how much we can help as medical records are private, except to advise you to give it to the police and to say that it may or may not have been intended for you. It seems quite a general address, as if the writer wanted to frighten someone, but wasn't certain who,' Alex said. 'There's a possibility that 'yours' may refer to the babies in the department. I think you need help from them immediately, for the sake of the babies there.'

Wilma nodded. 'That's what we thought, but we needed someone to confirm it. Ring them now, Ogden.'

Later, in the car, Alex said, 'What made you smell the paper? It wouldn't have crossed my mind.'

'It's strange. When we have an invoice from the butcher, I know as soon as I have taken it from the mailbox. It smells mildly of raw meat, and the chemist's are always slightly scented, from the body products they sell. I don't think I consciously noticed it until I took Ogden's letter in my hands. We really shouldn't have been touching it at all, but I didn't think of that until it was too late.' I added.

'I'm certain that letter is referring to the babies in the unit, not to Ogden's children,' Alex said, 'Whichever way, they have to get the police involved.'

CHAPTER 26

That evening was our breadmaking class and, for the first time, I didn't feel like going. I chatted with Alex who convinced me that it would be alright and we had already cancelled supper with Sally, so we shouldn't change our minds. I was thinking of the babies that may be in danger at the hospital and it depressed me.

At the class we were making naan bread. Nina was in good spirits and was laughing and joking with the others. I knew my attitude was wrong, but I couldn't forget that letter. I kept thinking of all the precious babies in hospital. At least it would be sorted out before Nina gave birth to her baby. I was wondering, too, how seriously the police would take the threat in the letter. I hoped Ogden would convince them of our worries.

We made our bread and left it to rise while we went across to the pub. I ordered my meal and then one of our group, who was scrolling on his phone, cried out. 'Listen to this. The police are guarding the Jenny Lind. Apparently, there's been some sort of threat.'

'Whoever would do anything like that?' asked Nina. The atmosphere changed and our group fell quiet.

'Terrorist or a nutter,' someone said.

At that point our food arrived and we dug in. My five bean chilli looked and smelt heavenly but I had no appetite. I fiddled with it while the atmosphere around the table improved. People were chatting again, the children forgotten.

But not by me. I suddenly felt angry at Nina. I felt full up inside as if something was going to burst out of me. I ran to the door and leaned against the outside wall gasping for air, my hand rubbing at the awful pain in my chest.

Alex came out. 'Jen… Jen. Just sit on this low wall for a while.' He steered me across.

I felt as if there was no space for air in my lungs. Perhaps I was dying. Someone else came over. 'Can I help?'

'Jen. It's okay, I'll call an ambulance,' Alex said.

'Hold back for a moment, do you mind? I think I recognise this. Jen, has this happened before?' someone asked.

I nodded. I couldn't speak. My lips and fingers were tingling.

'You're having a panic attack, right? Work with me. Breathe in and out of this paper bag,' she said.

Alex held it over my mouth and nose. Gradually the pain eased.

When the bag was removed, the woman, who I recognised then as one of our class members, said, 'What caused you to panic, Jen?'

'I'm not sure. I suddenly felt trapped. I needed to breathe.'

Alex gave me a strange look as if he didn't believe me.

When we were alone, Alex put his arm around me. 'Come on, I'll take you home.'

'No, I mustn't. If I run away now, I'll never return. I need to go back in. But we can talk later, okay?'

'Of course, sweetheart.'

When we arrived back at the table our food had gone cold, not surprisingly. It summed up the whole evening, really. I felt embarrassed at everyone fussing and didn't want to look at them, but it wasn't long before I could join in their conversation again.

As we walked back, my miracle healer walked beside me. 'Your attack seemed to come on suddenly. Do you have them often?'

'Not really. This is the third now. Hopefully there won't be a fourth.'

'Can you talk to Alex?'

'Yes, he's lovely like that.'

'I think that could be the remedy. Fingers crossed, eh?'

I smiled. 'Thank you.'

'I'm a nurse, so if you ever want to talk, just give me a call. Evenings are best.' She slipped a piece of paper into my bag.

'Thank you so much.'

When we arrived back at the Village, Alex took our bread into the communal kitchen while I went to "talk to Mungo". Like with the donkeys, it felt like he was listening intently and understood everything I said.

Alex was quite a while coming back, I guess he was giving me space. When he sat on the sofa beside me, he put his arm around me and I lay my head on his shoulder.

'Do you know what it was that caused the panic attack?'

'No, I think I should sit where there's more space. I felt trapped.'

Alex was quiet for a while.

I burst into tears and he held me while I cried.

'My poor Jen,' he said. 'Now how about a hot drink?'

'Cocoa, please.'

We interspersed our cocoa with kisses and I started to feel better.

'Poor Mungo, shouldn't we be walking him?' I asked.

'Jazz did it for us earlier. I thought you might need to talk.'

'Thanks, Alex. Please don't say anything to Meadow. She's really kind, but I'm not ready to talk to her yet.'

He agreed and walked me back to my apartment.

CHAPTER 27

After breakfast, I meandered to the gate to collect the mail and Alex joined me.

'How are you feeling?'

'Absolutely normal, although it's shocked me. I just hope it won't happen again. I've never felt quite that bad before. "Hysterical woman"…'

'You're not! It just shows what pressure you are putting on yourself at the moment, that's all.'

'I suppose… I've been thinking about that letter that Ogden received. I'm thinking it's from an addict who has a grudge against the department, rather than against one person in particular. I think that if it was recent, she or he would have addressed it to a specific person.

'It must have been handed in rather than sent as there was no address on the envelope and no stamp. So, we're looking for someone who went to the hospital either yesterday or the day before.' I put the post into a bag. 'The writing was shaky, but the spelling was okay. Whoever it was had a good grasp of English, so is probably reasonably intelligent.'

'And we don't know if it was an empty or real threat,' Alex added, 'which doesn't amount to a lot.'

'Do you think it could be in any way connected with our investigation?' I asked.

'It could be. I'm certain that Harriet or someone would have seen us on CCTV by now. But then, they wouldn't know who we are. As far as they are concerned, we could just be walkers.'

'I want to help Wilma and Ogden,' I said. 'I've never seen them as worried as that before. But I don't think we can do anything.'

'Can you ring them this morning to ask how they are feeling? They may want to talk.'

'I'll do that,' I said.

As it was, there was no answer when I phoned. I assumed they were both working.

Alex took me for a drive to the coast that afternoon. We were sheltered as we walked behind the sand dunes but the easterly wind hit us as we crossed them to the beach. The golden sands were empty apart from a few dog walkers. Mungo was having a wonderful time, running around after his ball, even venturing into the sea. My lips tasted salty and my nose ran. 'I've not been to the coast since I left our home here,' he said.

'Is it still painful?'

'Not so bad here, but if we went a bit further along, we would come to my old house, and a bit further to where Millie died.'

'Is that why we turned round when we did?' I asked.

He nodded. 'Yes. I don't think I'll ever be able to go back.'

'Do you think it would help if you did?'

'Possibly, but I don't know if I'm ready yet.'

I took hold of his hand. 'Do you think we could do it together one day?'

'I think so. But at the moment I'm frightened it might destroy me.'

'Have you thought any more about counselling?'

'You're a great one to ask that question.'

'I know. I was wondering if we should go together. All these things that we're pushing down inside us will escape and damage our relationship if we don't do something about them.'

'Would you mind if we asked about it at the church Stuart goes to? I've been talking to him about Millie and I think they could help.'

'I'm prepared to give it a go if you are. Do you think Stuart would take us on Sunday?'

'If he does, I'm not going to cry in the service, like you did,' he said.

'Don't count on it.'

The news that evening showed a video of police guarding the hospital's Jenny Lind department. The parents of the children there must have been so worried, I couldn't bear to think about it. I had a feeling deep in my stomach that the letter came from Harriet, but I couldn't justify it.

That evening, Alex told me that Meadow had asked him to go to the market on Saturday to help Stuart sell the hedgehog houses and bug hotels. She was concerned that someone may need help getting the hedgehog houses to their car and that it wasn't reasonable to expect Stuart to do that.

'That's a shame,' I replied, 'we were going to see Harriet tomorrow afternoon, and by the time you get back, it will be too late.'

'We'll have to go next weekend,' he said. 'Ruth is dead, but the customers are alive. They must come first. Anyway, who was it suggested I should sell the things I make?'

'I know, I just wanted to get it over and done with,' I said.

'I understand that, sweetheart, but work has to come first. Why don't you have a cooking session with Amber?'

'I think I will. You do know she brings the chief taster with her?'

'And he gives his opinion?'

'He doesn't like ginger.'

'That's sad, because children usually love gingerbread men. Could you make him a chocolate one?'

I laughed. 'It's not so cold tonight, I feel a bit too hot with all these clothes on.'

'You could strip them off.'

'You must be joking.'

'Oh dear. I was going to take you to Cromer on Boxing Day morning for the annual swim in the sea. You did bring a swimming costume with you, didn't you?'

I was trying to work out whether he was joking or not.

'Well, there's still plenty of time to get one. I'll ask Mark to order you one.'

'As it so happens, I have brought one with me, and there's no way I'd let Mark order me one online.'

At that point he laughed. 'We could go down just to watch if you like, but I think you may like to spend the day with your children.'

'I have a suspicion that Mark and Peter will be together and Lily will be with Jazz and Teddy.'

'In that case we'll have a cuddly Christmas morning.'

'Sounds good to me, but won't they need our help in the kitchen?'

'No. Clifford and Will make the Christmas Day meal. If Sally's at a loose end, she joins in. Did you realise that it's Stir Up Sunday this Sunday?'

'What's that?'

'The Sunday before Advent. It's traditionally when Christmas cakes and puddings are made. As Sunday is our day off, we usually make them on Monday afternoon. Everybody helps, and it will be busier this year as we're making extras for the refuge as well as the orders we have,' Alex said.

'I love it when we all get together for something like that, I've only used bought puddings before and we haven't worried about Christmas cake. It was too expensive to buy, especially as I didn't know whether the children would like it.'

'So, they've never had Christmas cake.'

'Unless they've had it a friend's. That doesn't make me a bad mother, you know!'

'You sound just like Amber.' I laughed.

On Saturday, Alex and Stuart sold all the hedgehog houses and bug hotels. They came home with a long list of orders. They were both jubilant, but I could see a lot of work ahead for Alex, even if nothing big needed doing on the site. I hoped he could manage it all.

Mark was very sweet and said that he would help after school and at weekends if he needed another pair of hands.

On Sunday, we climbed into Stuart's van to go to church. After the service, Stuart introduced us to the church counsellor and he suggested that we don't stir things up too much before Christmas, but start in the new year. We made our first appointment and left relaxed, feeling we were in safe hands.

On the way home, Alex said, 'I'll be sorry to see you go, Stuart.'

'Me, too,' I said.

'I'm staying a bit longer than I anticipated. The decorators haven't finished at my flat, so I'll be here for a couple more weeks. I'll be able to help you out with the hedgehog houses and bug hotels. That is, if you want me.'

'You're the answer to my prayers. Uh, oh, maybe I shouldn't have said it like that, but I did tell God I had too much to do over the next few weeks,' Alex said.

'You're right to do that. He helps out with all my problems.'

I felt uncomfortable. They were talking about God as if he were a friend. They'd be preaching to me soon!

The next morning at breakfast, Sally appealed for help with Christmas cakes and puddings that afternoon. 'You two boys,' she said to Alex and Stuart, 'have a lot of your own work to do, so I don't expect you to help, but at some point this afternoon, I expect you both to come in and stir the pudding mixture. Everyone has a go, it's lucky. So, we'll sort you out when you have your tea break.'

'I've never tasted Christmas cake,' Mark said, and I felt myself going red.

'It was one of the extras we couldn't afford,' I said.

'There's no need to defend yourself, lovey, you've done well with this pair.' This time Lily blushed, making a hasty retreat to catch the school bus.

Although I didn't think I would, I was looking forward to this afternoon and the beginning of Christmas preparations. We were all working on or thinking about our Secret Santa, but making puddings was an activity for the community and it marked a point of time in the Village's year.

As usual, everyone turned up. Sally immediately gave Peter the task of peeling the carrots to go into the Christmas pudding. The amount of each ingredient needed for the Christmas cakes was on a blackboard at one side of the room, with the Christmas puddings' ingredients on the other side. Apparently,

Mark and Peter had calculated the amounts and Sally had checked them.

The ingredients were weighed and part of them put into each of half a dozen large bowls. I couldn't help wondering if it would all work out in the end.

Amber was to help Meadow, but Will pointed out that she wouldn't have much to do because Meadow was a good stirrer. He almost got a wooden spoon across his backside for that one, but as Meadow said it was a waste of good ingredients to smear them on his trousers. Daniel was given a little bowl with raisins and other tasty bits in it and "supervised" from his highchair.

It was harder work than the chutney had been, because there was a lot of mixing to be done and the quantities were enormous, added to which the ovens were already heating up for the cakes. At four o'clock, Stuart and Alex joined us and helped with the stirring, and then had their tea.

'These cakes are going to take ages to bake and it looks as if you'll need to use the ovens more than once,' I said.

'That's alright, lovey, Clifford and Will are doing the second shift, so they'll come in at whatever time they are needed during the night. They don't have to work tomorrow. And they'll be checking on the puddings, too. They'll be rich and dark with all that grated carrot in them. If we need extra oven space, we can use the ones in the apartments.'

Not long after, Amber departed with Daniel for a nappy change and sleep. I noticed Meadow waving as he was leaving, and suddenly he put his arms out to her. Amber took him back to Meadow and she blew some raspberries on his face and kissed him. I could see by her expression how much she loved him and I took Amber's place beside her.

'He's a beautiful little boy,' I said. 'Have you been able to get his and Amber's Christmas presents or do you want me to shop for you?'

'I've ordered them online and hope they'll be here any day now. Alex got me wrapping paper and labels. How about your Secret Santa? I know I'm not supposed to say, but I've picked a difficult one. Have you any ideas for Teddy?'

'He could do with something to carry his gardening tools in. Does your sewing machine work?'

'Yes, I love sewing and it's something I can do. In that case, you can get me some suitable fabric from Honsham. I'm sure our upholstery lady will have something I can buy. Or better still, you can take me. I can thank her for the work she did on my mobility scooter.'

'You won't buy flowery bright coloured material, will you?'

She laughed. 'Of course, I won't. I'm quite excited now. I'll draw a design and decide how much I need. There's an old tent in the store, too, so I can use that on the outside to keep it waterproof.'

Cake and pudding mixtures were being ladled into tins and basins ready to be cooked. I helped Will with the washing up while Sally had a sit down.

'However are you going to cook supper tonight with every cooking area being used?' I asked Will.

'No need,' he said, 'Tonight we have fish and chips. Jazz will be collecting them in time for supper. It's the only time we have a takeaway here.'

We'd just finished the cleaning up when Jazz came in with a large parcel wrapped in white paper. It smelt glorious.

'Did Amber write to the fish and chip shop?' I asked Meadow.

'We decided against it because they already supply sausage and chips to the refuge every week, free of charge.'

'How generous,' I said. 'I'm looking forward to my supper. I've not had fish and chips for years.'

'Really?'

'Yes. It was far cheaper to cook at home and we lived on a tight budget.' She put her hand on mine.

'I hadn't forgotten, I just wondered if Ben…'

I shook my head. 'Never.'

CHAPTER 28

The following morning the communal kitchen smelt of Christmas. There were cakes on cooling trays and puddings in foil basins on the worktop.

'Will and Clifford were up until four o'clock this morning,' said Sally, 'so try not to disturb them for a while. I don't expect they'll surface much before lunchtime.'

Lily and Mark looked on in wonder. 'Did you really make all of those?' Mark asked.

'Yes, lovey, but Clifford and Will are the ones we need to thank. Without them we couldn't have done it. A few minutes less and they'd not be cooked inside, a few minutes more and they'd be dried out. They took them out at exactly the right time.'

'Mum,' said Mark, 'If you could cook perfectly anything you wanted, what would you choose?'

I thought for a while. 'I think it would be a soufflé. What about you, Meadow?'

'I love baking, so I think I would cook a courgette cake.'

'I'd love to make a proper crème caramel,' said Lily, 'Not the ones you buy in the shop, but a real one.'

'I could teach you how to do that, lovey, if you want,' Sally said.

'Oh, yes, please. I could do with some lessons.'

'Why don't we have a "bake off" between Christmas and New Year?' asked Amber.

We all looked at Meadow. 'It's our quiet time and it would be fun,' she said. 'We'll need a list of names of people who want to join in and Sally and Clifford could judge it. Can you come back during the day for that, Stuart?' she asked.

'Only if I can put my name on the list.'

'And I'll order extra indigestion tablets,' said Meadow.

'I'd like to enter,' Teddy said, 'but I'll probably get the booby prize.'

'I don't know about that,' Stuart said, and we all laughed.

It was cold and wet and I felt my spirits sink as the day passed. I wasn't looking forward to our breadmaking class.

At lunchtime, Alex took me to one side. 'Are you worried about having panic attack again tonight?'

'I don't think so. It's just that Nina's pregnancy seems to be going so well now and I'm a little bit jealous.'

'Would you rather stay at home?'

'The true answer is yes, but I don't think I can allow myself to run away. If I start doing that, I'll never go anywhere in case there's a pregnant woman there, and I love going to the playgroup with Amber and Daniel. There are pregnant women there, probably more than I actually know of.'

'That's a brave decision, but you can change your mind up to the time we go in the door tonight.'

'Thanks Alex.'

I stuck to my decision and found I felt nowhere near as bad as I had anticipated. At the pub Nina sat next to me. She was glowing.

'Is the police guard at the Jenny Lind worrying you?' she asked.

186

'Yes,' I said, 'I can't even imagine how bad the children's parents might be feeling. It's worrying enough having a child in hospital, let alone thinking of that extra danger.'

'Have your children ever been in hospital?' she asked.

'Not as inpatients, but Mark had an accident on his bike during the summer holidays and was taken by ambulance to A and E. It was awful seeing him strapped to a spinal board.'

'How bad was he hurt?'

'As it turned out, it was concussion. They glued a cut on the back of his head, but apart from a headache and a bit of dizziness, he seemed okay. He was back to his normal self within a week.'

'That's a relief. I'm so happy about this pregnancy that I haven't thought about the problems the baby might have. I would hate for him to be in hospital for long periods,' she said.

'You're a strong woman and you'll cope,' I replied.

'Thanks, Jen.'

On the way home, I asked Alex whether he'd had any further thoughts about Ogden's letter. The police had been guarding the children's hospital unit for a week.

'My main thought,' he said, 'is that the police don't have the resources to keep police officers there for months. Nothing has happened, so it could have been an empty threat or the writer is waiting to catch the unit without security.'

'I would have thought they had their own security department, so it's unlikely the unit will be left unguarded,' I said.

'There's lots of ways to get into that unit. I wouldn't have thought they could have enough security for every access point. If it's an insider writing the letter, he or she could get into the unit unchallenged,' he said.

'I don't think it was an insider because they would have known who to address the letter to.'

'True. And if the baby died recently the parents would know the name of the doctors and nurses who cared for it,' he said. 'I think the writer's baby died a long time ago, or the writer has taken so many drugs that their memory is impaired.'

'Harriet would fit into both those categories,' I said, 'but there must be a lot of other people in this area who do.'

'Let's hope she's at home and lucid when we visit on Saturday.'

I hoped the same. I was dreading talking to her about her baby and was at the point where I felt I couldn't wait much longer.

'Do you want to carry on investigating?' he asked, 'because we can drop it at any time.'

'I wish you wouldn't keep tempting me to take the easy way out. It's making me annoyed. I need to get it over and done with,' I said.

'Sorry. Do you fancy a drink?' he asked.

'I need something to help me sleep.'

CHAPTER 29

The following morning, I loaded Daniel and Amber into my car in readiness for the playgroup.

'Make the most of the journey,' I said, 'the car is going to auction tonight.'

'I didn't know that,' said Amber. 'Are you buying another one?'

I shook my head.

'You'll feel trapped without a car,' she said. 'When Chloe took hers home, I panicked. I didn't want to be stuck somewhere and not be able to get away, not even from here.'

I could feel the heat behind my eyes and knew I was close to tears.

'Pull up for a minute,' she said. I did. 'It's hard to drive when you're crying. I know all about that. It ain't the end of the world. I'm sure Alex or Meadow will let you use theirs.'

'I know. But if something goes wrong here, I've got nowhere to go and no means of getting there.'

'But you and Alex are together. He's lovely. What could go wrong?'

'Me. I have a temper and take offence at the smallest things. If Alex and I break up, I'd have to leave because it would be my fault, and then there's no home for me and my children.'

'Would you like help cleaning the car out this afternoon? At least I can be there if you get upset.'

'Thanks Amber,' I said, giving her a hug, 'I'd like that.'

'And I say it's time we go to playgroup. The little boy in the back won't like it if we arrive late.'

When we arrived, Daniel got so excited he was sick. Amber laughed. 'Poor little chap, so desperate to get to his friends.'

His bum shuffle had speeded up considerably since we started.

'He gets on his hands and knees now. I don't think it will be long before he's crawling.' Amber said.

She was right. When a child had the need to move, like he did, he would find the quickest way possible. The bum shuffle wasn't efficient enough and I expected to see him crawling by Christmas.

Amber pointed out a woman who was crying.

'You or me?' she asked.

I got up and went to her. I put my arm around her shoulders, which made her cry even more. When the tears had subsided, I introduced myself and she said her name was Megan.

'Do you want to talk about it?' I asked.

She nodded. 'I've been living with my boyfriend and his dad. My boyfriend works shifts. One night when my baby was about six months old, his father raped me. I thought I'd be okay as I was feeding my baby and I didn't think I could get pregnant then. I was wrong. I'm expecting twins.'

I waited for her to compose herself. 'My boyfriend thinks the babies are his. His father keeps coming into my room at night. I don't know what to do. If I tell my boyfriend, he'll be livid and chuck me out and if I say anything to his father, he'll bad mouth me to his son and he'll probably chuck me out anyway. I love my boyfriend and he's kind and helpful with the baby, but it's his father who's the problem. At this rate I'll be having babies every year.'

'I can't give you advice about what to do, I wouldn't know where to start.' I gave her a piece of paper with my telephone number on it. 'Ring me if you want to talk, or ask to speak to Amber over there, it's the same number just a different extension.'

'Thank you.'

I squeezed her hand. 'You have friends here, don't be afraid to call us.'

'Thanks.'

It was time to do my kitchen duties, so I disappeared off with Prue.

'You seem happy today,' I said.

'It's because of you. What you've done is the best thing that's ever happened to me. I know now why Stuart and I have always felt close, and I'm gradually introducing him to his nieces and great-nieces and nephews. He has a real way with children.'

'I think you're very lucky to have him as your brother.'

'Just a few weeks ago, I didn't even know I had a brother. Now my Christmas present list has got longer.'

'But Stuart's has increased much more than yours.'

She grinned. 'I don't think he minds.'

I left, feeling happy for Prue. On the way home, I told Amber about Megan.

'Perhaps she'd like to talk to me, I know what it's like to be raped by old men. I was lucky I didn't get pregnant. I don't know how I'd feel about having a rapist's baby. At least I loved Craig.'

'How do you feel about him, now he is in prison?'

'Addiction is sort of a sickness, I suppose. If I think of it like that, then I don't feel too bad, more sort of sorry for him. When I first met him, I thought we matched, but I didn't know nothing about his drug problem then. I wish Daniel had a dad who loves him and does "dad things" with him.'

'When you say that, I wonder if Ben, my ex, has some sort of addiction problem. He can't leave other women alone. He was away from home most evenings and weekends and he didn't do any "dad things" with Lily and Mark. They would have had a much richer childhood if he could have been bothered to spend time with them.'

'But they've grown up alright, you must have made up for him not being there.'

'I don't know. Do you remember how overweight Mark was when we came here. I think he used food to fill his Dad-hole, if you like, and Lily would hardly talk to me.'

'But you did the right thing bringing them here,' she said.

'Just like you did with Daniel.'

After a little while she said, 'I'm glad I'm helping you clean your car this afternoon. You shouldn't be doing it alone. Between us we could do inside and outside and make it look really posh.'

'I'd like that, but what about Daniel?'

'Jazz wants an afternoon with him, so it seems it's a good time.'

'In that case, I'd be very grateful.'

By lunchtime, the good feeling that Prue had left me with had dissolved. I didn't want to clear my car out.

After we'd eaten, Amber gave her baby to Jazz with a carrier bag of Daniel's things. 'He smells as if he needs his nappy changed, I'll do that and bring him back.'

Jazz laughed. 'I've changed a lot of nappies, we'll manage it together, won't we, Daniel?' Daniel grinned showing off all of his four teeth.

Will pointed out some boxes in the hallway. 'Are these what you want?'

'Thanks, Will. We'll put them in the recycling bin when we've finished with them.'

I couldn't think why Amber needed boxes, but understood as she sat them down beside my car.

I went to get my car keys. My car was like another room to my home, albeit an extremely untidy one.

'We can use one box for rubbish and one for things you want to keep,' Amber said. 'Looking inside, I reckon you'll want to throw more out than you keep, so we'll use the big one for rubbish.'

I smiled; she was right.

She was encouraging, too, and wouldn't throw out anything I valued, which didn't amount to much.

There were three linen bags which I kept in the car in case I forgot to take my own or ran out of space, two warm blankets, a bright yellow waistcoat with reflective strips, a map and some items from the glove box. The rest went into the rubbish box. Amber cleaned the inside of the windows, while I vacuumed the interior and then we washed and polished the outside together. By the time we were ready for tea, the car was immaculate and we felt proud of our work.

'I never bothered to clean it much,' I said to Amber, 'it was such a rubbish car that I didn't take any pride in it.' I couldn't help feeling that the same could be said of my marriage.

'Would you like me to come with you this evening, so you're not on your own?'

'That's really kind of you, Amber, but I think I'll be fine alone. I'll be following Alex and he'll bring me back,' I said.

'That's good,' she said smiling.

When Lily and Mark got home from school, I was sitting on the sofa with the box containing the contents of the car beside me.

'Are you okay, Mum?' Lily asked.

There was a lump in my throat so big that it stopped the words coming out. I just shook my head.

Mark kneeled down in front of me and held my hands. 'Are you sick?'

I shook my head again and the tears came. Lily sat beside me and put her arms around me. 'Is it the car?'

'Yes.'

'Can you tell us what's wrong? I've never seen it look so good.'

I nodded and told them what I had said to Amber this morning.

'You're not right there,' said Mark. 'You won't be paying for insurance or breakdown cover or road tax. You'll have enough money to hire a car if you need to leave. In fact, with what you earn now, you could take out a rental agreement on a new car if you wanted to.'

I looked at him, realised the wisdom of what he was saying and smiled.

'I can always use Alex's or Meadow's car while we're here, so I don't need a rental agreement, but of course I could hire a car. I could even take a taxi to collect it. Why didn't I think of that?'

'Because you need a cup of coffee,' Lily said, 'I'll make it.'

Mark moved beside me. 'I can't see you breaking up with Alex, you're too entwined.'

'But I'm always getting things wrong or saying the wrong thing. I upset him at times.'

'I think you're being rather negative. I don't think anything you'll do, short of having an affair, will cause such an enormous rift that it can't be mended. Alex loves you too much for that.'

I thought about our conversation. Mark was usually right, but I still had my doubts. I relaxed as we drank our coffee together.

'What I need to know,' Lily said, 'is whether you love that car so much you can't bear to part with it.'

'I hate that car and always have.'

We all laughed.

At supper Alex said how good the car looked. 'I assume Ben gave it to you and it's not still in his name.'

'I'm not that daft,' I said, 'and it's registered to me at this address.'

'That's a relief, and you'll bring the logbook and MOT certificate?'

'They're already in the car,' I said. The car was definitely going tonight – unless it broke down before we got to the auction house.

When we got home, I told Alex that I wouldn't sleep well and thought I could do with a walk. Jazz had already walked him, but Mungo carried on as if it was his first walk of the evening.

'I hope he's not going to want two walks every night now,' Alex said.

Suddenly one of the donkeys brayed and I jumped. 'Sorry, I didn't expect that,' I said.

'Are you going to tell me why you were crying earlier?' he asked.

I'd hoped he hadn't noticed, but I was wrong. I told him everything.

'It would take more than an argument for me to give up on you, Jen. Much more.'

He kissed me, and my insides felt a wave of electricity passing through them. How did he do that to me? I admitted to myself for the first time that I would be devastated if something came between us. I yearned to have his baby, but it was impossible and I would have to learn to accept that having him alone was adequate.

'Alex,' I said, 'I've just had a thought. What happens if the car doesn't sell?'

'I'll eat my hat. Didn't you notice all the old bangers there? They accepted them into the auction and they wouldn't have done that if they didn't think they'd sell. The mileage on yours is low and the bodywork and engine are sound, you'll have a cheque in the post next week.'

'And if I don't, I'll buy you a new hat for Christmas.'

'I might be glad of Meadow's indigestion tablets after all.'

Later that evening, after the children had gone to bed, I felt low. I hadn't wanted to get rid of the car, but it was an expense I couldn't afford and I didn't need it. It seemed like my get-out clause had been removed and I was helpless to do anything about it. I rummaged through the kitchen cupboard and found what I needed – a large bar of chocolate and a box of chocolate biscuits…

CHAPTER 30

The following morning, I regretted bingeing and purging all those biscuits and the chocolate. It was such a waste of food and my throat felt raw. I was certain it was doing my teeth no good either. I'd been okay for over a month and hoped it had gone away, but it was obvious it hadn't. I would have to tell Alex. That's what we agreed.

I had no desire to go to breakfast but knew Meadow would question me if I didn't. There suddenly seemed to be no privacy here. I had to go to breakfast and at least try to eat some toast. I chewed and chewed, but found swallowing difficult. This place was taking away my freedom.

When Alex asked if I was okay afterwards, I shook my head.

'Come over and talk to Mungo.' He took my arm and led me to his apartment.

Mungo was the non-judgemental being I needed to have on my side.

I started talking to him and he licked my face, stimulating the tears that I had been trying so hard to hold back.

'Can you tell him why you did it?' Alex asked, and it all tumbled out.

'I'm so sorry about the car,' he said, 'I thought I was helping you out of a financial hole, but instead I've given you more to grieve about. I didn't realise how important it is to get away if you need to. I was wrong.'

He went to the kitchen and came back with a key in his hand. 'This is my spare and it's for you. Take the car whenever you need it.'

'But…'

'No "buts". I'm happy to use Meadow's if you're out in mine. You're a good driver and I trust you. I'll call my insurance company and put your name on my insurance.'

When he'd finished his call, I asked, 'Are you angry with me?'

'Not at all. You told the truth and that was what we agreed. You've done well. How about if we both walk to the gate to collect the mail?'

I left, thankful that he wasn't disappointed in me. But as I passed the place where my car usually stood, I was fighting back the tears again.

We spent the afternoon together making Florentines, gingerbreads and flapjacks.

'I've always wanted to decorate gingerbread men, but I've only ever stuck in currants for eyes and scratched a mouth on the biscuits. Do you think I'll be any good at icing?' Alex asked.

'You've got a steady hand and an eye for design. I think you'll be fine.'

'I borrowed a piping bag and nozzle, so I could try.'

'Don't do it while it's still hot,' I said.

'Why not.'

'I don't know, that's what my Mum always said.'

'You don't talk much about your parents. Are they still alive?' he asked.

'Yes, but they live in Adelaide, near where my sister lives. They don't come home.'

'That's sad, do you keep in touch?'

'Oh yes,' I said, 'we used to Skype, but we keep in contact on Zoom now. They left before Lily was born, so they could get in while they were still young enough to meet the Australian entry regulations.'

'That must have been hard on you,' he said.

'Yes, I hadn't long married Ben and we were working through that difficult first year. My sister went first and kept saying what a great life she had there. Then Mum and Dad decided to go, too.'

'So that means your children have never met their grandparents and aunt?'

'Yes,' I said, 'and Ben's parents didn't approve of me, so they didn't speak to me after the wedding day. They've never even asked after the children.'

'Why don't you come to Sheffield with me and meet my daughters and in-laws when I next go there?'

'I don't think so. I'd feel like the girlfriend who is taken home to meet the parents. I've been there before.'

'But not with my in-laws. They are wonderful people and my girls can't wait to meet you,' he said.

'Let me think about it.'

Amber and I took Daniel to the playgroup in Alex's car. He was moving his hands about and making a strange noise. I couldn't work out what was wrong.

'Do you think he's alright?' I asked Amber.

'I think so. He seemed fine before we got him into the car.'

As we drove to our destination the noise got louder but, as soon we arrived, it stopped abruptly.

I asked him, 'Are you driving the car?' He studied me for a bit then smiled broadly.

'Are you driving the car?' Amber asked.

He replied, 'c'.

'Clever boy,' she said. 'That's what he was doing with his arms, driving.'

Of course, I had to tell him what a clever boy he was and he grinned.

'It must be because it's a different car,' I said, 'and he hasn't realised where we are yet.'

It was only a few minutes before he started wriggling and throwing his arms and legs about.

'He knows now,' Amber said.

I couldn't help but smile. It was wonderful watching a tiny person develop. We went inside and Amber put him straight on the mat. He looked thoughtful as he watched the other children, he did his bum shuffle, then leaned forward onto his hands. I thought he may be trying to copy the children who were crawling, but then he sat back and returned to his bum shuffle.

After a couple of songs, I looked around the room. Flip was there, but not Megan. I wondered where she was, but nobody has to come every week. Perhaps her child was unwell or she'd made arrangements to do something else.

I mentioned it to Prue at coffee time. 'I'm not aware of her missing a session before. I think she's glad to get away from home with her little one.'

I was sure she was and I wished I'd taken her phone number.

'You could always try asking the girl who takes the class. Megan may have told her in advance. You could ask for her phone number, but I don't think she'll pass on information like that.'

The organiser looked in her book. 'This is the first session she's missed, she's one of our more regular attendees. I'm afraid I can't give you her number because of data protection. She was crying last week, wasn't she?'

I nodded.

'I'll give her a ring now,' she said. But there was no reply.

'I'll try her again later. Is there a message to pass on?'

'Just to say I was thinking of her and could she give me a ring to let me know she's okay. Thanks.'

I explained to Amber, just in case she rang her. Amber was concerned, too.

Meanwhile, Daniel was having the time of his life emptying the toy box and distributing the toys. He hadn't been taught to share, but he seemed to like giving things away, a bit like his mother.

After lunch, Alex came over to me. 'I've got some bad news. Meadow wants me to go to market again on Saturday. I asked if there was anyone else, but Jazz has a family get-together, so he can't do it. She said this would be the last time.'

I sighed. 'This investigation is doomed. I've not seen any police around here for a couple of weeks. I think they've given up.'

'We could stop, too.'

I snapped back at him. 'Don't try it again, Alex. We'll have to carry on because, if we don't, the murderer will never be found. I hope it doesn't stretch over Christmas. I'd like to get it tied up now.'

Then I remembered that Prue had told me she and Stuart had sent off DNA samples to find out whether they have the same mother and she'd asked me if I would come with them to meet Elsie. I told Alex and said we hadn't set a date for the visit.

Prue told me in confidence that she would talk to the nurses. If they thought Elsie was well enough, she would like to take her home for Christmas lunch. She was worried she might be overwhelmed with children, so Prue had set aside a room that she could sit in if she just wanted to watch television in peace. I knew she would look after her well and it would probably do Elsie good. I smiled to myself, thankful that her family had been found.

CHAPTER 31

That evening, Megan telephoned me and apologised for not giving me her phone number. Her father-in-law was still after her and she needed to get away. I asked her if I could talk to a friend about her.

'If you think she can help,' she replied.

'She may not be able to, but she may know someone who can. Don't get your hopes up, it's just a possibility.'

She sounded desperate, so I went across to Meadow to talk about her.

'One of the neighbours had told her partner that she was screaming and shouting as if she was being attacked, but only on the nights he was working.' I could feel tears near the surface again. 'He went out one evening, but not to work. He parked the car around the corner and walked back and waited close to their home. He heard her screaming and let himself in. He found his father on top of her in the bedroom. There was so much noise that neither of them knew her partner was there. Megan had scratched his father's face, but he was a big man and too much for her.' By now I was close to tears.

'Her partner dragged him off and took Megan straight to the police station to report his father for rape. The police went to the house and took the old man to the station. The following morning, Megan and her partner started looking for somewhere else to live, but they had been paying the old man so much rent, that they didn't have enough for a deposit on a rented property. Do you have any ideas?'

'Make a coffee while I think about it,' Meadow said.

I hoped she could think of something because Megan was desperate and possibly in danger now. I didn't think she'd be eligible for a place in a refuge and anyway she wanted to stay with her partner.

I took the coffee through and hoped she'd thought of something.

'Do you think they'd come here for a couple of months? They could live rent-free and not have to pay for food. That should give them a chance to save a deposit. The only disadvantage is that we don't have any ground floor apartments free. There is one on the first floor, but it could be rather inconvenient. They can move in tomorrow if they wanted.'

'Not as inconvenient as living with the old man.'

I finished my coffee and went back to our apartment, where I telephoned her back. I spoke to her partner, too, who was clearly angry with his father. He could see that living under the same roof as him was no longer viable.

'I can't believe that a stranger could be so kind,' he said. 'We're not worried about it being on the first floor, we're just so grateful. Would late morning be okay? We need to be out of here while the police are still holding him.'

I said it would and returned to Meadow. She was delighted. 'Snowy and I built this community so people who have been hurt by the world could feel safe. There can be no doubt that the young couple and their child fall into that category, I'd love them to come.'

I said I would go around the flat with a duster and she would make an announcement at breakfast time.

'Is it alright if I tell Amber this evening?'

'Yes, and you had better ask Alex to put another highchair in the communal kitchen. They'll probably bring the baby's furniture for the apartment, but from what you say it's unlikely they'll have any other furniture. I'll chat to them tomorrow and see what we can do to help.'

I smiled. 'You're a big softie.'

'You're no better,' she replied. 'Now out of here and let an old lady relax.'

I kissed her on the cheek and left.

I managed to get all my work done prior to the arrival of Megan, her partner Tom and little Ruby. Jazz and I were assigned to greeting them and helping them move in. I was concerned that Ruby seemed to be an unhappy baby, quite the opposite to Daniel.

'Don't worry about her,' Megan said, 'she's tired and hungry and has just seen everything she knows get put in the car. She may take a bit of time to adjust.'

While Jazz and Tom were putting Ruby's cot together, I made a pot of tea and Megan fed Ruby. Before long the nursery was complete and Ruby asleep.

'Would you like me to put her in her room?' I asked. I took the sleeping baby and laid her in her own cot, with her toys around her.

'If you need a babysitter at any time, just ask,' I said.

'Hey, what about me?' Jazz said, 'I'm only upstairs.'

'You'll soon find out that Jazz is amazing with babies,' I said.

'With seven younger brothers and sisters, I'm used to looking after babies,' he said. It reminded me that I should ring Wilma and Ogden again to find out how they were coping.

'You probably need what's left of the morning to sort yourselves out.' I said.

'I'll pop round at lunchtime,' Jazz said, 'and take you to the communal kitchen, then after lunch, if Ruby is up to it, I'll show you around. Our next big project is making holly wreaths and it would be good if you could help us, Megan. It will give you a chance to get to know the community. Obviously, we'd be grateful of your help, too, Tom, but we know you're working shifts and need to sleep at strange times, so only volunteer if you feel you can manage it comfortably. We'll put the babies together with some toys and keep an eye on them. I'm sure Daniel and Ruby will get along well.'

We left them then to sort themselves out. I wanted to ask Megan if the police had charged the old man, but didn't want to seem nosy.

I'd told Alex not to put the two highchairs together in the communal kitchen as I had visions of Daniel giving all his food to Ruby. In the end, we decided to put them opposite each other, so they could see but not reach each other.

Daniel was excited to see another child at the table. He grinned and pounded on the tray of his high chair. However, Ruby whinged when she was brought in.

The community welcomed them and introduced themselves. The poor couple stood no more chance of remembering their names than I did when I arrived.

'Everyone,' Clifford announced, 'tomorrow and Friday we will be making holly wreaths. Peter has mossed the bases, so we'll be putting holly, berries and ornaments on them. We have plenty of leather gloves to protect your hands and there's a playpen with toys for the babies; we don't want them getting near the holly or the berries. We'd be grateful for as much help as we can get as some of the younger and agile men will be digging trees and Alex and Stuart will be working on hedgehog houses and bug hotels.'

'Last Saturday was the cut-off day for orders,' said Alex, 'and Stuart and I have finished the orders, so any made from now on will go on the stall for sale. I think we should be able to help from next week onwards.'

'I know what a holly wreath is, but I ain't ever made one,' Amber said.

'Don't worry, they're not difficult and we can show you what to do,' Clifford said.

I said, 'I've never made one, either.'

'We'll teach you along with the others who don't know,' he said.

While we were having coffee, I pulled an envelope out of my pocket, which had come this morning addressed to me. In it was a cheque for £540. I kept staring at it.

'What is it?' Alex asked. I thought he probably knew what it was, but I couldn't believe the amount of it.

'How much did you get for your car?' he asked. I passed the cheque over to him. 'And you thought it wouldn't sell.'

All I could say was 'Wow!' I was so pleased, this would make Christmas shopping for the children easier but, having been short of money previously, I would naturally be cautious.

Lily needed a new bike; I could get her a new, rather than a pre-used one. Mark hadn't said what he wanted, apart from some DIY tools. I would probably have to send Jazz out to get Lily's bike and perhaps Alex and I could go together to get the tools. I remembered that I had a refund of road tax and insurance still to come.

I wanted to get Alex a present but had no idea what to get him. He said he didn't want anything and I definitely wouldn't be buying him socks. Mark would probably be able to find out if there was anything he needed but, if not, I'd buy him a new jumper.

I'd probably also get something for Daniel and for Meadow, but Meadow was another of those people it was difficult to buy for. She had everything she needed, apart from Snowy, and I couldn't buy a replacement for him.

The following day after breakfast, I put on a warm sweater and my winter coat and hat, and tucked my scarf inside my coat. Clifford said it was cold in the barn as the door had to be left open to take foliage and wreaths in and out. When I collected the post, I had noticed the first trickle of cards among the letters. I hadn't asked what we did about cards and made a mental note to ask either Alex or Meadow.

At the barn, everyone else was there and working hard.

Clifford said, 'There's a space near Meadow, she'll show you what to do.' I noticed that Amber and Megan were on a table together and chattering away. Amber already had a completed wreath on the floor beside her table and had almost finished the next one.

When she saw me, she looked around the room, and called Clifford.

'Is the one beside me alright?'

He examined it. 'Yes, it's beautiful, carry on.'

Meadow showed me what to do and I collected together a small bunch of holly with conifer foliage behind it and bound it in with wire, then went to the next with some berries and wound it in. The smell of greenery in the barn was intoxicating. The next bundle had Christmas tree foliage and I went around the wreath, binding in the bundles and trying to keep the pattern symmetric. The further I got on the wreath, the more the holly pricked. There seemed to be nowhere I could hold it without pain.

'I'm glad I don't have to tie those bows,' I said, 'I'd make a terrible mess of it.'

She laughed. 'I think I would, too. Clifford and Will do them every year. Did you know Clifford is a qualified florist?'

'I suppose I should have guessed, but I didn't. How do you fix the cones and bows to the wreath?'

'You need stub wire.' She pulled out some thick wire already cut into lengths and showed me how to wrap it around the centre of the cone, 'then you just poke it through the moss base and weave it in at the back. You put the bow on, tying the remainder of the ribbon in a loop to hang on the door, like this.'

I looked up and saw Amber had a half a dozen finished wreaths laying around her table.

'How did she make so many in such a short time?'

'I don't know how she's doing it but she's working faster than the rest of us.'

As we looked, she placed another on the floor.

Clifford went over. 'You're doing well Amber and they're good quality. You work much faster than me.' She glowed. 'I'll show you where to put them now, as you're running out of floor space.'

She threaded her arm through them, took them to a box, and packed them vertically.

'She's found her forte, hasn't she?' Meadow said. I had to agree.

I looked at Daniel and Ruby playing together and smiled to myself. Daniel was busy giving Ruby all the toys, then they shuffled round and he gave them to her all over again. Perhaps Ruby would adopt a happy frame of mind here. Megan told me that she and Tom used to have her cot in their bedroom, and she would howl when the old man came into the room. She heard her mother screaming and joined in.

I was glad of the mid-morning break. As we left the barn, I looked at Amber's heap of beautiful wreaths and looked at my few mediocre ones and shook my head. I couldn't understand it.

During the break DI Watson walked through the communal kitchen door.

'Are you after anyone in particular?' I asked.

'You,' he said.

'I'll make you a coffee and we can use the communal lounge for a while.'

'I don't like to ask you,' he said when we were alone, 'but are you still investigating?'

'Yes, but we haven't got far. Are you any closer to finding the killer.'

'I've had officers questioning people she worked with after she was released. It seems that she was charming when they first met her and then turned nasty. It was an established pattern and she upset everyone she met, including the customers. I'm not surprised she didn't keep a job for long, she seemed a nasty piece of work.'

'She was the only person Meadow ever had to ask to leave.'

'I'm of the opinion that almost anyone who met her may have wanted to kill her,' he said.

'I'm surprised the media haven't established who she was previously,' I said.

'Me, too.' he said, 'I was expecting some bright young reporter would, but they didn't and there have been no leaks this time.'

CHAPTER 32

'Now I must get back to wreath-making.'

'Would it be alright if I came to see them? I have instructions to get one for the front door and one for the grave. You don't do Christmas trees, do you?'

'Come along, I'll show you where we're working.'

He ended up emptying his wallet, with two wreaths, a Christmas tree, a hedgehog house and two bug houses. I went to the office and put the cash in the safe.

Back in the barn, I thought through what he had said. He had much more power to interview people than I had. Why would I think that I might turn up something that he couldn't? I still hadn't located Annie Mosley. I knew she'd been released from prison, but I'd failed to trace her. If she had changed her name like Ruth did, I'd have no chance of finding her.

I wondered whether the DI had managed to get Harriet at a time when she was lucid. Even if she was high, she would probably say the same thing to me as she had to DI Watson. Something like, 'if I ever saw her I'd kill her'. Although woman-to-woman she might open up.

My thoughts were interrupted by Clifford talking to Amber. 'Had you thought of training to become a florist when Daniel gets older? You work quickly and have an artistic eye. The work's not well-paid, but if it's something you might enjoy it would be worth considering.'

'Tell you the truth,' she said, 'I ain't really thought about what I want to do. I'm going to evening classes next term. English and maths, 'cos I didn't get no exams.'

'You're doing the right thing. Think about it and talk to me if you want to know anything more.'

'Thanks,' she said.

'She thinks she's no good at anything, that should help her self-confidence,' Meadow said quietly. We were both smiling.

By lunchtime, I had slowed down.

Clifford announced, 'You only need do one hour this afternoon, production is higher than I had expected. If you don't feel able to come this afternoon, then please come tomorrow morning if you can.'

The babies were getting hungry and then I thought they would have their nap. I was tired, so I suggested to Amber that I sit with Daniel while he slept and she would be free to do more wreaths. I couldn't understand why she enjoyed making wreaths, I found it a chore.

Daniel slept for more than the hour that Amber worked, I think he had worn himself out playing with Ruby.

'How do you make those wreaths so quickly?' I asked.

'I love making stuff,' she said. 'It's the only thing I'm good at, except running. They were the only things I got good marks for at school. I think it was because making things came out of my head and I didn't have to learn it. I wasn't good at learning.'

'Well, you're really good at making wreaths. I'll be happy to sit with Daniel tomorrow if you want to carry on.'

'That would be good, thanks.'

I made my way to the workshop to find Alex and Stuart.

'Thanks for sending DI Watson here this morning, that's more we won't have to take to market on Saturday. What did he want?'

I told him and Stuart about our conversation.

'We're not getting anywhere,' said Alex. 'I'm thinking that we ought to try Harriet one more time and then let it go.'

'I'm not keen on dropping it,' I said, 'but I'm beginning to think there's a limit to the number of times we can drive over there. What do you think, Stuart?'

'I think Alex is right. I know Ruth's my mother, but she spread hatred everywhere. I've got to know her better through all this, and I can't help feeling that you've given it your best. Perhaps it's something we will never know.'

I nodded.

'Jen, we don't want to give you something more to grieve about. You've done your best and you can't expect more than that from yourself.'

'Thanks Stuart, but perhaps a couple more visits.'

'If you need more purpose, how about helping us with the varnishing?' Alex said.

'No way. I've already shown I'm not much good at wreath-making, I'd prefer not to show myself up again.'

'But Clifford said all the wreaths were saleable.'

'Mine probably were, but they took half an hour each. Amber was finishing one every ten minutes and hers were beautiful. I prefer to sit with Daniel and let her work. There's something else I need to ask,' I said, 'I didn't think to bring any Christmas decorations with me. Do we have any spares here?'

'Yes,' Alex said, 'And you can have a Christmas tree. There's large boxes of baubles and Meadow orders a lot of chocolate ones, but I can't have any of those. Or rather, Mungo can't.'

We both laughed.

At supper, Megan asked me if I would like to pop in for a hot drink. Tom was at work and Ruby would be asleep, so we had time to talk.

We talked generally about things and she wanted to know some things about the Village, very much as I had when I came. We got round to the subject of Christmas as she wondered what would happen. I told her that we all ate together as we did on other days, but we spent the afternoon together in the communal lounge, playing games, watching old films and generally enjoying each other's company, then we had supper and could go back to our apartments or stay in the lounge. It was up to individuals.

She asked me about Christmas decorations and I laughed. I told her that I'd only found out about them that afternoon.

'But you seem so settled. How long have you been here?'

'We only came for the summer holiday, but we've been here five months,' I said.

'It's so relaxing here,' she said, 'like a big family.'

'That was what Meadow and Snowy wanted. I'll warn you though, we often get together in the kitchen for a massive baking project. There will be chocolate logs to be cooked and made up just before Christmas, and there's Christmas cakes to ice.'

'Lovely,' she said, 'I studied catering at college and worked in the pub in Honsham as a cook, before I had Ruby. I love icing and decorating cakes.'

'I think you should tell Sally about that; she may well need your talents.'

'I'd love to help, but what about Ruby?'

'Daniel is chief taster but he'd probably let Ruby share the responsibility. If she's tired, I'm happy to sit with her here, and I know Amber wouldn't mind looking after two of them.'

'She's a lovely person, she cares about everyone.'

'Do you feel safe here?'

'I do. Teddy is next door and Jazz is upstairs and there's that big metal gate. Even if Tom's father found out where we are, he wouldn't be able to get to me.'

'Are you certain the twins you're expecting are the old man's?'

'I thought I was, but when I looked up the dates, they could be Tom's. We've talked about it and thought we'd wait till they arrived before deciding whether to do DNA tests. I might love them so much that I won't want to know.'

'That sounds sensible to me. Whatever the circumstances, the babies were conceived as innocents and will be born innocent.'

I noticed that Megan was getting tired. 'I'll be going now. It looks as if you need a good sleep.'

'I do, but Ruby will wake me at four for milk, so I never get a full night's sleep.'

'I know what that's like, both of mine did the same thing. I'll leave you now, you know where I am if you need anything.'

I went downstairs and put my head around Meadow's door. She was sound asleep on the settee. I gave her a gentle shake and told her it was time she went to bed.

'Wreath making is such hard work,' she said.

'Or is it talking all day that tires you out?'

'No, it was definitely making the wreaths,' she said with a smile.

'Would you like me to make you a hot drink while you get ready for bed?'

She said she would like Horlicks. When I took it into her bedroom, she appeared to be asleep again. I put it on the bedside table, kissed her cheek and left.

Stuart had asked me when it would be convenient to visit Elsie. I told them I would phone the home first, as I didn't want us to turn up without warning her in advance. I was worried the shock might kill her.

Initially I thought of phoning Ross, but remembered how abrupt he was when I last phoned him. If he thought we were mistaken, there would be no way he would want to inform Elsie of something that he believed to be untrue. It was strange though that if Claire was her granddaughter, as she claimed to be, she had made no effort to see her grandmother.

The following morning, I rang the home and explained the situation. They agreed to break the news to her gently and then tell her we would be coming on Sunday afternoon.

I was nervous, so when Stuart offered to take me and Alex to church, I decided to go. Alex, knowing I would be out in the afternoon, offered to come with me.

It was good to meet Stuart's brother and sister again and his parents. When Stuart explained that we were the people who identified his birth mother and helped Prue to find her brother, his parents were very supportive. When he told them he was going to meet his grandmother in the afternoon, they were delighted.

'Now, you know if she is well enough to go out, we're happy for her to spend a day with us,' his father said. I was full of gratitude to these kind people.

'If she's well enough,' Stuart said, 'she'll be spending Christmas day with Prue and her family.'

'That's wonderful,' said his mother, 'Not only have you found a family, she will have, too.'

'Have my brother and sister ever asked about their parents?' asked Stuart.

'Not to my knowledge,' his mother said.

'I'm rather concerned that, when they find out about me and my birth family, they may want to find them.'

'That's no problem at all. We'll help them with it,' his father said, 'won't we dear?'

'Of course,' his wife said, 'That's what we agreed when we adopted them.'

'That's generous of you,' I said.

That afternoon I got into Stuart's van with him. 'How are you feeling about meeting your grandmother?' I asked.

'Nervous. It's unusual for me as I hardly ever get nervous.'

'She's a lovely lady, bright and intelligent. She deserves to have people like you and Prue as grandchildren.'

We stopped at Prue's house and picked her up.

'How are you feeling?' Stuart asked her.

'Strange.'

'In what way?'

'I'm not certain,' she said.

A nurse greeted us at the door of the home. 'We've told Elsie about you both, and she's very excited.'

'What should we call her?' Prue asked.

'I think you're best to sort that out with her,' she said.

'We've put her in a different room, so she can be alone with you. Would you like tea or coffee?'

We told her our preferences and she showed us into a small room with just four chairs set out around a coffee table. I realised too late that I had forgotten to tell the nurse that Stuart was in a wheelchair.

Elsie smiled as we came in and opened her arms to her grandchildren. All three of them were crying and I felt a bit left out.

'You look like Ruth,' she said to Stuart. 'There's a resemblance in you, Prue, but not as strong as Stuart.' She picked up a photo album from the side of her chair and showed them a picture of Ruth holding a baby. 'This was you, Prue.'

'I've brought a photograph of me as a baby. There's no doubt we are the same child. Look at that birthmark,' Prue said.

'Ruth said she gave you up because of that but I thought at the time, it was because a baby would affect her nightlife.'

'And here's one of her with you, Stuart. Do you have spina bifida?'

'Yes,' he replied.

'I was furious when she gave you up. I told her that you'd end up in care all your life if she did.'

'I didn't, though. I was adopted by a wonderful couple who adopted two other disabled children. They saw me through university and sponsored me as I trained as a solicitor.'

'That's a much better upbringing than you would have had with Ruth,' Elsie said. 'She was a strange woman.'

'How about you, Prue?'

'I was adopted by a lovely couple, as well. I was so happy that I didn't even think of trying to contact my birth mother. It's only in the last few months that I've thought about it and Jen helped me to find out about her. I have three children and my youngest, Emily, had a stroke when she was sixteen. She has two pre-school children now and my other daughters have children, as well.'

'So that makes me a great-great-grandmother! No one else here can make that claim.'

'The reason I wanted to find my mother was to find out the family history, in case early strokes are in the family, especially high blood pressure.'

Elsie told her she need not worry about that as she didn't know of any at all.

They talked together for about half an hour, when Elsie started looking tired. They said their goodbyes and Elsie called me over.

'Thank you, Jen. This means so much to me.' I squeezed her hand, kissed her on the cheek and left.

Prue was talking to the nurse in the corridor, who told her they would get Elsie onto her bed to have a lay down. 'I don't think she slept at all last night; she was so excited.'

On the way home, Prue became weepy. I held her hand.

'If I'd known she was alone in a home so close, she could have come and lived with me. I'm sorry that I didn't search for my mother earlier.'

Stuart said, 'Don't let it worry you. I've known my mother's name for ten or more years. I didn't want to visit her in prison and lost her when she left and changed her name. If I had persevered with my search, I would have found my grandmother, too. At least we've found her before it's too late.'

We fell into the silence of our own thoughts, dropped Prue off and went back to the Village.

'Would you like to come in for a cup of tea?' I asked Stuart.

'I don't like to refuse, but I need to spend some time alone.'

I understood.

CHAPTER 33

We were walking Mungo that evening when Alex asked, 'When were you going to tell me how it went with Elsie this afternoon?'

'When you asked,' I said.

'That's not like you, you usually can't wait to get news out.'

'I was thinking,' I said, 'about how Stuart and Prue both said how guilty they felt about not visiting their grandmother before. When we got back, Stuart wanted to be alone.'

'He seemed quiet at supper. Were they okay with Elsie?'

'Yes, it all seemed to go well. They all cried, but I expected that. The first thing she did, when we went in, was to hug them. There's no doubt they are both Ruth's children, the photos of them as babies prove it.' I waited while Alex threw Mungo's ball. 'Elsie wanted to tell them all about Ruth as a child, and why she cut herself off from her daughter when she put Stuart up for adoption. I think she felt guilty for not insisting that Ruth cared for her own children. Prue pointed out that it could have been them that were killed rather than Harriet's baby. I think Elsie felt bad about giving up on her so early. If she had been closer, she could have stopped the murder.'

'But that argument doesn't hold water,' Alex said. 'If she stopped the first child being murdered and returned it to

Harriet, there was sure to be more further along the line. She wanted the perfect baby.'

'I know, but it's not my place to say,' I said.

'Yes, I suppose you were just an onlooker. Can you visit her some time on your own or do you think it would be better to let things settle?'

'I'll give it some thought,' I said.

We walked along in companionable silence, with Mungo sniffing around.

'Can I ask you something, Alex?'

'I suppose so.'

'Why do you shave your head?'

I wasn't expecting that. Well, the short answer is: I don't. Now don't try to apologise for making assumptions. My hair was thick and fair, until recently. When Millie died, I felt as if I was responsible for her suicide. Shortly afterward I noticed that I seemed to be losing more than I usually did when I combed it, then one morning I found tufts of it on my pillow. I examined my head in the mirror and there were patches of baldness. Within weeks, the patches had joined up and I had no hair left. I lost my eyebrows, too.'

'I'm sorry. I wouldn't have asked if I'd known. I was thinking how cold you must be in this weather and then you get sunburned in the summer. To me the solution was for you to grow it, but now I know you can't. I'm sorry.'

'It's hard for me. I had to explain to people who knew me with hair. Many of them thought I had cancer. I look at my baldness in the mirror every day and think I can see a little fluff, like baby hair, but I can't and I'm beginning to think that it will never come back.'

'I love you just as much with no hair as I would with hair.'

He kissed me roughly.

Afterwards he asked, 'So why do you perm yours so tightly?'

'Touché. It's my African ancestors.'

'How far back?'

'Three generations. My great-grandfather was in Nigeria when he met my great-grandmother and proposed to her. You can imagine his parents' reactions when he brought her back to this country. Things were so different then. His parents didn't speak to him again and he was bypassed in their wills. He didn't mind because he loved his black wife. I think their children had a lot of problems in those days, but they survived and married. Eventually the black element was compromised with marriage to white people, but I'm a bit of a throwback.'

'When I came to collect you on the afternoon you arrived, you'd been sleeping and your hair was everywhere. I wanted to run my fingers through it,' he said.

'So why have you never done it?'

'Come here.' As he combed my hair with his fingers, he kissed me. I groaned. The sensation was almost too much to handle. He told me how much he loved me. I loved him more and I knew that I would never find anyone more lovable than him. We broke off for air and then he kissed me again. I felt a head coming between our legs and laughed.

'Mungo wants to join in,' I said.

'He's a spoilsport. I haven't trained him not to do that yet.'

We returned to his apartment for hot chocolate.

That week was the last of our breadmaking class for the term. As soon as we walked in, Nina came over to ask how I was. I said I was fine; it was just another panic attack.

'Look at your poor hands,' she said, 'Whatever have you been doing?'

'Making holly wreaths. I couldn't get on with the big thick gloves, so I chose to work bare handed. Even then I didn't do very well. I'm not talented in that field, I'd rather be cooking any day.'

'I've never made a holly wreath. Are they difficult?'

'That's the strange thing. They're not. I can't understand why I struggled.'

The teacher came in and our conversation broke up.

As this was the last week before Christmas, we were making wholemeal rolls in the shape of a Christmas tree. We worked at preparing, mixing and kneading the dough accompanied by Christmas songs. Alex was singing along, obviously happy with his task.

'Do you think I'll have to make Christmas wreaths next week?' I asked.

'I will, so I could help you. Stuart and I stopped our production line this afternoon.'

'I'll be sad to see him go. I hope we can meet up with him again,' I said.

'There's something I needed to talk to you about. If we're using the church for counselling in the new year, I think we should become church members.'

'No,' I said.

'You know Millie and I used to attend church regularly, and it seemed to put shape into the week. I'll be going weekly and I'd like you to come with me.'

'You're not going to push me into it, are you?' He shook his head. 'The best I can say is that I'll think about it. Please don't make me feel guilty.'

At the pub, Christmas cards were distributed and we all had an early Christmas dinner. I loosened my belt after the Christmas pudding, only to see mince pies being brought out. I wrapped mine in a serviette and put it in my pocket, then we waddled back to the bread kitchen.

'At least we've done the most energetic part,' I said to myself.

'I heard that,' Alex said.

'I feel as if I could flop.'

When we arrived home, I asked Alex if we could go for a walk. He told me he was feeling bloated, so a delighted Mungo had a second walk.

'I assume you signed to say you would like the classes to continue next term,' he said.

'I did, they're such a nice group of people, I'll miss them if we don't carry on.'

'I wonder if the teacher can find enough different types of bread to keep us going for another term.'

'Quite frankly, I don't mind repeating some of those we've already done as long as you're with me,' I said.

'I suspect we will be making breads from other countries that we've never heard of before.'

'Countries we've never heard of?'

'No, I mean, the bread that we haven't…Oh, never mind!'

'Well, we haven't made a French stick yet, so I take your point.'

'Changing the subject, are we going to see Harriet on Saturday afternoon?'

'As long as it's the last time. I hate to keep going out there time and time again and I don't think it's doing you any good, sweetheart.'

'I promise it will be the last time,' I said. 'If she can't talk to us this time, then I am reluctantly prepared to drop the case.'

He turned me round and kissed me.

CHAPTER 34

The second attempt at wreath-making, for some reason, didn't seem anywhere near as hard as it had the previous week. My heap grew much quicker than it had before and the quality was improving, too. In fact, I was enjoying it. I had found an old pair of leather gloves which fitted much better than the ones provided and they helped considerably. Why hadn't I thought of that earlier?

By breaktime, I wasn't far behind Alex. Clifford commented that I was producing much better quality work, 'not that it matters to the customers,' he said, 'most of them have no taste at all. Look at that one with the gaudy plastic flowers on it – a special order – and the customer will be delighted.'

I couldn't help smiling. As a perfectionist, he seemed disappointed in his customers.

Meanwhile, Megan had offered to help Sally finish the Christmas cakes and she wasn't going to refuse.

'Have you thought of trying Amber, too?' I asked. 'She's probably done nothing like that before but she's artistic, although I don't think she'd acknowledge it.'

'That's a good thought, lovey, and the two babies together will keep each other happy,' she said.

'I think Amber needs as much opportunity as she can get to try different things. She's determined she's going to make a career for herself, so she can work to keep herself and Daniel.'

'She's a lovely girl, isn't she?' Sally said.

Meadow beckoned to me. 'I'm going to suggest that Amber goes out in the van next week with Clifford, to collect the gifts from the shopkeepers for the refuge. Can you look after Daniel?'

'I could,' I said, 'but Megan will probably keep him with Ruby if you ask. The babies get on so well together.'

'That sounds like a better solution,' she said. 'Did you know there's an extra market on Christmas Eve?'

'No, I didn't. So, there'll be a huge rush to get everything done in the days leading up to it.'

'That's right,' Meadow said. 'I would have preferred for Amber to be making wreaths rather than collecting gifts. But I couldn't do that to her, the refuge collection is her baby.'

'I'm not certain what Lily and Mark are doing next week. They break up from school tomorrow and love working with the residents. I assume that the children's parcels will need wrapping.'

'And the chocolate logs will need to be made, and vegetables dug before Christmas Eve.'

'Will the men still be digging Christmas trees?'

'Not unless someone has ordered a particular size, or one that will stand up a corner.'

'We'll be glad when Christmas day gets here,' I said. 'I was wondering what will happen about Secret Santa for Megan and Tom.'

'Don't worry, it's all in hand.'

I couldn't sleep on Friday night – I was worried about seeing Harriet. For some reason, I felt we would get to talk to her this time. As the night passed, the feeling grew stronger and I wondered if I might get myself into such a state that I'd have a panic attack. Some Horlicks at four o'clock did the trick.

The sky was dark when my alarm woke me. Not a night-time dark but rain clouds dark and I could hear the rain rattling my window. I sighed. I could do without getting soaked again this afternoon but, unless it improved, in all likelihood I would.

I thought of Clifford, Teddy and Jazz who would be putting up the market stall in the rain and told myself I shouldn't complain.

'Have you slept at all?' Alex asked me.

'A few hours.'

'After today you won't have to worry about visiting Harriet again,' he said.

I nodded. I was wondering what I was hoping for this afternoon. Interviewing Harriet would be of little use unless she confessed to killing Ruth and somehow, I couldn't see that happening.

After breakfast Alex walked with me to collect the mail. I was glad he was there.

'Have you left Jazz or Stuart a note of where we're going this afternoon?' I asked.

'Do you think it's necessary?'

'Yes, I do. We don't know who the lodger is or if they'll get aggressive. I'll do notes to both Jazz and Stuart and deliver them with the mail. What time do you think we'll be back?

'Four-thirty at the latest.'

'Okay.'

By the afternoon, the sun was trying to break through and my spirits rose. We parked the car about a quarter of a mile away and walked to Harriet's house.

A car stood in the drive, which I assumed belonged to the lodger.

'Are you sure you want to do this? Because we can always turn around and go home,' Alex said.

'Come on, we're doing it.'

We walked to the front door and hammered on it.

'Come on in, we've been expecting you,' Ross said.

CHAPTER 35

'What are you doing here? You've been lying to us.' I was furious, but I knew I had to control my anger.

'Come through and join us for tea and cake and I'll explain,' Ross said.

We sat at the kitchen table with Harriet and another woman.

'Hello,' she said, 'I'm Annie.'

'Not Annie Mosley?' She smiled and nodded.

'I'm forgetting my manners,' said Alex, 'This is Jen and I'm Alex. Harriet, you're looking much better than when we last saw you.'

'Sorry about that. I was having a bad day. Thank you for looking after me.'

Ross gave us each a cup of tea and we helped ourselves to cake.

'I owe you an explanation,' he said.

'You most certainly do!' I retorted. Alex put his hand on mine.

'I'll start at the beginning. When Harriet's husband killed himself, I felt so bad about what Ruth had done to her, that I contacted Harriet. We've been in touch ever since. Harriet's health was declining and I was worried about her living alone in this place. I'd seen Annie in prison and wrote to her suggesting that she might like to lodge with Harriet if she had nowhere else to go. I saw it as a solution to both their problems: Annie would have lodgings and Harriet would have company.'

'So why did you tell us you didn't know where either of them were?' I asked.

'I didn't want Harriet to be questioned. She would be better if she wasn't reminded of her son and husband. I didn't want her to live through it again.'

That seemed reasonable to me.

'You were caught on camera on your two previous visits, then there was a long break and I thought you might have given up.'

'What about Claire?' Alex asked.

'You were right about her, and I was annoyed that your research was better than mine. In all fairness, I had a publisher's deadline and didn't have as much time to spend on looking for Ruth's children as I would have liked. Yes, she was a friend who I asked to lie to you. I wanted to put you off.'

We talked some more, Ross telling us he'd set up the CCTV to give the women extra security.

I didn't feel, under the circumstances, that I could question Harriet. In any case, it wasn't long before she disappeared into the lounge and came back glassy-eyed.

'I suppose you'd like to know what happened on the day Ruth died,' Ross said.

'Have you found out already?'

'I've known all along,' he said, 'from the minute she was killed and I'm sorry I misled you.'

I was feeling tired and could hardly keep my eyes open, but I wanted to hear what he had to say.

'I had a phone call from Harriet in the early afternoon. She said that Ruth had turned up and accused her of being responsible for her prison sentence. She said that if Harriet hadn't had a baby, she wouldn't have stolen it and had to go to prison. Annie had come in and she and Ruth began to fight. They were rolling around on the floor, biting, scratching and kicking each other. I came straight over.

'I thought I was going to break up the fight but, when I walked in, I found Harriet holding a gun pointed at the two of them. I tried to take it away from her gently but, as I did, it went off. Annie was underneath, shouting "get that big lump off me."

'When I went over, I could see that Ruth had been shot in her upper left back. I turned her over, but her eyes were unresponsive. Harriet was drugged up. She took a knife out of a drawer and went over to her. I told her to leave her, but she wouldn't. She gouged her eyes out. She said it was so she could never see a baby again.

'Annie persuaded me not to call the police or ambulance as she didn't want to return to prison, so we wrapped Ruth in a sheet and took her to the outhouse while we decided what to do. Harriet was totally out of it and Annie and I cleaned up.' He rubbed his eyes. 'Annie knew where she could get a van and, when it was dark, I drove her to the garage the van was kept in. I thought she had an arrangement with the owner, but when I got in later, I saw she'd hot-wired it. We put Ruth in the back of the van, put Harriet in the front seat with Annie and myself. Annie drove the van to Honsham Forest Village. That was the last place I knew she had been, so it seemed logical to take her there. I took my car, so we could return the van afterwards.'

'You should change your security system,' Annie said, 'I climbed over the gate, pressed the exit button and the gate opened. I'd looked at the place on Google earlier and knew we shouldn't go far along the track or we'd be seen. That's why we dug the hole close to the gate. It was hard work digging out brambles and cutting through tree roots.'

Ross continued, 'Harriet was becoming more aware of her surroundings and put a baby doll she had brought with her in the sheet with Ruth. She seemed to think it was her dead baby. We put Ruth in the hole, covered her with soil, topped it with leaves and pulled the brambles back over the grave.' He stirred his tea. 'I really thought Annie was going to take the van back. She was wearing gloves but Harriet had taken hers off and would have left prints, so the van had to go.'

Ross put his head in his hands before continuing, 'I drove behind the van, until Annie pulled up by a field in a clearing in the woods. She put Harriet in the back of my car while I unloaded our spades from the van and put them in the boot.' He poured himself another cup of tea. 'She drove onto the field and set light to the van. For some reason this seemed to excite Harriet and I was glad I had turned on the child locks. Annie came back and joined us in the car, then we came back here to clean up. While we were cleaning, we found Ruth's silver chain necklace. It had come off during the fight. We wrapped it in tissues and binned it.'

'It was an accident,' Alex said, sleepily.

'It's time to get them into the outhouse,' Annie said. 'I'll take Jen and you can deal with Alex.'

I tried to stand to run away, but my head was spinning and all I wanted to do was to sleep. Annie put my arm round her shoulder and held it there, then put her other arm around my waist, walked me into the outhouse and plonked me on a chair. Alex was dumped on the other chair beside me. I heard the door shut and two bolts sliding across.

Alex roused me from my sleepiness by shouting, 'Give me your phone. Make yourself sick. Phone! We've been drugged.'

I vomited on the floor again and again, until my stomach was empty.

I could hear someone saying, 'Hello. Are you there?' The nearest phone mast must have picked up the call. Alex was out of it, so I grabbed the phone and told them where we were.

He slumped onto the floor. I sat him up and slapped his face on both sides. His eyes opened. Still fighting unconsciousness, I said, 'I'm going to make you sick.'

I stuck my fingers down his throat and he vomited over my hand and clothes. I repeated it twice.

'Try to stand up. Try harder, Alex. Open your eyes! We mustn't fall asleep.'

Eventually I managed to get him to his feet, leaning on the wall. 'Now Alex, we'll die if we fall asleep. Move your legs and walk with me.'

We staggered about. All I wanted to do was sleep. At one point, I felt Alex's head drop and smacked his face with my free hand. 'Keep walking Alex, help me. We can't die before Christmas.'

Alex mumbled something unintelligible. We seemed to stagger about endlessly until I heard vehicles outside. I shouted and Alex tried to shout, but only growled.

I shouted again and then heard the bolts being slid open and the place seemed full of police and ambulance men.

I could hear my voice slurring, 'we've been drugged.'

We were taken in two separate ambulances, with sirens blaring. I just wanted to go to sleep.

'Stay awake, Jen.' The paramedic kept talking to me and expecting me to reply. I don't know if I did and didn't care.

I remember being taken into A and E and a cannula being inserted into the back of my hand but little after that.

When I woke up, it was daylight and Meadow was sitting beside me.

'What are you doing here?'

'Clifford brought me,' she said.

'Is Alex alive? I tried to keep him awake.'

'Yes, Clifford is with him. You did a good job there.'

'He called the emergency services. I made myself vomit and then Alex.'

A nurse came over.

'How do you feel?'

'Like I have a massive hangover.'

'I'll bring you some paracetamol and the police will talk to you before you're discharged.'

'What about Lily and Mark?' I asked.

'They know you're here and that you're okay. Jazz slept in your apartment last night. Perhaps next time you'll listen when I tell you not to get involved in a case.'

'I hope there won't be a next time,' I said.

The nurse brought me some paracetamol and water, and then the police came in. I told them everything I could remember.

Meadow came back and then the doctor came to discharge me.

'Can I use your phone to ring Clifford, please?' I asked Meadow, not knowing where mine was.

It seemed the police were with Alex, but the doctor had said he could go home after they'd finished.

Before long, I was back in my apartment with Lily and Mark, all three of us in tears.

CHAPTER 36

After all the tears were mopped up and the smiles reappeared, Lily went off to see Teddy and Mark went to find Peter.

Left alone, I became aware of the headache again and went over to Alex's.

We sat together on the settee and Mungo came to me for a cuddle. 'How are you feeling?' I asked.

'I've got a hangover and, I'm not pointing fingers, but my face feels a bit like it did after you slapped me. I can't see any bruises though.'

'How much do you remember of the time in the outhouse?'

'After the door was bolted, I remember demanding your phone. I put it on hands-free and dialled 999. I vaguely remember something in my throat and throwing up. Then you telling me to keep walking or we'd die. That's about it.'

'Do you want me to fill you in on the rest?'

'Yes, please,' he said and I did so.

'What I don't understand is how we made contact with the police when there was no signal.'

'In an emergency, the nearest transmitter will pick up a 999 call. I left it on hands-free in case they told us to do something. Did they stay on the line? They couldn't call back as there was no signal,' he said.

'Probably, but I was too busy to listen. I'm sorry, but I had to smack your face to keep you conscious. I stuck my fingers down your throat, because you were too far gone to do it yourself, and you vomited all over my coat and shoes.'

'I'll buy you new ones. That's a small price to pay for you saving my life.'

I smiled, 'The hardest bit was getting you to your feet. I eventually managed to heave you against the wall and then shouted at you to walk. And, yes, I slapped your face to keep you awake.'

'Seriously, Jen, you saved my life.'

'But I probably wouldn't have been able to without you dialling 999. I didn't know the nearest transmitter would pick it up.'

'I'm not allowed to drive for seven days,' said Alex despondently, 'and I'd hoped to go to my in-laws for a few days before Christmas.'

'I'm in the same position. Can you ring them up and say you're not well enough to drive? You may have to make up a story and explain to them later.'

'You mean like Ross did?'

'No. That's not a good idea. Could you tell them you're a bit under the weather and you don't think you can drive that far at the moment?'

'That sounds better. Will you come with me the weekend after Christmas?' he asked.

'Okay. I was thinking. You know when we last went to see Ross and I slept all the way home.'

'Yes.'

'Meadow said my pupils were dilated when I arrived home. She thought I'd been taking drugs,' I said. 'The same thing happened to DI Watson and he put it down to stress and lack of sleep catching up with him.'

'Did you google Ross when you were searching for everyone else?'

'No. Can we do it now?' I asked.

We put his name in and came up with a number of newspaper articles about Ross sleeping with bereaved victims. There was an internal enquiry and he left the force.

I was shocked and then remembered how hard he found it to cope with other people's emotions.

'Do you think it was his way of comforting them?'

'Possibly. I still don't think he's a bad bloke though. I wondered why he felt that need to confess to us about what actually happened when Ruth was killed. It was an accident and he should have called the police.'

'Yes,' I said, 'but Harriet went straight in and cut her eyes out, he probably wouldn't have tried to stop her as she was a wild woman with a knife. Perhaps he thought she would get the blame, but I don't think she knew what she was doing. She could probably get off any sentence as she was mentally unbalanced because of the drugs.'

'But would a jury accept that? We're looking at a disgraced ex-police officer and a convict, connected to a drug addict. He probably couldn't risk it,' he said, 'and illegally disposing of a body.'

'I wonder why he even told us. I'd accepted what he said up to that point about not giving us information because he didn't want Harriet disturbed.'

'I accepted it, too,' he said. 'It makes no sense.'

I shrugged my shoulders. 'Do you think he was trying to kill us as well?'

'Perhaps we'll never know. Let's go for a short walk with Mungo before lunch to clear our heads.'

I couldn't help thinking about Ross's confession and then it dawned on me. 'He'd drugged us enough to kill us, and he thought we should know everything before we died.'

'I don't know, I don't think he was planning to kill us, sweetheart. I think the drugs were stronger than he had anticipated. I think he wanted us to know, so he could bring the case to an end. He knew they'd disposed of the body illegally and that he and Annie would both be punished for that, but he'd rather take his punishment than live the rest of his life feeling guilty. After all, as soon as there was any question about him having sex with victims, he owned up. I think he's basically an honest bloke.'

'You mean he knew that we would inform the police when we came round, but it gave him a bit more time with Harriet and Annie before he was arrested? He would have known about the 999 call getting through even if there was no signal and assume that one of us had a mobile.'

'But he probably thought we didn't know about that. Perhaps the only way we'll ever know is to talk to him later or wait until the court case,' Alex said.

'I think we should stop worrying about it and put it behind us. We've a busy week ahead of us with Christmas coming. We need to prepare our Secret Santa as well as help in the kitchen with the chocolate logs. I hope Sally doesn't want me icing Christmas cakes, I don't think I'll be any good at it.'

'Mark and Lily would probably both do well with that. Have you asked them whether they want to spend an afternoon helping out?' Alex asked.

'We can mention it to them at lunchtime,' I said. 'You're not bad with a piping bag either,' I said.

'Now, don't start volunteering me. If you do, I'll volunteer you.'

I put on a look of mock horror. We put Mungo back in Alex's apartment and went to the communal kitchen for our Sunday lunch.

'I was hoping I wouldn't have to stay in hospital for lunch. As hard as they try, it would be a let-down after Clifford and Will's cooking,' I said.

'I didn't think I'd fancy eating much with a monstrous hangover,' Alex said, 'but I'm starving.'

The meat and the roast potatoes smelt delicious and the whole of the communal kitchen was warm and welcoming, as were our friends. They wanted to know what had happened, but all we were able to tell them was that our cups of tea were drugged. We couldn't let any other information seep out as the media would get hold of it and neither of us fancied being responsible for leaks.

We were both expected at the police station in the afternoon and DI Watson had said he would collect us personally. I was concerned that he may be angry with us, but Alex said it was more likely that he was grateful to have a solution to the case.

When we left the communal kitchen, Alex said he didn't think he would go for a long walk this afternoon – he had phone calls to make, and it had started raining.

'I couldn't have gone anyway,' I said, 'I have to wash my coat and clean my shoes.'

'I hope I haven't ruined them,' he said, 'because neither of us can drive into town to get replacements.'

'I think Jazz would take us, but I couldn't go there barefoot or in wellies.'

I went back to the apartment and settled down for a quiet read, but fell asleep on the second page. The doctor was right, there must still be some drugs in my system.

CHAPTER 37

Prue telephoned me to see how I was and I told her that I was fine, all things considered.

'But did you find out who killed my mother?' she asked.

'Are you and Stuart ganging up against me? I told him this morning that I didn't know who killed her.'

'That's okay, just wanted to check that you're not trying to protect us from the truth.'

I knew I wasn't. I didn't know who actually shot Ruth, but I was certain it was accidental.

'When are you due to get your DNA test results through?'

'Before Christmas, they said. It doesn't make any difference one way or the other. Stuart is my little brother whatever they say. We have the same mother.'

'Are you ready for Christmas?' I asked.

'Apart from the decorations, some shopping and cooking. The problem with Christmas is that a lot of the food preparation has to be done at the last minute.'

'I'm ashamed to say it, but our last Christmas meal came from the freezer. I had to buy when items were on special offer and store them until Christmas,' I said.

'That's hard. You can sit back and enjoy this Christmas. I assume someone else is cooking it this year?'

'Yes, it will be pure luxury, but we're all sharing in the preparation of the vegetables on Christmas Eve afternoon. I don't think that will be too bad, though, because we'll be working at it together.'

'How is little Ruby? Still an unhappy baby?' she asked.

'She's good and much happier than she was when she came here. Daniel's responsible for that, and she relates well to the adults here, too.'

'I was wondering when you'd be able to come over for a coffee. I think we're looking sometime between Boxing Day and New Year.'

'Can I call you back on that? We're having a bake off and I don't know what the schedule is, or perhaps you could come over here, there always seems to be something going on.'

We wished each other a happy Christmas and left it at that.

At breakfast on Monday, Sally asked for help with Christmas cakes that morning. I'd made sure everyone knew that I wouldn't be any good at cake decorating.

'Don't you worry, lovey. Come over after you've finished your chores and you can make the marzipan.'

'Make marzipan? I didn't know you could make marzipan.'

Lily said, 'Did you think it grew like that?' She laughed.

'I suppose you knew because you made it with Wilma?'

'Yes.'

'Are you going out this morning?' Sally asked her, 'Because you and Mark would be welcome to help.'

'Okay,' they said together.

It looked as if I would spend some time with my children this holiday after all.

I'd set aside the following morning for wages, so I had a bit of extra admin to do, but I was through it by coffee break.

When I went to the kitchen, Mark and Lily showed me the marzipan they'd already made.

'You're thinking it should be yellow, aren't you?' Mark said.

'I've only ever seen yellow marzipan; I suppose they must colour the stuff we buy in packets. There's no rule to say it should be yellow,' I said.

'Have you thought about how much we've learned since the beginning of the summer holidays? I don't mean book learning, but learning about life,' said my thoughtful son.

'I hadn't thought about it before, but you're right. When we moved here it was like moving to a different world.'

'Are you glad you came?' he asked.

'I almost chickened out at the last minute. I couldn't have dreamed life could be like this.'

'Nor me,' said a voice behind me. It was Amber.

'Are you happy, too?'

'Yes. Clifford reckons we should collect the stuff from the shops Wednesday morning 'cos it'll take ages to wrap up the kiddies' Christmas presents and we shouldn't be troubling the shopkeepers when they're busy. Clifford and Teddy are at the market on Friday, so we'll take the stuff to the refuge on Thursday morning. You don't need to come to that, we can do that on our own.'

Meadow had a word with me as she left the kitchen. 'Can you give Amber a week's pay for her work on the wreaths? She worked quicker and better than three of us. Don't say anything to her, just pop it through her door in cash, with a payslip.'

I smiled. 'She'll be pleased with that.'

I stayed in the communal kitchen, while Lily and Mark showed me how to make marzipan. When it was all done, Sally came over. She told us the weight of marzipan for each cake and Lily chopped it into lumps. We moulded the chunk into a ball, rolled it out and then spread apricot jam on top, picked it up over the rolling pin and turned it onto the cake. We did sixty between us.

DI Watson came to collect us in the afternoon. He seemed much more relaxed. 'I think you may like to know that Harriet wrote the letter to the Jenny Lind. She could only vaguely remember doing it and had no intention of following it up. I've spoken to Ogden and Wilma and explained. They were extremely forgiving about it.'

'Have you any idea why Ross decided to tell us everything, when we would have naturally assumed he knew nothing about it?'

'Yes. He said that the fear that he could be found out at any time was more than he could cope with. He was struggling to concentrate on his writing and wanted the guilt from Ruth's killing over and done with. He said he'd drugged you to allow a couple of hours to talk over the situation with Annie and Harriet and to give them the chance to run away if they wanted to. He'd decided it was his time to give himself up.'

'But the drugs were much stronger than he anticipated,' I said, 'Alex was hallucinating.'

'That's the thing about street drugs,' he said. 'Harriet always had them from the same supplier, but the quality was variable. The drugs he gave you were almost pure. You could both have been killed.'

'We know, but we're alive. Will he automatically be charged for what he did to us or can we say we don't want to press charges?' asked Alex.

I looked at him and wondered why he was saying that.

I thought about Ross and how he tried to protect Harriet by burying Ruth's body. I thought about how he tried to protect her from our questions, and how he put Annie in Harriet's house in the hope of solving problems that each of them had. If Harriet had left Ruth's body alone it would have been seen as an unfortunate accident, but Harriet wrecked that possibility when she took a knife to it.

All along, Ross had tried to do the right thing but circumstances had changed that. I didn't want to press charges either, if I had the option. I decided that when we returned, I would call Stuart and have a chat with him about it.

I remembered the sixty Christmas cakes waiting to be iced and was glad I was out of the way for a while. They needed a professional finish and that was something I couldn't give them.

The following morning Sally asked for volunteers to make the sponge for the chocolate logs. When I went into the basement to collect ingredients, I saw the beautifully iced and decorated Christmas cakes.

'How did you manage to get those cakes iced so quickly?' I asked Megan.

'Fondant icing is quick and easy and there were five of us. We soon finished.'

I didn't think fondant icing was quick and easy. I'd tried to use it once on a cake and the cake looked as if it had a sheet draped over it.

'I made a Swiss roll at school. It was awful. The cake cracked and I'm worried the same thing might happen today,' I said. Megan placed herself between Amber and me to give us the guidance we needed. I noticed that Clifford was supervising Lily and Mark. We started by beating the egg whites until they were stiff and adding sugar to the yolks. The mixtures came together and we poured them into our trays. Immediately we had to repeat the process so we could reuse the oven space and get everything cooked.

A mouth-watering chocolate smell came from the ovens. I was hoping that mine wouldn't come out as a biscuit, tooth-breakingly hard, and it didn't. We turned them out onto clean tea towels and used those to help roll them up. I couldn't remember doing that at school and mine didn't feel as if it cracked.

Once it had cooled, we unrolled it and covered it with chocolate filling, then re-rolled without having the tea towel inside. The last thing was to make up the topping and spread it on the Swiss roll.

I looked at my offerings when I had finished them and was satisfied they looked every bit as good all the others.

I glanced over at Daniel and Ruby and saw them happily licking spoons which had some of the topping on them, their smiling faces covered in chocolate. Ruby seemed to be settled with us now.

I would have liked to taste one of my chocolate logs to make sure I hadn't left an ingredient out, but had to trust that it would be okay.

We took them on boards to the basement, cleaned up our workstations and left Sally and Will to sort out lunch.

CHAPTER 38

On Wednesday, Amber left Daniel with Megan and we rode in the van with Clifford. Amber had phoned the businesses in advance so they knew we would be coming, and had made a list of places we were to visit. Together with Meadow, they had sorted it out to make a logical journey. We had put the kitchen's large cool boxes in the back, so that the meat could be kept separate at a safe temperature.

I was stunned at the generosity of people, not just the traders but the public who had donated food and little luxuries. We left the supermarket with large boxes, and it was the same in the chemist. The chemist's boxes contained not only toiletries, but women's essentials and nappies.

I went into the upholsterer's with Amber because I wanted to meet her. She was a lively woman whose artistry shone through the items she'd made. There were cushions, rucksacks of different sizes and designs for children, baby carriers and women's bags that were true designer items.

'I could have sold all of these ten times over,' she said, putting them into boxes. 'Making these has done me a favour. I often get surplus fabric and breaks between commissions; I shall be making more of these. It's good use of time and saves on waste.'

'You could put them in a gallery. People would queue up for these. Women I knew in London spent ages hunting for things that were different. They're beautifully made,' I said.

'Thank you. I was thinking of selling them online, but I'll look into galleries in towns where there are a lot of second homes. That way I can build up a stock and let the gallery buyers select which ones they think they can sell.'

I was impressed by the upholsterer and thought she would do well in her business.

The owner of the hardware shop had prepared boxes of Christmas decorations. 'I've put in boxes of batteries,' he said. 'You can never have too many batteries at Christmas. There are pretty fairy lights here that can be used all year round in their rooms. One moment, I'll just get a Christmas tree stand for you.' He went to the end of the shop and picked one up. 'It will be lighter to move around than a pot, if there's not a lot of room. I've put in some small artificial Christmas trees, so the children can have them in their rooms. There's plenty of decorations for all of them.'

'Thank you so much,' I said, pulling a tissue out of my pocket and blowing my nose.

We collected wooden boxes of fruit from the greengrocer and boxes of stationery, colouring books, colouring materials and toys from the post office. The postmaster handed me a box of rolls of Christmas paper, gift cards and sticky tape.

Finally, the butcher pulled a trolley of meat from the back of the shop and filled our cool boxes. The van was full and I was shattered.

'We'll wrap the presents this afternoon,' Amber said, 'Meadow's helping and then we're taking them tomorrow afternoon, but you don't have to be around for that. The refuge knows Clifford and I can tell them who I am.'

I thought of the quiet, almost wordless girl that Amber had been only four months ago, having learnt from her various foster homes that the best way to stay in one place was to keep your mouth shut and not look anyone in the eye. Even then, she was moved on to other homes. The community had taught her a different way of life and she was blossoming.

Clifford drove us back and we first put all the meat in the walk-in fridge.

'Do we need to get everything out?' I asked Amber.

'Yes, we need to sort out the groceries from the gifts. The fruit can stay in the van. There's Christmas cakes and puddings from here, but the vegetables we're giving are heavy and will need to be near the bottom. What about the Christmas tree, Clifford?'

'Don't you worry about that I'll strap it to the roof.'

That afternoon, those of us who weren't involved in the outdoor work met to sort and wrap. Amber had a list of Christian names of the mothers and their children, name, age and gender, and we wrapped and labelled accordingly. When we opened the chemist's box there was a full box of toiletries gift sets. My eyes were hot and I pulled a tissue out and blew my nose. Amber was excited, but Sally was wiping her eyes.

Prue had dropped off a box of her own beautiful cakes and biscuits. I struggled with the generosity of these people who were giving to strangers.

Amber's system was good. When we sorted the groceries, she told us to put the heavy items together and the lighter ones could sit above them.

When everything was wrapped, family items were put into paper sacks with the mother's name on it. They were put into the van, after the vegetables, with Amber setting aside a space for the cool boxes, cakes and Christmas puddings.

I could only imagine the faces of those mothers when they saw the contents of the van.

I would be glad of a day of routine the following day to get the admin up-to-date before Christmas.

DI Watson came to see us the following morning while we were loading the van for the refuge with cakes, puddings and cool items.

'You should have come to the station,' he said. 'We're always prepared to rattle a bucket for something like that. We could have provided enough cash for the mums to have a gift token in their Christmas card; I don't expect that they'll all have their benefits sorted out. Take this to go towards next year,' he said, placing a twenty-pound note in my hand.

He helped us finish loading and then I took him back to my apartment.

'That idea was from the partner of the criminal you caught here, Craig.'

'I remember, the girl with the baby.'

'Yes. So why do you want to see me?' I made him a cup of tea and put some handmade biscuits on a plate.

'I wanted you to know that Ross, Harriet and Annie have been bailed. Ross was in a bit of a state. He was prepared to take the punishment himself without involving Harriet and Annie, but I couldn't let him do that. Before long someone would ask how he managed to get Penelope into the van on his own.' He bit into a biscuit. 'This is good.'

I smiled at the compliment.

'He made it clear that Annie was at the burial site simply to do him a favour and look after Harriet. Her probation is over, so it's possible she'll be fined just for burglary and a few other charges. Harriet is unlikely to be punished at all. Once the jury know what Penelope had done to her in the past and see how addicted she is as a result, they will be a hard lot if they find her guilty. She had a licence for the gun, so she owned it legally,' he said.

'It sounds as if Ross has arrived at the point where his conscience is so bad that he wants to be punished,' I said.

'That's true. He's near to breaking point. Although he was pushed out of the force, and that was right, I still think he's a basically good guy.'

'I've noticed that he can't cope well with emotions. Was it consensual sex?'

'Yes. The victims never accused him of rape and he wanted to ease their pain for a while. In that sense it worked, it's not professional though. The women at that time were vulnerable.' he said. 'He owned up to that too; reported himself. The victims hadn't complained, but he couldn't live with his conscience.'

'Do you think he would mind if I phoned him? I want him to know we don't hold anything against him.'

'I don't have any objections. You won't be called as witnesses.'

'And what about you?' I asked. 'When do you retire?'

'Tomorrow is my last day. I'm hoping it will be a quiet one, but Christmas Eve never is. Mind you, it's better than being at my daughter's. My wife went last night, and not only are they doing the food preparation but they're also keeping our three grandchildren occupied. I didn't fancy doing any of that, so I decided to finish my shift tomorrow and then leave. They'll all be too busy to take me to the pub and fill me up with alcohol, which can only be a good thing,' he said.

'You mean that you avoided a party with free drinks?'

He nodded.

'I probably would have done the same,' I said, 'I don't like hangovers, even if they're from drugs I didn't know I'd taken.'

We both laughed.

'Look pop round anytime when you're getting under the wife's feet,' I said.

'I certainly will. You may need some help with your next investigation!'

'I hope there won't be a next one.'

We shook hands and I wished him a long and happy retirement.

Shortly afterward, Amber arrived back from the refuge and knocked on my door.

'You should have seen their faces when we gave them the sacks of presents. One of them cried.'

I smiled at her excitement.

'But the place they're living in ain't good. The house is clean, but a lot of the rooms have two sets of bunks, because there ain't enough room for beds. The mums sleep on the bunks, too. There's one room for each family. Me and Daniel would be okay, but some of them have three children and they could be teenage boys. They're grateful for a safe place to live. I understand that, but some of them have been waiting for ages for the council to house them,' she said.

'I'm afraid it's the way things are today. There aren't enough houses available for everyone who needs one.'

'I suppose not. It's hard to believe that me and Daniel could have been living somewhere like that this Christmas. I was lucky,' she said. 'I have to collect Daniel and Ruby won't like that.'

CHAPTER 39

'How will you manage to get everything to market tomorrow?' I asked Clifford. 'The cakes and Christmas puddings alone, the van already seems full.'

He smiled, 'We have stacking crates for them. Stuart is coming for supper and we'll load up his van. He and Prue will be helping with that side of things. The cakes and puddings are all labelled, so we know who should be collecting what.'

'Do you have enough people to serve?' I asked.

'Yes, Jazz, Teddy and I make a good team and Stuart will be there with Prue helping him. Presumably you'll be helping Alex with the decorations or will you be preparing vegetables?'

'Is there a choice?' I asked.

'Yes, but I think your children will choose to help Alex. I think Will may want to, as well. There's not much cooking done on Christmas Eve. I gather Sally has made the pizza in advance, so it's just a case of heating it up. Will did extra vegetables yesterday, and in the evening we have our leftovers meal, so we don't leave uneaten food over Christmas.'

I had made my Secret Santa sweets earlier in the week. I knew that both Alex and Amber would be cooking this evening and either of them would be glad of my help. I decided that Amber probably needed it most with little Daniel around and made up my mind that was where I would be.

I didn't think I'd see much of the children then, as Mark would be with Peter and Lily with Jazz and Teddy.

I couldn't help thinking back to this day last year, when I upset Lily and she wouldn't talk to me and strung it out over Christmas. That phase in her behaviour had gone and she was much more of a friend to me than she had ever been.

I suddenly realised that I was looking forward to Christmas for the first time since the children were small.

The evening with Amber was good fun. She was still on a high after this morning, and then when I told her that we had a twenty pound donation towards gift vouchers for the women, she became even more excited. I had put it in the petty cash with a note about it, so it would still be there next Christmas.

'I reckon that we're going to provide easter eggs for the children there,' she said.

'People will donate if the supermarket puts out a collection basket,' I said.

'I'm hoping everyone at the refuge has a good Christmas. Do you think they will?'

Daniel had picked up his mother's excitement and was laughing and making excited noises.

'Well, we've done our best but very often times like Christmas bring back memories.'

'I've just got the ingredients out and he knows I'm going to cook. He's hoping for something nice.'

'Have you started cleaning his teeth yet?' I asked.

'No. Do they make baby's toothbrushes?'

'Yes,' I said, 'and toothpaste, too.'

'I'm not a bad mother.'

'I know you're not. It's the sort of thing I would be mentioning to my daughter if she had a baby. I'm just being your mum.'

She turned to me and hugged me. 'Thanks, Mum, it's the sort of advice I need.'

'We'd best start cooking or Daniel will fall asleep before the biscuits come out of the oven.'

We soon managed the first trays, and they looked and smelt lovely when they came out of the oven. Suddenly a little voice distracted us. 'Mum, Mum.'

'Oh Daniel, you're such a clever boy. He's never said that before.' She picked him up and hugged him.

'Mum, Mum.'

'He wants a biscuit, but they're too hot as yet,' she said. By this time, I had them on the cooling rack.

'One of them has broken. If you took a piece and blew on it, I think it would be cool enough for him.'

Daniel's eyes were round as he watched his mother. He took a bite and laughed, starting the pair of us up.

'Let's get the next lot in,' she said.

'I've brought a basket for you to put them in to make it a proper gift.'

'Thanks. I ain't thought about that. Do I just lay them in it?'

'No, I've brought some bags and ribbon and tie-on labels. You're going to have to make them look good.'

'I can't write on the labels because I can't spell,' she said.

'That's not a problem, just copy the name from the recipe. Don't put the biscuits in a bag until they are completely cold. You could leave it until tomorrow morning.'

Daniel was quiet and I turned around to look at him and saw he was fast asleep.

'I think my little boy needs his bed. Can you get the rest of the biscuits out of the oven when they're done, please? I'll go and get him ready for bed.'

'Of course.'

While she was doing that, I made up the next batch and put them in the oven.

Finally, when they were all baked, I made us each a welcome mug of Ovaltine.

'Most of the foster parents I had only gave me like a tiny present, but their children had lots. I wasn't jealous, it was what my life was. I had Christmas with them and they looked after me, but I always felt like I shouldn't be there, I didn't belong. I never looked forward to Christmas like the others,' she said.

'How do you feel about it this year?'

'It's funny, I'm a bit excited. It's been good working with everyone to get ready, I feel like I belong here,' she said.

'You do,' I said. 'That's why you'll be in the kitchen tomorrow preparing vegetables. It shouldn't take long.'

'I don't mind as long as I'm not doing the whole lot,' she said.

When our drinks were finished, I went back to my apartment.

Mark and Lily were both in.

'You smell nice,' I said to Mark. 'What have you been cooking?'

'If I tell you, Peter will kill me.'

'I won't ask again. Will I find out on Christmas Day?'

He grinned. 'I hope so. You know I've been thinking about Amber organising those things for the refuge. She did really well.'

'She's a kind girl,' I said.

'And I love Daniel to bits,' he said.

That remark surprised me, but then he did seem to look after the small children at Wilma and Ogden's.

The following morning, I woke to bright sunshine. It promised to be a good day. When I opened the front door, there was a potted Christmas tree outside. I looked around and every apartment had one.

'Mum,' said Mark, 'We've never had a real tree before. This is so good. What are we going to do about decorations?'

'You'll find out later,' I said.

When we arrived at the communal kitchen, we saw two bags of chocolate tree decorations sitting at each place setting.

'At least we have something to put on our tree,' said Lily, 'But we'll need more than that to fill it up.'

'Don't worry about it,' said Alex. 'It will be sorted out later.'

Mark asked Sally who provided the chocolate decorations and when he learned that it was Meadow, he went over and kissed her.

Lily, suddenly remembering her manners, thanked Meadow.

After breakfast, Meadow said to everyone, 'Come back here shortly because there's vegetables to be prepared for tomorrow and decorations to be put up. Then you're free for the rest of the day, except Sally and Will.'

'Can we do decorations, please?' Mark asked on behalf of Lily, too.

'You're both in my team,' said Alex, 'and so is your mother. Everyone else is in the other team. We're quite short of people because of those at the market, but we should be able to manage.'

As we walked back to the apartment, Lily asked, 'Do you know what Alex's team will be doing?'

'I know no more than you,' I said.

When we returned, Alex called us into the lounge and told us we would be putting up the Christmas decorations. There was an enormous Christmas Tree in one corner of the communal lounge.

'How do we reach the top?' Lily asked.

'I pick you up and sit you on my shoulders,' he replied.

'I don't like that idea,' she said.

Alex laughed. 'Of course, I don't, we use ladders.'

There were crates of baubles and other decorations in the centre of the room. 'Would you two like to be responsible for the tree?'

'Yes please,' Mark replied, 'I've never decorated a tree as big as this before.'

'Right,' he said to Lily, 'It's time for a strategy meeting.'

They spent five minutes talking about what they were going to do. I watched the pair of them and thought back six months, when they wouldn't even talk to each other, and how the Village had brought out the best in us. Lily was almost fifteen and with the friends she had in London, I could see her failing at school or even being expelled. Then it would be a downward spiral as she and her friends dressed older than their age and experimented with drink, sex and drugs. I'd never looked at it objectively before and it shocked me.

Mark had been the fat boy of the class with only one friend. He was bullied and unhappy. It wouldn't have been long before he started failing at school, became depressed and relied on me for everything. I would never have been his friend, and would have hated to see him alienated. And what might depression lead to? I didn't want to think of the consequences. This place had changed everything and been a real blessing to us.

Alex broke into my thoughts, 'What are you thinking about?'

'That life for all of us is much better now,' I said.

Alex passed me his handkerchief. 'Have a good blow, sweetheart,' he said and kissed me on the forehead.

The children's meeting seemed to have finished and Lily disappeared while Mark sorted through the decoration's boxes sorting out the baubles.

'We're going for a silver, pink and purple colour scheme,' he said.

'Okay,' said Alex, 'Can you sort out the rest of the decorations, Jen, and I'll bring in the greenery?'

I was still sorting through, when he came in with a huge bag of foliage. Lily returned with a couple of tote bags and they slung them across their bodies and filled them with baubles.

'There are metallic sprays outside – all colours. It's essential we use them out there as they're toxic. There are some masks on the table. The ivy berries always look beautiful sprayed. Oh, and spray on the tarpaulin, we don't want metallic paving slabs,' Alex said.

When I went outside, I saw that the tarpaulin had spray paint marks on it already.

'Tactics meeting,' Alex said. 'Are we going to use a single colour for each of the walls or do we mix them in the same colour range as the tree? I vote we mix them.'

'No disagreement there,' I said, 'but will there be enough?'

'Hopefully, but if not, we'll have to spray extra foliage for colour.' We settled down to our spraying.

'Are you worried about your children up ladders?' he asked.

'Not really. They're both sensible.' I said, crossing my fingers.

By lunchtime, the lounge was decorated and looking beautiful. As we took the remainder of the decorations and greenery outside, I noticed that there was a Christmas table cloth on the communal kitchen table and Will, Amber and Megan were finishing off table arrangements. They looked wonderful and it felt like Christmas was almost here.

'The rest of the decorations and greenery go outside on the patio,' Alex said, 'I brought out the rest of the sprays, so people can help themselves to whatever they want, to decorate their own apartments.'

'I'll let the children take ours,' I said, 'and I'll sort out Meadow's when she tells me what she wants.'

'There's one rule,' Alex said, 'whatever isn't used in your apartment you bring back out. The men who're at the market will need some, as well. They should be back soon after lunch. Everything sells out quickly on Christmas Eve.'

'We've forgotten something,' I said.

Alex looked puzzled.

'Mistletoe.'

'We don't usually have that. I think Meadow's been caught once too often!'

I had a lot of fun. It was so different from last year where we had just the same old decorations, and the artificial Christmas tree that came out of the loft already decorated.

Meadow told me she liked just greenery to decorate her home and a mixture of baubles for the tree with any type of fairy lights. She was easy to please, but when her apartment was done, I had to admit it looked lovely.

When the men arrived back from the market, they emptied the crates out of the van and sat down for a late lunch.

Everything was done now, apart from decorating their apartments. Will started on his and Clifford's. When Lily had finished ours, she went to help Jazz and Teddy with their apartments, while Mark drifted off to Peter's.

This felt strange. I'd not been alone on Christmas Eve afternoon since before the children were born, so I went over to see Alex. He was still working at his decorations.

'Here to help,' I called out.

'I'm still sorting out the holly,' he said. 'Would you mind starting on the tree?'

'Do you have a colour scheme?'

'Not really, sweetheart. There are some decorations that the girls made when they were younger. I still like to put those on the tree, but nothing chocolatey or Mungo will have the tree over. I need some lights, but not the ones that flicker. Any colour except blue.'

'Don't you like blue?'

'I don't mind blue as a colour, but blue lights remind me of that day on the beach when they found Millie,' then he burst into tears.

I went over and put my arms around him. 'Is it worse at Christmas?'

'Yes, we're having fun together, or pretending to, and she's not here to share it. It would be so different if I'd noticed how depressed she was. We could be having a family Christmas, just like we always did.'

There was nothing I could say, so I just sat beside him with my hand rubbing his back. Mungo came over and started licking his face. He held him tightly for a time and kissed his head.

'Sorry,' he said.

'There's no need to be sorry. Christmas is a time of laughter and tears. I've already blubbed today and don't expect you'll be the last this holiday.'

He blew his nose then said, 'I could do with a coffee.'

By the time I'd made it, he was looking more cheerful again.

'What would I do without you?' he said and kissed me.

'Where did you put the chocolate baubles?' I asked.

'Oh no!' Mungo was standing with his paws on the kitchen table. 'Leave it,' he commanded. Mungo sloped off to his bed.

'Did he get any?' I asked.

'No, the bag protected them but he's broken a few.' Alex stretched up and put them in the top of one of the cupboards.

We drank our coffee and started to work again.

When it was all done, it looked beautiful. We took the leftovers out and Alex suggested we have a glass of wine.

'It's not suppertime yet,' I said. 'Isn't that the way to ruin?'

'You may have to prove it to me. We've worked so hard the past few weeks and made a lot of people happy. I can't see a problem with relaxing the rules over the holiday period. Or are you going to the midnight service at Honsham?'

'No, I'll give that a miss, I need my sleep. Does anyone go from here?' I asked.

'Sometimes Jazz does, but he's been at the market today. I think he'll be tired.'

'So will Stuart and Prue from what I heard. There were almost two hundred cakes and puddings to be collected, they must have been run off their feet.'

'It's better that way than to be standing around thinking how cold you are,' said Alex.

'I suppose so.' I said. 'What happens with our secret Santas? Do we put them under the tree?'

'Yes, you can do it this evening or tomorrow morning. We usually open them after lunch,' he said.

As it was almost suppertime, I nipped back to the apartment and then went on to the community kitchen for leftovers supper. These were my favourite suppers of the week, when we sat in the lounge and ate together informally. The babies' highchairs were brought into the communal lounge so they could eat with us.

Meadow had arranged for a travelling cot to be put in the office, so they could be laid down in there if they fell asleep when we were all together.

'I can't imagine what it will be like this evening at Wilma's,' Lily said, 'trying to get all those excited children to sleep.'

It brought back memories of a time that I cherished.

CHAPTER 40

Everyone seemed happy at suppertime.

'Don't eat too much supper,' said Clifford, 'you'll eat a lot more food than normal in the next few days.'

'Take no notice of him,' said Will. 'Eat as much as you can to stretch your stomach in readiness for the big day. Anyway, it would be terribly wasteful to put all those lovely leftovers in the bin. Anyone for seconds or thirds?'

Meadow said to me, 'I've never seen this room looking like it is at the moment. Whose idea was the colour scheme?'

'Lily and Mark's,' I said, 'I thought it might be too pastel for you.'

'It's good to have young ideas and yes, I love it. It wouldn't work in my apartment, but it works well in here.'

'Do you think it contrasts or complements the bright coloured sofas?' I asked.

She banged her spoon on her dish a few times. 'Quiet everyone. Let's give Lily and Mark a round of applause for this delightful colour scheme. We've not had a colour-coordinated Christmas before. Well done, you two.'

Both of the children blushed.

It seemed that everyone was relaxing in anticipation of the restful days ahead. The past week had been a hard one.

'Are you looking forward to the big day?' I asked Meadow.

'I am. And although we have our traditions, it's unexpected every year because of the different mix of residents.'

'I feel sorry for Ross,' I said.

'You mean Ruth's stepbrother? Wasn't he the one who buried Nicole's body?'

I nodded. 'I've talked to him on the phone since he's been bailed, and everything he'd done was to protect or help others. He knew it was unlawful, but he felt a strong need to help the mother of the dead baby. He put other people before the law.'

'Was he putting you before the law when he tried to kill you?'

'He didn't try to kill us. It wasn't his fault that the batch of drugs was stronger than he thought. He expected us to tell the police later what had happened so he didn't have to live with the guilt he was feeling. He needed us to sleep for a few hours to give the women a chance to escape. He was going to take the blame for everything. I happen to think he should be commended for that.'

'I suppose so, but the law is the law.'

'That's where we differ,' I said with a smile. 'Did you know I'm helping Stuart and Prue to arrange Ruth Carpenter's funeral?'

'Doesn't that make you feel uncomfortable? She's a child-killer and children are high on your agenda.'

'Not anymore. In a way, she's helped me come to terms with my early menopause. I'm not feeling jealous of pregnant women or women with young children anymore.' It seemed strange to say out loud something that had been moving around in my subconscious.

'And you're certain of that?'

'Yes. I'll be going into the new year a different person.'

'I'm glad for you, my dear,' she said.

That evening, I went around to Alex's to walk Mungo with him. As he went to get poo bags, I saw an enormous stash of them. 'Are you expecting Mungo to have an upset stomach?' I asked.

'He may well do, but the hardware shop does a special offer before Christmas, for a year's supply of bags. They were very cheap.'

'That's nice of them.'

'They want to keep Honsham clean,' he said, 'and it's their contribution towards it.'

'But Mungo doesn't go into town,' I said.

'What you mean to say is that you've not noticed me putting him into the car. The people in the hardware store love him and it's good for him to meet strangers.'

I smiled and we left for our walk. The moon was full and bright and it wasn't long before my fingers and toes were numb.

'It looks as if God has decorated the Village with frost just for us,' I said. 'What are the chances of seeing Father Christmas flying past?'

'Fairly slim,' he said, 'You can't see much beyond the trees above us. Would you rather walk in the open tonight?'

'No, I like being in the woods at night.'

'You're a very different woman from the frightened person who arrived here in July, sweetheart.'

'I know. I don't think I've ever changed as much as I have over those few months.'

He turned towards me, pulled me close and kissed me. 'I love you, Jen.'

'And I love you, Alex.'

We kissed again and then went inside for our nightcap.

CHAPTER 41

I woke up a number of times during the night and looked at my alarm. When the children were young, they would have been up anytime from two o'clock, and I was constantly telling them to go back to bed as Father Christmas might come back.

When they went to school, the joy was taken out of Christmas. All the other children wrote letters to Santa with long lists of what they wanted for Christmas. First Lily, and then Mark, realised that Santa took little notice of their letters. The gifts he brought them were nothing like the gifts that he delivered to other children. I didn't have the money and Ben never thought to give me extra for the children's presents. He wasn't there to see their pretend excitement when they opened their presents. I knew Amber would understand – she'd been through it, too.

The final time I woke it was seven o'clock. Breakfast wasn't until eight-thirty that morning. It was a special day. I made myself a coffee and took it back to bed with me.

There was no noise from Lily or Mark. They'd both had late nights and Christmas morning was just like any other morning to them, so they had no reason to get up early. They didn't realise that this year I'd had the money to buy the things they had asked for, not that they'd asked for much. Lily needed an adult's bike; she probably thought it would be an old one which had been done up. Mark was expecting a screw driver set, not the lovely power tools that I was giving him. I didn't choose them, but gave Alex the money to buy them and that money went a long way. I'd had enough left to buy them some smaller presents that I put under the tree.

I'd bought Alex a lovely warm jumper, some toys for Daniel and Ruby, glace fruits for Meadow and a book on parenting for Amber.

I'd never before been able to buy so much for my family and I'd never had so many friends to buy for. In fact, since I had the children, I'd not had any friends to buy for in my old life. It was quarter to eight before I went to wake up the children.

Lily looked at me, still half asleep, and then jumped up. 'I was dreaming I was back in London, but we're in the Village and we're going to have a fun day.'

'I did try to make it fun for you in London,' I said.

'I know Mum, but I don't think I knew what fun was until we moved here. Thanks for being brave enough to bring us and let us stay here.'

After that sentence from my daughter, I didn't think that the day could get better. I knocked on Mark's door.

'I'm up, just getting dressed.'

'Are you collecting eggs today?'

'No, Mum, they don't lay when the days get short.' Why hadn't I noticed that?

I went to the kitchen, rinsed my cup out and poured myself another. Mark came through and made himself a coffee and Lily followed shortly afterward.

'Mum, who are the presents under the tree for?'

'Have a look.'

'Wow! There's three each for us, Lil.'

They sat on the floor together, opening their gifts.

'Thanks Mum,' said Lily. 'I love them! It's the best Christmas ever.'

Mark came over and kissed me and I felt a tear hit my wrist.

'Mark, are you crying?'

'Not really.'

We stood together and hugged each other.

'We've both got something for you.' They handed their presents to me and to each other. Lily had bought me a new pair of jeans, 'You can take them back and swap them if they don't fit.'

'But I'm not a size twelve. I'm a sixteen.'

'I think you're a twelve, try them on.'

I came out of my bedroom wearing the new jeans which fitted beautifully, a huge smile on my face.

'You need to open mine now,' said Mark.

It was a beautiful cashmere jumper in my favourite colour, red, also size twelve. I stripped off my old baggy jumper and put my new one on. It fitted well and felt lovely on my skin.

I stood up and went to the mirror. 'I think Santa has brought me a new body,' I said surprised. 'But you two couldn't afford to buy these out of your pocket money.'

'I helped Alex out in my spare time, and he paid me for the work I did,' said Mark.

'I knew that Wilma usually paid someone to do the family ironing. She said that if I did it well, she would pay me what she normally pays someone else.'

'I spent two whole Saturdays ironing and she paid me for it.'

I was pleased that the children wanted to give me decent presents.

'I'm impressed by your initiative,' I said.

'Now I have a surprise for you both. Your main presents are outside.'

'Wait? You mean these aren't our main presents?'

They opened the door. This time there were two tear-stained faces.

'Thanks so much. You're the best Mum ever,' said Mark. He put his hands around my waist and picked me up.

'Hey, put me down.' We all laughed.

'I think it's time we went over for breakfast,' Lily said.

CHAPTER 42

I thought people might be quiet as they relaxed from the hard work they'd been doing but Will was as bubbly as a schoolboy on Christmas Day. The babies soon picked up on the atmosphere and became excited, too.

'Who's doing the cooking?' I asked Meadow.

'It tends to be Sally, Will and Clifford but Megan has offered to help out if anyone needs some time off. Tom is home today and will look after Ruby. The morning is used for delivering presents to our special friends, but the trouble is that they are delivering, too, so there's a lot of running around in circles.' We listened to Will getting excited about Christmas pudding.

Clifford said, 'I often send him to deliver our presents, just to get him out of the kitchen. He can be too much at times.'

'That's why you love me isn't it, darling?'

'I have to admit it was your childlike enthusiasm that attracted me to you in the first place.'

'And it was your cool calm attitude that attracted me,' said Will. 'It would be no good me marrying a man like me. We'd fall apart in tears every few days and the days in between we'd be hysterically silly. And why do I have to wait until coffee time to open my present?'

'We agreed, remember? It's the best time for us to take a break from the kitchen and we can have a little tipple at the same time.'

'Oi,' said Sally, 'I can't have intoxicated men in my kitchen.'

'Look at the height of him,' said Clifford, 'gravity will pull the alcohol to his feet. It stands very little chance of going to his head.'

'That's true, isn't it? I've never been drunk,' Will said.

'To be quite honest, it's difficult to tell if you're drunk or sober most of the time,' laughed Clifford, and Will punched him so hard on his arm that he nearly fell off his chair.

The atmosphere was jovial and relaxed, more than I'd experienced before in the communal kitchen.

When Sally and Will stood to clear away the dishes, Mark said, 'Sit down. Lily and I will do that.'

They cleared the table, put the crockery in the dishwasher and Mark rolled up his sleeves and started scrubbing the pots.

'Did you know they were going to do that?' Meadow whispered. I shook my head, feeling a sudden surge of pride.

In London, I had never seen anything in them to be proud of. Was it because I didn't look properly or was there nothing for me to see?

When the kitchen was cleaned up and everything washed, I walked back to the apartment with Lily and Mark. 'Do you have presents to deliver?' I asked.

'We both have presents for Alex and I have one each for Teddy and Jazz,' Lily said.

'And I have one for Peter and one for Sally. I wanted to thank her for putting up with Peter and I spending so much time in his room that we ignored her.'

'That's kind,' I said, 'But I'm sure she wouldn't think you were ignoring her.'

'She brings us hot drinks and biscuits. One evening we were so engrossed, we didn't hear her come in, so I didn't thank her until I left.

'Another time she was asleep in her chair and I wondered if I'd stayed too late, but when I looked at the time it was only nine o'clock.'

'I think it could be because she had a hard day on her feet. She's not as young as me,' I said.

'And sometimes you fall asleep in the chair,' he said.

I didn't reply, just smiled to myself.

We decided to catch Alex first. I knocked on his door while the children started singing 'Rudolph the red nosed reindeer' and I joined them.

'Welcome,' he said, smiling at our singing. 'Come on in.'

Mungo darted to the children and they both bent down and fussed him. We sat in the lounge, the children taking the settee and Alex and I the chairs. He had a fire - the apartment seemed warm and cosy - and Mungo plonked himself in front of it.

'I have to watch him,' Alex said, 'sometimes the sparks from the fire land on his back. He has such a dense coat that he doesn't know they're there. I only know when I smell burning hair, and I have to put the spark out. That's why I light a fire only on special occasions.'

'Can we have a fire tomorrow morning, Mum? We didn't have a fireplace in London.' Mark said.

'I don't know, we haven't any wood.'

'I can sort that out for you, and show you where the wood pile is,' Alex said.

'Yes, but…'

'Do you know how to lay a fire?' Alex asked.

'I've no idea,' I said honestly. 'I grew up in centrally heated houses, so I've never had to do it.'

'I'll come in and show you all.'

Alex collected parcels from the Christmas tree and we rummaged through our bags to find his.

The children had been thoughtful in their choice of presents. Mark bought him a new tee-shirt with 'handyman' on it and Lily bought him a pair of Christmas pyjamas. Both gifts made him laugh. He was grateful for the jumper I had bought him and rewarded me with a kiss.

'Get a room!' Lily and Mark said in unison.

Alex poked his tongue out at them. 'How did you know what size I wore?'

'Simple,' Mark said, 'Do you remember when I brought in the jumper you'd left outside? I noted the size then.'

Alex had bought me a beautiful but unusual gold chain, which he helped me put on.

Mark opened his present and saw a toolbox filled with hand tools. He pulled a tissue from his pocket and wiped his eyes.

'Thank you so much,' he said, Alex hugged him. 'I hope I'm not going to do this later when I open my Secret Santa.'

'That would be embarrassing for you, but I think it's good for men to cry,' Lily said.

'Thanks, Sis.'

'Look at these, Mum,' Lily said. I saw a pair of tasteful earrings that I knew would suit Lily. 'They're nine carat gold. I've never had gold before. Can I use your mirror?' She put them in and admired them. 'They're exactly right for me and I love them. Thank you so much, Alex.'

'They're antique,' he said.

'And magnificent,' she replied. 'I'll look after them really well.'

We sat and chatted until there was a knock at the door. 'I think it's time we moved on and delivered the rest of our presents.'

I went next to Tom and Megan's. 'I've brought a gift for Ruby,' I said.

'Come on in,' Ruby was sitting on the floor playing with a doll.

'Gosh, you've made this apartment homely,' I said.

'We'd been collecting things for our own home, but we had no use for them when we were living at Tom's father's house. We brought them with us, and rather than leaving them in the car, we decided to get them out. This place feels like a real home now.'

'Is it the apartment or the community that makes you feel good?'

'Both really, but without the community we would never have a decent Christmas.'

I gave them Ruby's present and she watched them opening it. As soon as she saw it was a soft toy pig, she reached out for it and hugged it. 'P-p-p,' she said.

'She's telling us it's Peppa Pig,' Megan said.

'Will you have a coffee with us? asked Tom. 'The pot's on.'

'Yes, I'd like to, thank you.' Tom went into the kitchen. 'How are you feeling now, Megan?'

'Much better. I don't know how I'm ever going to be able to thank Meadow and all the lovely people here who've kept me safe, made me feel a part of the family and, more than that, restored Ruby's happy nature.'

'Amber, Meadow and Alex know your story, but no one else and we don't gossip here. But Sally has commented on how much Ruby has changed. She will have realised that something was wrong before you came here. Jazz will, too. I think Ruby's change has been thanks enough,' I said.

'I still wonder if I should have pressed charges against Tom's father.'

'If nothing else, he needs to be on the sex offenders list, so that future complaints will be treated seriously. You're lucky to have a partner like Tom who loves you.'

'I know, and he's so good with Ruby, too.'

'Are you talking about me?' he asked.

'Yes,' Megan said, 'just saying how much I love you. You were so sensitive and understanding about my problem with your father.'

'When I heard you screaming, it tore me apart. You've never been one to scream, but it was horrific. I can't understand why you didn't tell me before.'

'I wasn't certain how you'd take it. You seemed to get on so well with your father.'

'Surely you know how much I love you and little Ruby. Both of you were miserable, and now look at the pair of you.' Ruby was holding her pig and laughing, and Megan was radiant.

'How are you getting on here?' I asked Tom.

'Not bad at all. It would be so much better if I didn't have to leave for work, but I have a week off now, so hopefully I'll get to know people better.'

'There's a bake-off next week. Why don't you put your name down for it? Megan won't be able to enter because of her training.'

'I don't know about that,' he said, 'I'm not too good with baking.'

'All the instructions will be given and other contestants will help you. It's a bit of fun and you'll get to know the others better.'

'Put like that, I feel as if I should. I'll join in and make a fool of myself.'

'Good,' I said.

'Before you leave, I've something to give you,' Megan said.

She gave me a small, beautifully decorated cake. On the top it said, "Thank you".

'I've made one for Meadow as well. Is it alright for us to knock on her door, or do we have to ring first?'

'Just knock and go in. There'll be a constant flow of people going through today.'

We said our goodbyes and I went downstairs to Meadow.

'I'm so glad to see you,' she said. 'I have a gift for you. Open it.'

I did and found a gold bracelet. She opened mine.

'This is lovely,' she said, 'I think I'll put it on now' She changed into her new bright multi-coloured cardigan and stood in front of the mirror. 'It's longer than most of mine and will keep the cold out of my kidneys when I'm stretching up.'

'When do you stretch up, Meadow?'

'When I'm putting my washing out.'

'But I'm here to do that for you.'

'Only until I get rid of my crutches.'

'We'll see,' I said.

'Hey, you can't say that. It's my phrase.'

Our conversation was disturbed by Tom, Megan and Ruby and then Amber arrived with Daniel. I gave her and Daniel my presents and she gave me one in exchange. At that point I decided to leave to visit the donkeys with some carrots and take Mungo for a walk before lunch.

Alex joined me. I remembered what Sally had said when I went to get the carrots from the kitchen, 'Those donkeys will think it's Christmas Day, the number of carrots that have been given to them, lovey.'

I smiled. It was only one day of the year.

CHAPTER 43

Lunchtime was later than usual and my stomach rumbled as we walked. 'I don't know if I'll ever get used to that noisy stomach of yours,' Alex said.

'It's only when it's empty or upset,' I said. 'There was no sign of the children at the apartment, when I went back in.'

'Does that surprise you?' he asked.

I shook my head. 'It seems strange they're not around on Christmas morning, I suppose they have more interesting people to be with than me.'

'Do I hear a little self-pity? At some time, they'll break away, but at the moment you know where they are and that they're safe.'

'True. Last Christmas, Lily was an intolerant misery and wasn't talking to me. I felt relieved when she went up to her room. Mark tended to treat Christmas day as any other day, apart from the Christmas pudding. We ended up watching the same old films that are shown every Christmas.'

'You did your best and shouldn't feel guilty. You couldn't make it any better.'

'I suppose so.'

'When the girls were teenagers,' Alex said, 'they seemed to deliberately gang up against us at Christmas. We gave them practically everything they asked for and more besides, but we'd nearly always end up with a row over the dinner table. I sometimes wondered if we'd spoilt them but, hearing what you've just said, perhaps it's just hormones in girls. By the way, how are your hormones?'

'I haven't asked them recently,' I said.

'Sounds as if they're jogging along nicely.'

'Do you know what I'm disappointed about?'

'No,' he said, 'tell me.'

'It was a beautiful clear night last night with no light pollution and I didn't see Santa.'

'You're still feeling bad about that, sweetheart? That's a shame. Did you notice the elf who was helping Amber make her wreaths?'

'So that was her secret,' I said. 'Come on, let's get back, put Mungo away and go for lunch.'

'Mungo's allowed into the communal lounge this afternoon. It's the one time of the year when he can come in.'

'I don't know what the babies will think of that,' I said.

With that, we separated. I went back to the empty apartment, combed my hair and admired my new body in the mirror. I could hardly believe it was me.

The enticing smell of turkey pulled me into the communal kitchen. The table looked beautiful with gold placemats, crackers, flower arrangements and wine glasses. Sally, Clifford and Will were all working.

'Is there anything I can do?' I asked.

'No, lovey, sit down at the table.'

Alex came in shortly afterwards. 'Would you like me to be the wine waiter?'

'Yes, please, lovey. Same as last year.'

'Would you like red or white wine, or grape or apple juice?' He went around the table asking everyone and pouring their drink for them.

Clifford was slicing the turkey and the beef. Will put tureens of steaming vegetables on the table and asked us in turn what meat we would like, adding Yorkshire puddings and roast potatoes to our plates. We helped ourselves to vegetables and gravy.

Afterwards there was Christmas pudding with cream, brandy sauce or brandy butter. I had to undo the button on my new jeans. We pulled the crackers and put paper crowns on.

Then we moved into the lounge, and Clifford came in with hot mince pies and Will followed with a coffee tray.

It was the best meal I'd ever eaten.

The children were tidying up in the kitchen with Tom and Alex. With four of them working, it didn't take long.

I was beginning to fall asleep when Meadow clapped her hands. 'Come on folks, it's no good sleeping through the best day of the year. It's time for Secret Santa.'

As each one of us opened our parcels, we tried to guess who they were from. Meadow opened hers first.

'It's my mobility scooter.' She held a perfect wooden replica on the palm of her hand. 'You must have made this, Alex. It's perfect.'

'Not guilty,' he said.

'Surely no one else could have done it?' She looked puzzled.

'It was me,' said Mark.

I took a deep breath in. 'Was it really?'

'I'll confirm that,' said Alex.

'I'm stunned,' said Meadow. 'Thank you so much.'

She may have been stunned, but I was gob-smacked.

Alex said to me, 'He's got a good eye for the overall picture as well as the detail. He'll go a long way in life.'

I was too shocked to say anything.

The tool carrier Meadow had made for Teddy was a big hit, as were the sweets I made for Peter. Clifford gave me an awesome flower arrangement.

Will opened his tiny parcel. Inside was a card saying your gift will come through the door. We all looked towards the door and Peter came in, carrying a large gingerbread house.

'I made it with Mark,' he said.

Will was so excited. He put it on the table and turned it round. 'This must be the best Christmas present I've ever had. Did you two really make it?

'Yes,' said Mark. Peter had put his ear defenders on as Will's voice rose in excitement.

'I've never had a gingerbread house before, this is wonderful.'

I looked at Sally and saw she was in tears. Jazz was beside her, holding her hand.

Megan had a small parcel with a card inside which read, "Stay in the Village until you have found your ideal home."

Tom also had a card which said, "The Trust will pay the landlord's deposit on your new home".

They hugged each other and Meadow.

Amber was the last person to open her parcel, a pen and ink portrait of Daniel. I could see she was tearful and Lily went over and hugged her.

'Did you draw this?' she asked.

'With a bit of help from my art teacher,' she said.

This time it was me with my mouth open. Alex said, 'Do they take after you or Ben?'

'Ben was useless at art, but my grandmother was a sculptor, so I guess it's come through my side of the family. I was quite good at art at school, but I didn't take it any further.'

'There's still plenty of time,' he said.

With the parcel-opening out of the way, Mark said, 'Would anyone like more coffee?' He and Lily went into the kitchen and made another pot.

Clifford turned the television on. It was part of the way through "The Towering Inferno". We all groaned. 'Shall I try a different channel?'

'No,' said Meadow, 'they'll all have the same old films or cartoons. We all know how it started, so leave it on.'

As it happened, people weren't really watching. Some went to sleep and others were chatting. As foodstuffs were put away, Alex went to collect Mungo.

The babies were on the floor and Mungo went straight over to them. We all watched as Daniel got hold of his ear and Ruby looked on. Eventually she summoned up the courage to touch him. He laid down on the floor with them and went to sleep. For them, he was a new toy. Not long afterwards Ruby, Daniel and Mungo were asleep in a heap. Jazz was taking photographs, so he snapped away at them from different angles.

'We don't really need the travelling cot,' Meadow said, 'We've got one in here.'

When the film was over, Clifford switched off the television and put a CD of Christmas songs on.

We were moving around between seats, chatting to each other. Amber was tearful.

'Is anything wrong?' I asked her.

'No. It's just that I ain't never been a proper part of a family. It's a real Christmas here, it's a shame that Daniel and Ruby are too young to remember it. Meadow gave me a laptop this morning and Jazz said he'll send me copies of all the photos, so I can tell Daniel who everyone is when he gets older.'

'Are you thinking of moving out?'

'No, but Ruby won't be here for ever, or Jazz, and your children will grow up and leave home. So, it's good to remember.'

While we were drinking more tea and coffee, Meadow clinked her teaspoon against her cup. 'Next we'll play charades.' A groan came from the room. 'It's no good being like that, there are some people here who have never played and may enjoy it.' She smiled and then went on to explain the rules. 'Who wants to go first?'

'I will.' Another groan went up, 'Make it easy, Will,' said Clifford. 'No one here has your background as an actor.'

Will did his piece, acting out a film title that I didn't have a clue about. It seemed that no one else did either. In the end, we all gave up and he had to tell us. I was no wiser when I heard the answer.

'Will anyone volunteer to do a television programme or a book?' Teddy stood up and did EastEnders. Lily guessed correctly then for her turn she did Harry Potter and the Goblet of Fire, which Mark guessed. Alex guessed that his was the Blue Planet.

Alex stood up and then kneeled in front of me. 'Jen, the woman who saved my life.'

'You're not supposed to speak.' I whispered.

'Jen, the woman who saved my life and means everything to me… Will you marry me?'

What? Was this a charade or was he proposing to me? I looked down at him and saw him holding a jewellery case with a ring inside it. The diamonds sparkled at me but, even then, I was sure he was joking.

The room was silent. Then I looked into his eyes and knew. 'Yes,' I blurted out, feeling hot and tears spilling off my chin. He slipped the ring onto my finger and everyone cheered and clapped. Then he held me tight to him.

The children came across and hugged us both, 'At long last, I'll have a proper dad,' Mark said. 'Can I still call you Alex?'

'Of course.'

Clifford and Will came in with champagne.

'Let's get the happy family together for a photo,' said Jazz.

I had swollen eyes and my hair needed a comb but I didn't care. I smiled at the camera.

'Champagne for the fiancés,' said Clifford, offering us a tray. 'Now, Lily and Mark, what would you like?'

He passed them their fruit juice and went around the room distributing drinks.

Meadow tapped on her cup again. 'This is a wonderful day and a first for the Village. Alex and Jen are well-suited, and yes, I did know in advance that this was to happen. Why else would we play charades? Let's toast Alex and Jen.'

'Alex and Jen,' came the reply.

'And,' said Meadow, 'Lily and Mark.'

'Lily and Mark.'

People came over to congratulate us, and I thought back to the day we arrived when I had made up my mind I would never get involved with another man. I was deeply happy for the first time for years.

After the congratulations, Alex said to me, 'I'd planned to wait longer, but I thought it would be good to ask you earlier so we could start the application to adopt a baby.'

'I don't need a baby anymore,' I replied. 'Things have changed. I've changed and I have everything here that I could ever want.'

We kissed in front of the people we loved.

Acknowledgements

Special thanks go to my sister, Helen, who constantly encouraged me to write my book. Also to Michael Heppell without whom I would never have published.

Thanks go to my editor, Jane Walters, my typesetter Matt Bird and my beta readers, Marie Breame, Sue Lambert, Heather Wakefield and Helen Worvill.

Special thanks go to my online writing group for their critique and my accountability group, Dynamics, who kept me going and were generous with their advice at all times.

Finally, I have to thank my dogs, Freddie and Janie who listened patiently to me and kept me sane.

About the Author

Lorna Clark was born in Norfolk, UK. She remembers her childhood as idyllic, running free with her sisters on her parents' farm. The only thing which spoilt it was school, where she felt confined.

At seventeen she left school, trained as an accountant and later moved to Hampshire to teach business studies. However, at forty-five, she returned to Norfolk, with her dogs, to help her elderly parents with their plant nursery.

After her father's death, Lorna cared for her mother until she died during lockdown. With time on her hands, she took extra writing courses and vowed to have her first novel, 'Strawberries and Suspicions', published while she was seventy. 'Breadcrumbs and Bones' followed six months later.

Her experience of living on farms and a plant nursery has been woven into the Honsham Forest Village novels.

Living in a 'wonderful village community' has influenced the theme of *belonging* which runs through all her writing.

She has two dogs, a dachshund and a chihuahua, who are beside her as she writes and love to cuddle up on her lap in the evening.

If you would like to know more about Honsham Forest Village, please go to www.lornajclark.co.uk

Strawberries and Suspicions

Strawberries and Suspicions

A Honsham Forest Village Cosy Crime

Lorna Clark

Lorna Clark's debut novel
Now available from Amazon.

Printed in Great Britain
by Amazon

21848573R00169